The Collected Supernatural and Weird Fiction of Richard Middleton

The Collected Supernatural and Weird Fiction of Richard Middleton

Forty-One Short Stories of the Strange and Unusual Including 'Children of the Moon', 'The Coffin Merchant', 'The Wrong Turning', 'A Railway Journey', 'The Last Adventure', 'A Railway Journey' and 'Blue Blood'

Richard Middleton

LEONAUR

The Collected
Supernatural and Weird
Fiction of
Richard Middleton
Forty-One Short Stories of the Strange and Unusual Including 'Children of the
Moon', 'The Coffin Merchant', 'The Wrong Turning', 'A Railway Journey', 'The Last
Adventure', 'A Railway Journey' and 'Blue Blood'
by Richard Middleton

FIRST EDITION

Leonaur is an imprint of Oakpast Ltd

Copyright in this form © 2022 Oakpast Ltd

ISBN: 978-1-915234-94-0 (hardcover)
ISBN: 978-1-915234-95-7 (softcover)

http://www.leonaur.com

Publisher's Notes

Contents

Introduction

The other day I said to a friend, "I have just been reading in proof a volume of short stories by an author named Richard Middleton. He is dead. It is an extraordinary book, and all the work in it is full of a quite curious and distinctive quality. In my opinion it is very fine work indeed."

It would be so simple if the business of the introducer or preface-writer were limited to such a straightforward, honest, and direct expression of opinion; unfortunately that is not so. For most of us, the happier ones of the world, it is enough to say "I like it," or "I don't like it," and there is an end: the critic has to answer the everlasting "Why?" And so, I suppose, it is my office, in this present instance, to say why I like the collection of tales that follows.

I think that I have found a hint as to the right answer in two of these stories. One is called *The Story of a Book*, the other *The Biography of a Superman*. Each is rather an essay than a tale, though the form of each is narrative. The first relates the sad bewilderment of a successful novelist who feels that, after all, his great work was something less than nothing.

He could not help noticing that London had discovered the secret which made his intellectual life a torment. The streets were more than a mere assemblage of houses, London herself was more than a tangled skein of streets, and overhead heaven was more than a meeting-place of individual stars. What was this secret that made words into a book, houses into cities, and restless and measurable stars into an unchanging and immeasurable universe?

Then from *The Biography of a Superman* I select this very striking passage:—

Possessed of an intellect of great analytic and destructive force, he was almost entirely lacking in imagination, and he was there-fore unable to raise his work to a plane in which the mutually combative elements of his nature might have been reconciled. His light moments of envy, anger, and vanity passed into the crucible to come forth unchanged. He lacked the magic wand, and his work never took wings above his conception.

Now compare the two places; "the streets were more than a mere assemblage of houses;" . . . "his light moments . . . passed into the crucible to come forth unchanged. He lacked the magic wand." I think these two passages indicate the answer to the "why" that I am forced to resolve; show something of the secret of the strange charm which *The Ghost-Ship* possesses.

It delights because it is significant, because it is no mere assemblage of words and facts and observations and incidents, it delights because its matter has not passed through the crucible unchanged. On the contrary, the jumble of experiences and impressions which fell to the lot of the author as to us all had assuredly been placed in the athanor of art, in that furnace of the sages which is said to be governed with wisdom. Lead entered the burning of the fire, gold came forth from it.

This analogy of the process of alchemy which Richard Middleton has himself suggested is one of the finest and the fittest for our purpose; but there are many others. The "magic wand" analogy comes to much the same thing; there is the like notion of something ugly and insignificant changed to something beautiful and significant. Something ugly; shall we not say rather something formless transmuted into form! After all, the Latin Dictionary declares solemnly that "beauty" is one of the meanings of "forma"

And here we are away from alchemy and the magic wand ideas, and pass to the thought of the first place that I have quoted: "the streets were more than a mere assemblage of houses," The puzzle is solved; the jig-saw—I think they call it—has been successfully fitted together, There in a box lay all the jagged, irregular pieces, each in itself crazy and meaningless and irritating by its very lack of meaning: now we see each part adapted to the other and the whole is one picture and one purpose.

But the first thing necessary to this achievement is the recognition of the fact that there is a puzzle. There are many people who go through life persuaded that there isn't a puzzle at all; that it was only the infancy and rude childhood of the world which dreamed a vain dream of a picture to be made out of the jagged bits of wood, There never has been a picture, these persons say, and there never will be a picture, all we have to do is to take the bits out of the box, look at them, and put them back again. Or, returning to Richard Middleton's excellent example: there is no such thing as London, there are only houses. No man has seen London at any time; the very word (meaning "the fort on the lake") is nonsensical; no human eye has ever beheld aught else but a number of houses; it is clear that this "London" is as mythical and monstrous and irrational a concept as many others of the same class. Well, people who talk like that are doubtless sent into the world for some useful but mysterious process; but they can't write real books. Richard Middleton knew that there was a puzzle; in other words, that the universe is a great mystery; and this consciousness of his is the source of the charm of "The Ghost Ship."

I have compared this orthodox view of life and the universe and the fine art that results from this view to the solving of a puzzle; but the analogy is not an absolutely perfect one. For if you buy a jig-saw in a box in the Haymarket, you take it home with you and begin to put the pieces together, and sooner or later the toil is over and the difficulties are overcome: the picture is clear before you. Yes, the toil is over, but so is the fun; it is but poor sport to do the trick all over again. And here is the vast inferiority of the things they sell in the shops to the universe: our great puzzle is never perfectly solved.

We come across marvellous hints, we join line to line and our hearts beat with the rapture of a great surmise; we follow a certain track and know by sure signs and signals that we are not mistaken, that we are on the right road; we are furnished with certain charts which tell us "here there be water-pools," "here is a waste place," "here a high hill riseth," and we find as we journey that so it is. But, happily, by the very nature of the case, we can never put the whole of the picture together, we can never recover the perfect utterance of the Lost Word, we can never say "here is the end of all the journey." Man is so made that all his true delight arises from the contemplation of mystery, and save by his own frantic and invincible folly, mystery is never taken from him; it rises within his soul, a well of joy unending.

Hence it is that the consciousness of this mystery, resolved into the form of art, expresses itself usually (or always) by symbols, by the part put for the whole. Now and then, as in the case of Dante, as it was with the great romance-cycle of the Holy Graal, we have a sense of completeness. With the vision of the Angelic Rose and the sentence concerning that Love which moves the sun and the other stars there is the shadow of a catholic survey of all things; and so in a less degree it is as we read of the translation of Galahad. Still, the Rose and the Graal are but symbols of the eternal verities, not those verities themselves in their essences; and in these later days when we have become clever—with the cleverness of the Performing Pig—it is a great thing to find the most obscure and broken indications of the things which really are.

There is the true enchantment of true romance in the Don Quixote—for those who can understand—but it is delivered in the mode of parody and burlesque; and so it is with the extraordinary fantasy, *The Ghost-Ship"* which gives its name to this collection of tales. Take this story to bits, as it were; analyse it; you will be astonished at its frantic absurdity: the ghostly galleon blown in by a great tempest to a turnip-patch in Fairfield, a little village lying near the Portsmouth Road about half-way between London and the sea; the farmer grumbling at the loss of so many turnips; the captain of the weird vessel acknowledging the justice of the claim and tossing a great gold brooch to the landlord by way of satisfying the debt; the deplorable fact that all the decent village ghosts learned to riot with Captain Bartholomew Roberts; the visit of the parson and his godly admonitions to the Captain on the evil work he was doing; mere craziness, you will say?

Yes; but the strange thing is that as, in spite of all jocose tricks and low-comedy misadventures, Don Quixote departs from us with a great light shining upon him; so this ghost-ship of Richard Middleton's, somehow or other, sails and anchors and re-sails in an unearthly glow; and Captain Bartholomew's rum that was like hot oil and honey and fire in the veins of the mortals who drank of it, has become for me one of the *nobilium poculorum* of story. And thus did the ship put forth from the village and sail away in a great tempest of wind—to what unimaginable seas of the spirit!

The wind that had been howling outside like an outrageous dog had all of a sudden turned as melodious as the carol-boys of a Christmas Eve.

We went to the door, and the wind burst it open so that the handle was driven clean into the plaster of the wall. But we didn't think much of that at the time; for over our heads, sailing very comfortably through the windy stars, was the ship that had passed the summer in landlord's field. Her portholes and her bay-window were blazing with lights, and there was a noise of singing and fiddling on her decks. "He's gone," shouted landlord above the storm, "and he's taken half the village with him!" I could only nod in answer, not having lungs like bellows of leather.

I declare I would not exchange this short, crazy, enchanting fantasy for a whole wilderness of seemly novels, proclaiming in decorous accents the undoubted truth that there are milestones on the Portsmouth Road.

Arthur Machen.

The Story of a Book

The history of a book must necessarily begin with the history of its author, for surely in these enlightened days neither the youngest nor the oldest of critics can believe that works of art are found under gooseberry-bushes or in the nests of storks. In truth, I am by no means sure that everybody knew this before the publication of *The Man Shakespeare*, and for the sake of a mystified posterity it may be well to explain that there was once a school of criticism that thought it indecent to pry into that treasure-house of individuality from which, if we reject the nursery hypotheses mentioned above, it is clearly obvious that authors derive their works.

That the drama must needs be closely related to the dramatist is just one of those simple discoveries that invariably elude the subtle professional mind; but in this wiser hour I may be permitted to assume that the author was the conscious father of his novel, and that he did not find it surprisingly in his pocket one morning, like a bad shilling taken in change from the cabman overnight.

Before he published his novel at the ripe age of thirty-seven the author had lived an irreproachable and gentlemanly life. Born with at least a German-silver spoon in his mouth, he passed, after a normally eventful childhood, through a respectable public school, and spent several agreeable years at Cambridge without taking a degree. He then went into his uncle's office in the City, where he idled daily from ten to four, till in due course he was admitted to a partnership, which enabled him to reduce his hours of idleness to eleven to three.

These details become important when we reflect that from his childhood on the author had a great deal of time at his disposal. If he had been entirely normal, he would have accepted the conventions of the society to which he belonged, and devoted himself to motoring, bridge, and the encouragement of the lighter drama. But some deep-rooted habit of his childhood, or even perhaps some remote hereditary taint, led him to spend an appreciable fraction of his leisure time in the reading of works of fiction. Unlike most lovers of light literature, he read with a certain mental concentration, and was broad-minded enough to read good novels as well as bad ones.

It is a pleasant fact that it is impossible to concentrate one's mind on anything without in time becoming wiser, and in the course of years the author became quite a skilful critic of novels. From the first he had allowed his reading to colour his impressions of life, and had obediently lived in a world of blacks and whites, of heroes and heroines, of villains and adventuresses, until the grateful discovery of the realistic school of fiction permitted him to believe that men and women were for the most part neither good nor bad, but tabby. Moreover, the leisurely reading of many sentences had given him some understanding of the elements of style.

He perceived that some combinations of words were illogical, and that others were unlovely to the ear; and at the same time, he acquired a vocabulary and a knowledge of grammar and punctuation that his earlier education had failed to give him. He read new novels at his writing-table, and took pleasure in correcting the mistakes of their authors in ink. When he had done this, he would hand them to his wife, who always read the end first, and, indeed, rarely pursued her investigation of a book beyond the last chapter.

We buy knowledge with illusions, and pay a high price for it, for the acquirement of quite a small degree of wisdom will deprive us of a large number of pleasant fancies. So it was with the author, who found his joy in novel-reading diminishing rapidly as his critical knowledge increased. He was no longer able to lose himself between the covers of a romance, but slid his paper-knife between the pages of a book with an unwholesome readiness to be irritated by the ignorance and folly of the novelist. His destructive criticism of works of fiction became so acute that it was natural that his unlettered friends should suggest that he himself ought to write a novel. For a long while he was content to receive the flattering suggestion with a reticent smile that masked his conviction that there was a difference between criticism and creation. But as he grew older the imperfections in the books, he read ceased to give him the thrill of the successful explorer in sight of the expected, and time began to trickle too slowly through his idle fingers. One day he sat down and wrote "Chapter 1." at the head of a sheet of quarto paper.

It seemed to him that the difficulty was only one of selection, and he wrote two-thirds of a novel with a breathless ease of creation that made him marvel at himself and the pitiful struggles of less gifted novelists. Then in a moment of insight he picked up his manuscript and realised that what he had written was childishly crude. He had felt his story while he wrote it, but somehow or other he had failed to get his emotions on paper, and he saw quite clearly that it was worse and not better than the majority of the books which he had held up to ridicule.

There was a certain doggedness in his character that might have made him a useful citizen but for that unfortunate hereditary spoon, and he wrote "Chapter 1." at the head of a new sheet of quarto paper long before the library fire had reached the heart of his first luckless manuscript. This time he wrote more slowly, and with a waning confidence that failed him altogether when he was about half-way through. Reading the fragment dispassionately he thought there were good pages in it, but, taken as a whole, it was unequal, and moved forward only by fits and starts. He began again with his late manuscript spread about him on the table for reference. At the fifth attempt he succeeded in writing a whole novel.

In the course of his struggles, he had acquired a philosophy of composition. Especially he had learned to shun those enchanted hours when the labour of creation became suspiciously easy, for he had found by experience that the work he did in these moments of inspiration was either bad in itself or out of key with the preceding chapters. He thought that inspiration might be useful to poets or writers of short stories, but personally as a novelist he found it a nuisance. By dint of hard work, however, he succeeded in eliminating its evil influence from his final draft. He told himself that he had no illusions as to the merits of his book.

He knew he was not a man of genius, but he knew also that the grammar and the punctuation of his novel were far above the average of such works, and although he could not read Sir Thomas Browne or Walter Pater with pleasure, he felt sure that his book was written in a straightforward and gentlemanly style. He was prepared to be told that his use of the colon was audacious, and looked forward with pleasure to an agreeable controversy on the question.

He read his book to his friends, who made suggestions that would have involved its rewriting from one end to the other. He read it to his enemies, who told him that it was nearly good enough to publish;

he read it to his wife, who said that it was very nice, and that it was time to dress for dinner. No one seemed to realise that it was the most important thing he had ever done in his life. This quickened his eagerness to get it published—an eagerness only tempered by a very real fear of those knowing dogs, the critics. He could not forget that he had criticised a good many books himself in terms that would have made the authors abandon their profession if they had but heard his strictures; and he had read notices in the papers that would have made him droop with shame if they had referred to any work of his. When these sombre thoughts came to him, he would pick up his book and read it again, and in common fairness he had to admit to himself that he found it uncommonly good.

One day, after a whole batch of ungrammatical novels had reached him from the library, he posted his manuscript to his favourite publisher. He had heard stories of masterpieces many times rejected, so he did not tell his wife what he had done.

2. THE SLEEPY PUBLISHER

The publisher to whom our author had confided his manuscript stood, like all publishers, at the very head of his profession. His business was conducted on sound conservative lines, which means that though he had regretfully abandoned the three-volume novel for the novel published at six shillings, he was not among the intrepid revolutionaries who were beginning to produce new fiction at a still lower price. Besides novels he published solid works of biography at thirty-one and six, art books at a guinea, travel books at fifteen shillings, flighty historical works at twelve-and-sixpence, and cheap editions of *Montaigne's Essays* and *Robinson Crusoe* at a shilling. Some idea of his business methods may be derived from the fact that it pleased him to reflect that all the other publishers were producing exactly the same books as he was.

And though he would admit that the trade had been ruined by competition and the outrageous royalties demanded by successful authors, and, further, that he made a loss on every separate department of his business, in some mysterious fashion the business as a whole continued to pay him very well. He left the active part of the management to a confidential clerk, and contented himself with signing cheques and interviewing authors.

With such a publisher the fate of our author's book was never in doubt. If it was lacking in those qualities that might be expected to commend it to the reading public, it was conspicuously rich in those merits that determine the favourable judgment of publishers' readers. It was above all things a gentlemanly book, without violence and without eccentricities. It was carefully and grammatically written; but it had not that exotic literary flavour which is so tiresome on a long railway journey.

It could be put into the hands of any schoolgirl, and at most would merely send her to sleep. The only thing that could be said against it was that the author's dread of inspiration had made it grievously dull, but it was the publisher's opinion that after a glut of sensational fiction the six-shilling public had come to regard dullness as the hall-mark of literary merit. He had no illusions as to its possible success, but, on the other hand, he knew that he could not lose any money on it, so he wrote a letter to the author inviting him to an interview.

As soon as he had read the letter the author told himself that he had been certain all along that his book would be accepted. Nevertheless, he went to the interview moved by certain emotional flutterings against which circumstance had guarded him ever since his boyhood. He found this mild excitation of the nervous system by no means unpleasant. It was like digesting a new and subtle liqueur that made him light-footed and tingled in the tips of his fingers. He recalled a phrase that had greatly pleased him in the early days of his novel. "*As the sun colours flowers, so Art colours life.*" It seemed to him that this was beginning to come true, and that life was already presenting itself to him in a gayer, brighter dress.

He reached the publisher's office, therefore, in an unwontedly receptive mood, and was tremendously impressed by the rudeness of the clerks, who treated authors as mendicants and expressed their opinion of literature by handling books as if they were bundles of firewood.

The publisher looked at him under heavy eyelids, recognised his position in the social scale, and reflected with satisfaction that his acquaintances could be relied on to purchase at least a hundred copies. The interview did not at all take the lines that the author in his innocence had expected, and in a surprisingly short space of time he found himself bowed out, with the duplicate of a contract in the pocket of his overcoat. In the outer office the confidential clerk took him in hand and led him to the door of an enormous cellar, lit by electricity and filled from one end to the other with bales and heaps of books.

"Books!" said the confidential clerk, with the smile of a game-keeper displaying his hand-reared pheasants.

17

"There are a great many," the author said timidly.

"Of course, we do not keep our stock here," the clerk explained. "These are just samples." It was sometimes necessary to remind inexperienced writers that the publication of their first book was only a trivial incident in the history of a great publishing house. The author had a sad vision of his novel as a little brick in a monstrous pyramid built of books, and the clerk mentally decided that he was not the kind of man to turn up every day at the office to ask them how they were getting on.

The author was a little dazed when he emerged into the street and the sunshine. His book, which an hour before had seemed the most important thing in the world, had, become almost insignificant in the light of that vast collection of printed matter, and in some subtle way he felt that he had dwindled with it. The publisher had praised it without enthusiasm and had not specified any of its merits; he had not even commented on his fantastic use of the colon. The author had lived with it now for many months—it had become a part of his personality, and he felt that he had betrayed himself in delivering it into the hands of strangers who could not understand it.

He had the reticence of the well-bred Englishman, and though he told himself reassuringly that his novel in no way reflected his private life, he could not quite overcome the sentiment that it was a little vulgar to allow alien eyes to read the product of his most intimate thoughts. He had really been shocked at the matter-of-fact way in which everyone at the office had spoken of his book, and the sight of all the other books with which it would soon be inextricably confused had emphasised the painful impression. This all seemed to rob the author's calling of its presumed distinction, and he looked at the men and women who passed him on the pavement, and wondered whether they too had written books.

This mood lasted for some weeks, at the end of which time he received the proofs, which he read and re-read with real pleasure before setting himself to correcting them with meticulous care. He performed this task with such conscientiousness, and made so many minor alterations—he changed most of those flighty colons to more conventional semicolons—that the confidential clerk swore terribly when he glanced at the proofs before handing them to a boy, with instructions to remove three-quarters of the offending emendations.

A week or two later there happened one of those strange little incidents that make modern literary history. It was a bright, sunny afternoon; the publisher had been lunching with the star author of the firm, a novelist whose books were read wherever the British flag waved and there was a circulating library to distribute them, and now, in the warm twilight of the lowered blinds he was enjoying profound thoughts, delicately tinted by burgundy and old port. The shrewdest men make mistakes, and certainly it was hardly wise of the confidential clerk to choose this peaceful moment to speak about our author's book.

"I suppose we shall print a thousand?" he said.

"Five thousand!" ejaculated the publisher. What was he thinking about? Was he filling up an imaginary income-tax statement, or was he trying to estimate the number of butterflies that seemed to float in the amber shadows of the room?

The clerk did not know. "I suppose you mean one thousand, sir?" he said gently.

The publisher was now wide awake. He had lost all his butterflies, and he was not the man to allow himself to be sleepy in the afternoon. "I said five thousand!"

The clerk bit his lip and left the room.

The author never heard of this brief dialogue; probably if he had been present, he would have missed its significance. He would never have connected it with the flood of paragraphs that appeared in the Press announcing that the acumen of the publisher had discovered a new author of genius—paragraphs wherein he was compared with Dickens, Thackeray, Flaubert, Richardson, Sir Walter Besant, Thomas Browne, and the author of *An Englishwoman's Love-letters*. As it was, it did not occur to him to wonder why the publisher should spend so much money on advertising a book of which he had seemed to have but a half-hearted appreciation. After all it was his book, and the author felt that it was only natural that as the hour of publication drew near the world of letters should show signs of a dignified excitement.

3. THE CRITIC ERRANT

There are some emotions so intimate that the most intrepid writer hesitates to chronicle them lest it should be inferred that he himself is in the confessional. We have endeavoured to show our author as a level-headed English-man with his nerves well under control and an honest contempt for emotionalism in the stronger sex; but his feelings in the face of the first little bundle of reviews sent him by the press-cutting agency would prove this portrait incomplete. He noticed with a vague astonishment that the flimsy scraps of paper were trembling in

19

his fingers like banknotes in the hands of a gambler, and he laid them down on the breakfast-table in disgust of the feminine weakness. This unmistakable proof that he had written a book, a real book, made him at once happy and uneasy. These fragments of smudged prints were his passport into a new and delightful world; they were, it might be said, the name of his destination in the great republic of letters, and yet he hesitated to look at them.

He heard of the curious blindness of authors that made it impossible for them to detect the most egregious failings in their own work, and it occurred to him that this might be his malady. Why had he published his book? He felt at that moment that he had taken too great a risk. It would have been so easy to have had it privately printed and contented himself with distributing it among his friends. But these people were paid for writing about books, these critics who had sent Keats to his gallipots and Swinburne to his fig-tree, might well have failed to have recognised that his book was sacred, because it was his own.

When he had at last achieved a fatalistic tranquillity, he once more picked up the notices, and this time he read them through carefully. The *Rutlandshire Gazette* quoted Shakespeare, the *Thrums Times* compared him with Christopher North, the *Stamford-bridge Herald* thought that his style resembled that of Macaulay, but they were unanimous in praising his book without reservation. It seemed to the author that he was listening to the authentic voice of fame. He rested his chin on his hand and dreamed long dreams.

He could afford in this hour of his triumph to forget the annoyances he had undergone since his book was first accepted. The publisher, with a large first edition to dispose of, had been rather more than firm with the author. He had changed the title of the book from *Earth's Returns*—a title that had seemed to the author dignified and pleasantly literary—to *The Improbable Marquis*, which seemed to him to mean nothing at all. Moreover, instead of giving the book a quiet and scholarly exterior, he had bound it in boards of an injudicious heliotrope, inset with a nasty little coloured picture of a young woman with a St. Bernard dog.

This binding revolted the author, who objected, with some reason, that in all his book there was no mention of a dog of that description, or, indeed, of any dog at all. The book was wrapped in an outer cover that bore a recommendation of its contents, starting with a hideous split infinitive and describing it as an exquisite social comedy written from within. On the whole it seemed to the author that his book was flying false and undesirable colours, and since art lies outside the domesticities, he was hardly relieved when his wife told him that she thought the binding was very pretty.

The author had shuddered no less at the little paragraphs that the publisher had inserted in the newspapers concerning his birth and education, wherein he was bracketed with other well-known writers whose careers at the University had been equally undistinguished. But now that, like Byron, he found himself famous among the bacon and eggs, he was in no mood to remember these past vexations. As soon as he had finished breakfast, he withdrew himself to his study and wrote half an essay on the Republic of Letters.

In a country wherein fifteen novels—or is it fifty?—are published every day of the year, the publisher's account of the goods he sells is bound to have a certain value. Money talks, as Mr. Arnold Bennett once observed—indeed today it is grown quite garrulous—and when a publisher spends a lot of money on advertising a book, the inference is that some one believes the book to be good. This will not secure a book good notices, but it will secure it notices of some kind or other, and that, as every publisher knows, is three-quarters of the battle.

The average critic today is an old young man who has not failed in literature or art, possibly because he has not tried to accomplish anything in either. By the time he has acquired some skill in criticism he has generally ceased to be a critic, through no fault of his own, but through sheer weariness of spirit. When a man is very young, he can dance upon everyone who has not written a masterpiece with a light heart, but after this period of joyous savagery there follows fatigue and a certain pity. The critic loses sight of his first magnificent standards, and becomes grateful for even the smallest merit in the books he is compelled to read. Like a mother giving a powder to her child, he is at pains to disguise his timid censure with a teaspoonful of jam.

As the years pass by, he becomes afraid of these books that continue to appear in unreasonable profusion, and that have long ago destroyed his faith in literature, his love of reading, his sense of humour, and the colouring matter of his hair. He realises, with a dreadful sense of the infinite, that when he is dead and buried this torrent of books will overwhelm the individualities of his successors, bound like himself to a lifelong examination of the insignificant.

Timidity is certainly the note of modern criticism, which is rarely roused to indignation save when confronted by the infrequent out-rage of some intellectual anarchist. If the critics of the more important journals were not so enthusiastic as their provincial *confreres*, they were at least gentle with *The Improbable Marquis*. A critic of genius would have said that such books were not worth writing, still less worth reading. An outspoken critic would have said that it was too dull to be an acceptable presentation of a life that we all find interesting. As it was, most of the critics praised the style in which it was written because it was quite impossible to call it an enthralling or even an entertaining book.

Some of the younger critics, who still retained an interest in their own personalities, discovered that its vacuity made it a convenient mirror by means of which they would display the progress of their own genius. In common gratitude they had to close these manifestations of their merit with a word or two in praise of the book they were professing to review. *The Improbable Marquis* was very favourably received by the Press in general.

It was, as the publisher made haste to point out in his advertisements, a book of the year, and, reassured by its flippant exterior, the libraries and the public bought it with avidity. The author pasted his swollen collection of newspaper-cuttings into an album, and carefully revised his novel in case a second edition should be called for. There was one review which he had read more often than any of the others, and nevertheless he hesitated to include it in his collection.

"This book," wrote the anonymous reviewer, "is as nearly faultless a book may be that possesses no positive merit. It differs only from seven-eighths of the novels that are produced today in being more carefully written. The author had nothing to say, and he has said it."

That was all, three malignant lines in a paper of no commercial importance, the sort of thing that was passed round the publisher's office with an appreciative chuckle. In the face of the general amiability of the Press, such a notice in an obscure journal could do the book no harm.

Only the author sat hour after hour in his study with that diminutive scrap of paper before him on the table, and wondered if it was true.

4. FAME

It was some little time before the public, the mysterious section of the public that reads works of fiction, discovered that the publisher, aided by the normal good-humour of the critics, had persuaded them to sacrifice some of their scant hours of intellectual recreation on a work of portentous dullness. Therefor the literary audience has its sense of humour—they amused themselves for a while by recommending the book to their friends, and the sales crept steadily up to four thousand, and there stayed with an unmistakable air of finality. If the book had had any real literary merit its life would have started at that point, for the weary comments of reviewers and the strident outcries of publishers tend to obscure rather than reveal the permanent value of a book.

But six months after publication *The Improbable Marquis* was completely forgotten, save by the second-hand booksellers, who found themselves embarrassed with a number of books for which no one seemed anxious to pay six-pence, in spite of the striking heliotrope binding. The publisher, who was aware of this circumstance, offered the author five hundred copies at cost price, and the author bought them, and sent them to public libraries, without examining the motive for his action too closely. There were moments when he regarded the success of his book with suspicion. He would have preferred the praise that had greeted it to have been less violent and more clearly defined.

Of all the criticisms, the only one that lingered in his mind was the curt comment, "The author had nothing to say, and he has said it." He thought it was unfair, but he had remembered it. At the same time, in examining his own character, he could not find that masterfulness that seemed to him necessary in a great man. But for the most part he was content to accept his new honours with a placid satisfaction, and to smile genially upon a world that was eager to credit him with qualities that possibly he did not possess. For if his book was no longer read his fame as an author seemed to be established on a rock. Society, with a larger S than that which he had hitherto adorned, was delighted to find after two notable failures that genius could still be presentable, and the author was rather more than that.

He was rich, he had that air of the distinguished army officer which falls so easily to those who occupy the pleasant position of sleeping partner in the City, and he had just the right shade of amused modesty with which to meet inquiries as to his literary intentions. In a word, he was an author of whom any country—even France, that prolific parent of presentable authors—would have been proud. Even his wife, who had thought it an excellent joke that her husband should have written a book, had to take him seriously as an author when she found that their social position was steadily improving. With feminine tact she gave him a fountain-pen on his birthday, from which he was meant to conclude that she believed in his mission as an artist.

Meanwhile, with the world at his feet, the author spent an appreciable part of his time in visiting the second-hand bookshops and buying copies of his book absurdly cheap. He carried these waifs home and stored them in an attic secretly, for he would have found it hard to explain his motives to the intellectually childless. In the first flush of authorship he had sent a number of presentation copies of his book to writers whom he admired, and he noticed without bitterness that some of these volumes with their neatly turned inscriptions were coming back to him through this channel.

At all the second-hand bookshops he saw long-haired young men looking over the books without buying them, and he thought these must be authors, but he was too shy to speak to them, though he had a great longing to know other writers. He wanted to ask them questions concerning their methods of work, for he was having trouble with his second book. He had read an article in which the writer said that the great fault of modern fiction was that authors were more concerned to produce good chapters than to produce good books. It seemed to him that in his first book he had only aimed at good sentences, but he knew no one with whom he could discuss such matters.

One day he found a copy of *The Improbable Marquis* in the Charing Cross Road, and was glancing through it with absent-minded interest, when a voice at his elbow said, "I shouldn't buy that if I were you, sir. It's no good!"

He looked up and saw a wild young man, with bright eyes and an untidy black beard. "But it's mine; I wrote it," cried the author.

The young man stared at him in dismay. "I'm sorry; I didn't know," he blurted out, and faded away into the crowd. The author gazed after him wistfully, regretting that he had not had presence of mind enough to ask him to lunch. Perhaps the young man could have told him how he ought to write his second book.

For somehow or other, at the very moment when his literary position seemed most secure in the eyes of his wife and his friends, the author had lost all confidence in his own powers. He shut himself up in his study every night, and was supposed by an admiring and almost timorous household to be producing masterpieces, when in reality he was conducting a series of barren skirmishes between the critical and the creative elements of his nature. He would write a chapter or two in a fine fury of composition, and then would read what he had written with intense disgust.

He felt that his second book ought to be better than his first, and he doubted whether he would even be able to write anything half so good. In his hour of disillusionment, he recalled the anonymous critic who had treated *The Improbable Marquis* with such scant respect, and he wrote to him asking him to expand his judgment. He was prepared to be wounded by the answer, but the form it took surprised him. In reply to his temperate and courteous letter the critic sent a postcard bearing only five short words—"Why did you write it?"

This was bad manners, but the author was sensible enough to see that it might be good criticism, especially as he found some difficulty in answering the question. Why had he written a book? Not for money, or for fame, or to express a personality of which he saw no reason to be proud. All his friends had said that he ought to write a novel, and he had thought that he could write a better one than the average. But he had to admit that such motives seemed to him insufficient. There was, perhaps, some mysterious force that drove men to create works of art, and the critic had seen that his book had lacked this necessary impulse. In the light of this new theory the author was roused by a sense of injustice. He felt that it should be possible for anyone to write a good book if they took sufficient pains, and he set himself to work again with a savage and unproductive energy.

It seemed to him that in spite of his effort to bear in mind that the whole should be greater than any part, his chapters broke up into sentences and his sentences into forlorn and ungregarious words. When he looked to his first book for comfort, he found the same horrid phenomenon taking place in its familiar pages. Sometimes when he was disheartened by his fruitless efforts he slipped out into the streets, fixing his attention on concrete objects to rest his tired mind. But he could not help noticing that London had discovered the secret which made his intellectual life a torment.

The streets were more than a mere assemblage of houses, London herself was more than a tangled skein of streets, and overhead heaven was more than a meeting-place of individual stars. What was this secret that made words into a book, houses into cities, and restless and measurable stars into an unchanging and immeasurable universe?

The Biography of a Superman

"O limèd soul that struggling to be free
Art more engaged!"

Charlies Stephen Dale, the subject of my study, was a dramatist and, indeed, something of a celebrity in the early years of the twentieth century. That he should be already completely forgotten is by no means astonishing in an age that elects its great men with a charming indecision of touch. The general prejudice against the granting of freeholds has spread to the desired lands of fame; and where our profligate ancestors were willing to call a man great in perpetuity, we, with more shrewdness, prefer to name him a genius for seven years.

We know that before that period may have expired fate will have granted us a sea-serpent with yet more coils, with a yet more bewildering arrangement of marine and sunset tints, and the conclusion of previous leases will enable us to grant him undisputed possession of Parnassus. If our ancestors were more generous, they were certainly less discriminate; and it cannot be doubted that many of them went to their graves under the impression that it is possible for there to be more than one great man at a time! We have altered all that.

For two years Dale was a great man, or rather the great man, and it is probable that if he had not died, he would have held his position for a longer period. When his death was announced, although the notices of his life and work were of a flattering length, the leader-writers were not unnaturally aggrieved that he should have resigned his post before the popular interest in his personality was exhausted.

The Censor might do his best by prohibiting the performance of all the plays that the dead man had left behind him; but, as the author neglected to express his views in their columns, and the common-sense of their readers forbade the publication of interviews with him, the journals could draw but a poor satisfaction from condemning or upholding the official action. Dale's regrettable absence reduced what might have been an agreeable dash of personalities to an arid discussion on art. The consequence was obvious. The end of the week saw the elevation of James Macintosh, the great Scotch comedian, to the vacant post, and Dale was completely forgotten.

That this oblivion is merited in terms of his work I am not prepared to admit; that it is merited in terms of his personality I indignantly wish to deny. Whatever Dale may have been as an artist, he was, perhaps in spite of himself, a man, and a man moreover, possessed of many striking and unusual traits of character. It is to the man Dale that I offer this tribute.

Sprung from an old Yorkshire family, Charles Stephen Dale was yet sufficient of a Cockney to justify both his friends and his enemies in crediting him with the Celtic temperament. Nevertheless, he was essentially a modern, insomuch that his contempt for the writings of dead men surpassed his dislike of living authors. To these two central influences we may trace most of the peculiarities that rendered him notorious and ultimately great. Thus, while his Celtic aestheticism permitted him to eat nothing but raw meat, because he mistrusted alike "the reeking products of the manure-heap and the barbaric fingers of cooks," It was surely his modernity that made him an agnostic, because bishops sat in the House of Lords. Smaller men might dislike vegetables and bishops without allowing it to affect their conduct; but Dale was careful to observe that every slightest conviction should have its place in the formation of his character. Conversely, he was nothing without a reason.

These may seem small things to which to trace the motive forces of a man's life; but if we add to them a third, found where the truth about a man not infrequently lies, in the rag-bag of his enemies, our materials will be nearly complete. "Dale hates his fellow-human-beings," wrote some anonymous scribbler, and, even expressed thus baldly, the statement is not wholly false. But he hated them because of their imperfections, and it would be truer to say that his love of humanity amounted to a positive hatred of individuals, and, *pace* the critics, the love was no less sincere than the hatred.

He had drawn from the mental confusion of the darker German philosophers an image of the perfect man—an image differing only in inessentials from the idol worshipped by the Imperialists as "efficiency." He did not find—it was hardly likely that he would find—that his contemporaries fulfilled this perfect conception, and he therefore felt it necessary to condemn them for the possession of those weaknesses, or as some would prefer to say qualities, of which the sum is human nature.

I now approach a quality, or rather the lack of a quality, that is in itself of so debatable a character, that were it not of the utmost importance in considering the life of Charles Stephen Dale I should prefer not to mention it. I refer to his complete lack of a sense of humour, the consciousness of which deficiency went so far to detract from his importance as an artist and a man. The difficulty which I mentioned above lies in the fact that, while everyone has a clear conception of what they mean by the phrase, no one has yet succeeded in defining it satisfactorily.

Here I would venture to suggest that it is a kind of magnificent sense of proportion, a sense that relates the infinite greatness of the universe to the finite smallness of man, and draws the inevitable conclusion as to the importance of our joys and sorrows and labours. I am aware that this definition errs on the side of vagueness; but possibly it may be found to include the truth. Obviously, the natures of those who possess this sense will tend to be static rather than dynamic, and it is therefore against the limits imposed by this sense that intellectual anarchists, among whom I would number Dale, and poets primarily rebel. But—and it is this rather than his undoubted intellectual gifts or his dogmatic definitions of good and evil that definitely separated Dale from the normal men—there can be no doubt that he felt his lack of a sense of humour bitterly.

In every word he ever said, in every line he ever wrote, I detect a painful striving after this mysterious sense, that enabled his neighbours, fools as he undoubtedly thought them, to laugh and weep and follow the faith of their hearts without conscious realisation of their own existence and the problems it induced. By dint of study and strenuous observation he achieved, as any man may achieve, a considerable degree of wit, though to the last his ignorance of the audience whom he served and despised, prevented him from judging the effect of his sallies without experiment. But try as he might the finer jewel lay for beyond his reach. Strong men fight themselves when they can find no fitter adversary; but in all the history of literature there is no stranger spectacle than this lifelong contact between Dale, the intellectual anarch and pioneer of supermen, and Dale, the poor lonely devil who wondered what made people happy.

I have said that the struggle was lifelong, but it must be added that it was always unequal. The knowledge that in his secret heart he desired this quality, the imperfection of imperfections, only served to make Dale's attack on the complacency of his contemporaries more bitter. He ridiculed their achievements, their ambitions, and their love with a fury that awakened in them a mild curiosity, but by no means affected their comfort. Moreover, the very vehemence with which he demanded their contempt deprived him of much of his force as a critic, for they justly wondered why a man should waste his lifetime in attacking them if they were indeed so worthless.

Actually, they felt, Dale was a great deal more engaged with his audience than many of the imaginative writers whom he affected to despise for their sycophancy. And, especially towards the end of his life when his powers perhaps were weakening, the devices which he used to arouse the irritation of his contemporaries became more and more childishly artificial, less and less effective. He was like one of those actors who felt that they cannot hold the attention of their audience unless they are always doing something, though nothing is more monotonous than mannered vivacity.

Dale, then, was a man who was very anxious to be modern, but at the same time had not wholly succeeded in conquering his aesthetic sense. He had constituted himself high priest of the most puritanical and remote of all creeds, yet there was that in his blood that rebelled ceaselessly against the intellectual limits he had voluntarily accepted. The result in terms of art was chaos. Possessed of an intellect of great analytic and destructive force, he was almost entirely lacking in imagination, and he was therefore unable to raise his work to a plane in which the mutually combative elements of his nature might have been reconciled. His light moments of envy, anger, and vanity passed into the crucible to come forth unchanged. He lacked the magic wand, and his work never took wings above his conception.

It is in vain to seek in any of his plays or novels, tracts or prefaces, for the product of inspiration, the divine gift that enables one man to write with the common pen of humanity. He could only employ his curiously perfect technique in reproducing the wayward flashes of a mind incapable of consecutive thought. He never attempted—and this is a hard saying—to produce any work beautiful in itself; while the confusion of his mind, and the vanity that never allowed him to ignore the effect his work might produce on his audience, prevented him from giving clear expression to his creed. His work will appeal rather to the student of men than to the student of art, and, wantonly incoherent though it often is, must be held to constitute a remarkable human document.

It is strange to reflect that among his contemporary admirers Dale was credited with an intellect of unusual clarity, for the examination of any of his plays impresses one with the number and mutual destructiveness of his motives for artistic expression. A noted debater, he made frequent use of the device of attacking the weakness of the other man's speech, rather than the weakness of the other man's argument. His prose was good, though at its best so impersonal that it recalled the manner of an exceptionally well-written leading article. At its worst it was marred by numerous vulgarities and errors of taste, not always, it is to be feared, intentional.

His attitude on this point was typical of his strange blindness to the necessity of a pure artistic ideal. He committed these extravagances, he would say, in order to irritate his audience into a condition of mental alertness. As a matter of fact, he generally made his readers more sorry than angry, and he did not realise that even if he had been successful, it was but a poor reward for the wanton spoiling of much good work. He proclaimed himself to be above criticism, but he was only too often beneath it. Revolting against the dignity, not infrequently pompous, of his fellowmen of letters, he played the part of down with more enthusiasm than skill. It is intellectual arrogance in a clever man to believe that he can play the fool with success merely because he wishes it

There is no need for me to enter into detail with regard to Dale's personal appearance; the caricaturists did him rather more than justice, the photographers rather less. In his younger days he suggested a gingerbread man that had been left too long in the sun; towards the end he affected a cultured and elaborate ruggedness that made him look like a duke or a market gardener. Like most clever men, he had good eyes.

Nor is it my purpose to add more than a word to the published accounts of his death. There is something strangely pitiful in that last desperate effort to achieve humour. We have all read the account of his own death that he dictated from the sick-bed—cold, epigrammatic, and, alas! characteristically lacking in taste. And once more it was his fate to make us rather sorry than angry.

In the third scene of the second act of *Henry V.*, a play written by an author whom Dale pretended to despise, Dame Quickly describes the death of Falstaff in words that are too well known to need quotation. It was thus and no otherwise that Dale died. It is thus that every man dies.

The Ghost-Ship

Fairfield is a little village lying near the Portsmouth Road about half-way between London and the sea. Strangers who find it by accident now and then, call it a pretty, old-fashioned place; we who live in it and call it home don't find anything very pretty about it, but we should be sorry to live anywhere else. Our minds have taken the shape of the inn and the church and the green, I suppose. At all events we never feel comfortable out of Fairfield,

Of course, the Cockneys, with their vast houses and noise-ridden streets, can call us rustics if they choose, but for all that Fairfield is a better place to live in than London. Doctor says that when he goes to London his mind is bruised with the weight of the houses, and he was a Cockney born. He had to live there himself when he was a little chap, but he knows better now. You gentlemen may laugh—perhaps some of you come from London way—but it seems to me that a witness like that is worth a gallon of arguments.

Dull? Well, you might find it dull, but I assure you that I've listened to all the London yarns you have spun tonight, and they're absolutely nothing to the things that happen at Fairfield. It's because of our way of thinking and minding our own business. If one of your Londoners were set down on the green of a Saturday night when the ghosts of the lads who died in the war keep tryst with the lasses who lie in the churchyard, he couldn't help being curious and interfering, and then the ghosts would go somewhere where it was quieter.

But we just let them come and go and don't make any fuss, and in consequence Fairfield is the ghostiest place in all England. Why, I've seen a headless man sitting on the edge of the well in broad daylight, and the children playing about his feet as if he were their father. Take my word for it, spirits know when they are well off as much as human beings.

Still, I must admit that the thing I'm going to tell you about was queer even for our part of the world, where three packs of ghost-hounds hunt regularly during the season, and blacksmith's great-grandfather is busy all night shoeing the dead gentlemen's horses. Now that's a thing that wouldn't happen in London, because of their interfering ways, but blacksmith he lies up aloft and sleeps as quiet as a lamb. Once when he had a bad head, he shouted down to them not to make so much noise, and in the morning, he found an old guinea left on the anvil as an apology. He wears it on his watchchain now. But I must get on with my story; if I start telling you about the queer happenings at Fairfield I'll never stop.

It all came of the great storm in the spring of '97, the year that we had two great storms. This was the first one, and I remember it very well, because I found in the morning that it had lifted the thatch of my pigsty into the widow's garden as clean as a boy's kite. When I looked over the hedge, widow—Tom Lamport's widow that was—was prodding for her nasturtiums with a daisy-grubber. After I had watched her for a little, I went down to the "Fox and Grapes" to tell landlord what she had said to me. Landlord he laughed, being a married man and at ease with the sex. "Come to that," he said, "the tempest has blowed something into my field. A kind of a ship I think it would be."

I was surprised at that until he explained that it was only a ghost-ship and would do no hurt to the turnips. We argued that it had been blown up from the sea at Portsmouth, and then we talked of something else. There were two slates down at the parsonage and a big tree in Lumley's meadow. It was a rare storm.

I reckon the wind had blown our ghosts all over England. They were coming back for days afterwards with foundered horses and as footsore as possible, and they were so glad to get back to Fairfield that some of them walked up the street crying like little children. Squire said that his great-grandfather's great-grandfather hadn't looked so dead-beat since the Battle of Naseby, and he's an educated man.

What with one thing and another, I should think it was a week before we got straight again, and then one afternoon I met the land-lord on the green and he had a worried face. "I wish you'd come and have a look at that ship in my field," he said to me; "it seems to me it's leaning real hard on the turnips. I can't bear thinking what the missus will say when she sees it"

I walked down the lane with him, and sure enough there was a ship in the middle of his field, but such a ship as no man had seen on the water for three hundred years, let alone in the middle of a turnip-field. It was all painted black and covered with carvings, and there was a great bay window in the stern for all the world like the squire's drawing-room. There was a crowd of little black cannon on deck and looking out of her port-holes, and she was anchored at each end to the hard ground. I have seen the wonders of the world on picture-postcards, but I have never seen anything to equal that.

"She seems very solid for a ghost-ship," I said, seeing the landlord was bothered. "I should say it's a betwixt and between," he answered, puzzling it over, "but it's going to spoil a matter of fifty turnips, and missus she'll want it moved." We went up to her and touched the side, and it was as hard as a real ship. "Now there's folks in England would call that very curious," he said.

Now I don't know much about ships, but I should think that that ghost-ship weighed a solid two hundred tons, and it seemed to me that she had come to stay, so that I felt sorry for landlord, who was a married man. "All the horses in Fairfield won't move her out of my turnips," he said, frowning at her.

Just then we heard a noise on her deck, and we looked up and saw that a man had come out of her front cabin and was looking down at us very peaceably. He was dressed in a black uniform set out with rusty gold lace, and he had a great cutlass by his side in a brass sheath. "I'm Captain Bartholomew Roberts," he said, in a gentleman's voice, "put in for recruits. I seem to have brought her rather far up the harbour."

"Harbour!" cried landlord; "why, you're fifty miles from the sea."

Captain Roberts didn't turn a hair. "So much as that, is it?" he said coolly. "Well, it's of no consequence."

Landlord was a bit upset at this. "I don't want to be unneighbourly," he said, "but I wish you hadn't brought your ship into my field. You see, my wife sets great store on these turnips."

The captain took a pinch of snuff out of a fine gold box that he pulled out of his pocket, and dusted his fingers with a silk handkerchief in a very genteel fashion. "I'm only here for a few months," he said; "but if a testimony of my esteem would pacify your good lady, I should be content," and with the words he loosed a great gold brooch from the neck of his coat and tossed it down to landlord.

Landlord blushed as red as a strawberry. "I'm not denying she's fond of jewellery," he said, "but it's too much for half a sackful of turnips." And indeed, it was a handsome brooch.

The captain laughed. "Tut, man," he said, "it's a forced sale, and you deserve a good price. Say no more about it;" and nodding good-day to us, he turned on his heel and went into the cabin. Landlord walked back up the lane like a man with a weight off his mind. "That tempest has blowed me a bit of luck," he said; "the missus will be main pleased with that brooch. It's better than blacksmith's guinea, any day."

Ninety-seven was Jubilee year, the year of the second Jubilee, you remember, and we had great doings at Fairfield, so that we hadn't much time to bother about the ghost-ship, though anyhow it isn't our way to meddle in things that don't concern us. Landlord, he saw his tenant once or twice when he was hoeing his turnips and passed the time of day, and landlord's wife wore her new brooch to church every Sunday. But we didn't mix much with the ghosts at any time, all except an idiot lad there was in the village, and he didn't know the difference between a man and a ghost, poor innocent!

On Jubilee Day, however, somebody told Captain Roberts why the church bells were ringing, and he hoisted a flag and fired off his guns like a loyal Englishman. 'Tis true the guns were shotted, and one of the round shot knocked a hole in Farmer Johnstone's barn, but nobody thought much of that in such a season of rejoicing.

It wasn't till our celebrations were over that we noticed that anything was wrong in Fairfield. 'Twas shoemaker who told me first about it one morning at the "Fox and Grapes."

"You know my great great-uncle?" he said to me.

"You mean Joshua, the quiet lad," I answered, knowing him well.

"Quiet!" said shoemaker indignantly. "Quiet you call him, coming home at three o'clock every morning as drunk as a magistrate and waking up the whole house with his noise."

"Why, it can't be Joshua!" I said, for I knew him for one of the most respectable young ghosts in the village.

"Joshua it is," said shoemaker; "and one of these nights he'll find himself out in the street if he isn't careful."

This kind of talk shocked me, I can tell you, for I don't like to hear a man abusing. his own family, and I could hardly believe that a steady youngster like Joshua had taken to drink. But just then in came butcher Aylwin in such a temper that he could hardly drink his beer. "The young puppy! the young puppy!" he kept on saying; and it was some time before shoemaker and I found out that he was talking about his ancestor that fell at Senlac.

"Drink?" said shoemaker hopefully, for we all like company in our misfortunes, and butcher nodded grimly.

"The young noodle," he said, emptying his tankard.

Well, after that I kept my ears open, and it was the same story all over the village. There was hardly a young man among all the ghosts of Fairfield who didn't roll home in the small hours of the morning the worse for liquor. I used to wake up in the night and hear them stumble past my house, singing outrageous songs. The worst of it was that we couldn't keep the scandal to ourselves, and the folk at Green-hill began to talk of "sodden Fairfield" and taught their children to sing a song about us:

"*Sodden Fairfield, sodden Fairfield, has no use for bread-and-butter,*
Rum for breakfast, rum for dinner, rum for tea, and rum for supper!"

We are easy-going in our village, but we didn't like that.

Of course, we soon found out where the young fellows went to get the drink, and landlord was terribly cut up that his tenant should have turned out so badly, but his wife wouldn't hear of parting with the brooch, so that he couldn't give the captain notice to quit. But as time went on, things grew from bad to worse, and at all hours of the day you would see those young reprobates sleeping it off on the village green. Nearly every afternoon a ghost-wagon used to jolt down to the ship with a lading of rum, and though the older ghosts seemed inclined to give the captain's hospitality the go-by, the youngsters were neither to hold nor to bind.

So, one afternoon when I was taking my nap I heard a knock at the door, and there was parson looking very serious, like a man with a job before him that he didn't altogether relish. "I'm going down to talk to the captain about all this drunkenness in the village, and I want you to come with me," he said straight out.

I can't say that I fancied the visit much myself and I tried to hint to parson that as, after all, they were only a lot of ghosts, it didn't very much matter.

"Dead or alive, I'm responsible for their good conduct," he said, "and I'm going to do my duty and put a stop to this continued disorder. And you are coming with me, John Simmons." So I went, parson being a persuasive kind of man.

We went down to the ship, and as we approached her, I could see the captain tasting the air on deck. When he saw parson, he took off his hat very politely, and I can tell you that I was relieved to find that he had a proper respect for the cloth. Parson acknowledged his salute and spoke out stoutly enough. "Sir, I should be glad to have a word with you."

"Come on board, sir; come on board," said the captain, and I could tell by his voice that he knew why we were there. Parson and I climbed up an uneasy kind of ladder, and the captain took us into the great cabin at the back of the ship, where the bay-window was. It was the most wonderful place you ever saw in your life, all full of gold and silver plate, swords with jewelled scabbards, carved oak chairs, and great chests that look as though they were bursting with guineas. Even parson was surprised, and he did not shake his head very hard when the captain took down some silver cups and poured us out a drink of rum. I tasted mine, and I don't mind saying that it changed my view of things entirely. There was nothing betwixt and between about that rum, and I felt that it was ridiculous to blame the lads for drinking too much of stuff like that. It seemed to fill my veins with honey and fire.

Parson put the case squarely to the captain, but I didn't listen much to what he said; I was busy sipping my drink and looking through the window at the fishes swimming to and fro over landlord's turnips. Just then it seemed the most natural thing in the world that they should be there, though afterwards, of course, I could see that that proved it was a ghost-ship.

But even then, I thought it was queer when I saw a drowned sailor float by in the thin air with his hair and beard all full of bubbles. It was the first time I had seen anything quite like that at Fairfield.

All the time I was regarding the wonders of the deep parson was telling Captain Roberts how there was no peace or rest in the village owing to the curse of drunkenness, and what a bad example the youngsters were setting to the older ghosts. The captain listened very attentively, and only put in a word now and then about boys being boys and young men sowing their wild oats. But when parson had finished his speech, he filled up our silver cups and said to parson, with a flourish, "I should be sorry to cause trouble anywhere where I have been made welcome, and you will be glad to hear that I put to sea tomorrow night. And now you must drink me a prosperous voyage." So, we all stood up and drank the toast with honour, and that noble rum was like hot oil in my veins.

After that Captain showed us some of the curiosities he had brought back from foreign parts, and we were greatly amazed, though afterwards I couldn't clearly remember what they were. And then I found myself walking across the turnips with parson, and I was telling him of the glories of the deep that I had seen through the window of the ship. He turned on me severely. "If I, were you, John Simmons," he said, "I should go straight home to bed." He has a way of putting things that wouldn't occur to an ordinary man, has parson, and I did as he told me.

Well, next day it came on to blow, and it blew harder and harder, till about eight o'clock at night I heard a noise and looked out into the garden. I dare say you won't believe me, it seems a bit tall even to me, but the wind had lifted the thatch of my pigsty into the widow's garden a second time. I thought I wouldn't wait to hear what widow had to say about it, so I went across the green to the "Fox and Grapes," and the wind was so strong that I danced along on tiptoe like a girl at the fair. When I got to the inn landlord had to help me shut the door; it seemed as though a dozen goats were pushing against it to come in out of the storm.

"It's a powerful tempest," he said, drawing the beer. "I hear there's a chimney down at Dickory End."

"It's a funny thing how these sailors know about the weather," I answered. "When Captain said he was going tonight, I was thinking it would take a capful of wind to carry the ship back to sea, but now here's more than a capful."

"Ah, yes," said landlord, "it's tonight he goes true enough, and, mind you, though he treated me handsome over the rent, I'm not sure it's a loss to the village. I don't hold with gentrice who fetch their drink from London instead of helping local traders to get their living."

"But you haven't got any rum like his," I said, to draw him out.

His neck grew red above his collar, and I was afraid I'd gone too far; but after a while he got his breath with a grunt.

"John Simmons," he said, "if you've come down here this windy night to talk a lot of fool's talk, you've wasted a journey."

Well, of course, then I had to smooth him down with praising his rum, and Heaven forgive me for swearing it was better than captain's. For the like of that rum no living lips have tasted save mine and parson's. But somehow or other I brought landlord round, and presently we must have a glass of his best to prove its quality.

"Beat that if you can!" he cried, and we both raised our glasses to our mouths, only to stop half-way and look at each other in amaze. For the wind that had been howling outside like an outrageous dog had all of a sudden turned as melodious as the carol-boys of a Christmas Eve.

"Surely that's not my Martha," whispered landlord; Martha being his great-aunt that lived in the loft overhead.

We went to the door, and the wind burst it open so that the handle was driven clean into the plaster of the wall. But we didn't think about that at the time; for over our heads, sailing very comfortably through the windy stars, was the ship that had passed the summer in landlord's field. Her portholes and her bay-window were blazing with lights, and there was a noise of singing and fiddling on her decks. "He's gone," shouted landlord above the storm, "and he's taken half the village with him!" I could only nod in answer, not having lungs like bellows of leather.

In the morning we were able to measure the strength of the storm, and over and above my pigsty there was damage enough wrought in the village to keep us busy. True it is that the children had to break down no branches for the firing that autumn, since the wind had strewn the woods with more than they could carry away. Many of our ghosts were scattered abroad, but this time very few came back, all the young men having sailed with captain; and not only ghosts, for a poor half-witted lad was missing, and we reckoned that he had stowed himself away or perhaps shipped as cabin-boy, not knowing any better.

What with the lamentations of the ghost-girls and the grumblings of families who had lost an ancestor, the village was upset for a while, and the funny thing was that it was the folk who had complained most of the carryings-on of the youngsters, who made most noise now that they were gone. I hadn't any sympathy with shoemaker or butcher, who ran about saying how much they missed their lads, but it made me grieve to hear the poor bereaved girls calling their lovers by name on the village green at nightfall. It didn't seem fair to me that they should have lost their men a second time, after giving up life in order to join them, as like as not Still, not even a spirit can be sorry for ever, and after a few months we made up our mind that the folk who had sailed in the ship were never coming back, and we didn't talk about it anymore.

And then one day, I dare say it would be a couple of years after, when the whole business was quite forgotten, who should come trapesing along the road from Portsmouth but the daft lad who had gone away with the ship, without waiting till he was dead to become a ghost. You never saw such a boy as that in all your life. He had a great rusty cutlass hanging to a string at his waist, and he was tattooed all over in fine colours, so that even his face looked like a girl's sampler. He had a handkerchief in his hand full of foreign shells and old-fashioned pieces of small money, very curious, and he walked up to the well outside his mother's house and drew himself a drink as if he had been nowhere in particular.

The worst of it was that he had come back as soft-headed as he went, and try as we might we couldn't get anything reasonable out of him. He talked a lot of gibberish about keel-hauling and walking the plank and crimson murders—things which a decent sailor should know nothing about, so that it seemed to me that for all his manners captain had been more of a pirate than a gentleman mariner. But to draw sense out of that boy was as hard as picking cherries off a crab-tree. One silly tale he had that he kept on drifting back to, and to hear him you would have thought that it was the only thing that happened to him in his life.

"We was at anchor," he would say, "off an island called the Basket of Flowers, and the sailors had caught a lot of parrots and we were teaching them to swear. Up and down the decks, up and down the decks, and the language they used was dreadful. Then we looked up and saw the masts of the Spanish ship outside the harbour. Outside the harbour they were, so we threw the parrots into the sea and sailed out to fight. And all the parrots were drowned in the sea and the language they used was dreadful." That's the sort of boy he was, nothing but silly talk of parrots when we asked him about the fighting. And we never had a chance of teaching him better, for two days after he ran away again, and hasn't been seen since.

That's my story, and I assure you that things like that are happening at Fairfield all the time. The ship has never come back, but somehow as people grow older, they seem to think that one of these windy nights she'll come sailing in over the hedges with all the lost ghosts on board. Well, when she comes, she'll be welcome. There's one ghost-lass that has never grown tired of waiting for her lad to return. Every night you'll see her out on the green, straining her poor eyes with looking for the mast-lights among the stars. A faithful lass you'd call her, and I'm thinking you'd be right.

Landlord's field wasn't a penny the worse for the visit, but they do say that since then the turnips that have been grown in it have tasted of rum.

A Hungerford Interlude

Bradford stood on Charing Cross footbridge and gazed steadfastly into the water, a pleasant enough occupation, and infinitely preferable to the odour of the onions which were being cooked for his supper at his lodgings.

While he was thus engaged, he became aware of a man who was pacing nervously up and down the wooden planking, as a timid passenger might pace the deck of a ship. Now those who use this deplorable bridge do so in a steady business-like fashion, covering the ground rapidly, with minds intent on catching trains or, if incorrigibly lazy, stopping frankly like Bradford to look, after a common human weakness, over the edge.

But this one did neither, and Bradford turned round to look at this unconventional monster, who neither was honestly idle nor went about his business.

The stranger was not one of those men of strongly-marked features whom novelists love to describe; just an ordinary looking member of the caste of pointed beards. And now you know him very well.

After a few more turns up and down he approached Bradford and asked, "How long do you propose to remain here?"

"Why?" said Bradford, naturally enough.

The man hesitated a little before replying. "You see," he said timidly, "the fact is I wish to jump over the edge."

"Oh!" said Bradford, and after a pause, "What for?"

The timidity of the stranger increased until Bradford found it painful to see. He stuttered and mouthed a long harangue without Bradford being able to catch anything except the two words "My wife." Then he stopped.

"Your wife," said Bradford encouragingly, but the stranger read another meaning in his voice.

"Oh no," he cried with passion. "It is not that. Heaven forbid.

43

She—she—my wife says, in fact, well." He wandered in a confused tangle of words.

"Well?" said Bradford patiently.

"My wife says I have broken her heart and so"—with a pain-pitiful reminiscence of the Surrey Theatre—"and so I must die!"

Bradford suppressed a primitive desire to laugh and tried to grapple with the unreality of the scene. "Your wife says that," he said feebly.

The man shook with impatience. "She says that I have broken her heart, and so I say I must die."

Bradford meditated. The man was so timid and, in a way, so matter-of-fact. He talked of suicide as one talks of duty, half-heartedly, but nevertheless as a thing to be done. Still, he might be joking. "Are you serious?" he asked.

The man shook his head. "I know," he said with the sigh of an unsuccessful artist. "I know that my manner is sadly lacking in conviction. But really you know it does sound so silly to talk of death and that sort of thing even when one has quite made up one's mind."

That was just how Bradford was feeling himself. "It does indeed," he said frankly. "But will not your wife relent?"

"My wife is a queen of women," said the other proudly. "It is I who have repented. I have broken her heart. I must die."

Bradford thought vaguely of the police, but how could he betray this timid trust? Then he had an idea.

"You know," he cried, "the worst of it is I can swim!"

"Well?" said the man.

"I should have to rescue you for the sake of my own respect, and in the effort, I might be drowned. That," he said, finding the stranger's style infectious, "that would be unjust."

The would-be-suicide looked melancholy.

"What a nuisance," he said at last. "Still," more hopefully, "you might turn your back for a minute, you know."

"No," said Bradford firmly. "It won't do. If you do it at all now you will ruin my whole life. I will think I might have stopped you."

The stranger sighed, "I suppose you are right."

"Yes," said Bradford, warming to his part. "I am very sorry to hinder you in any way, but you see you shouldn't have told me."

"What a nuisance," repeated the man.

"You can go back and no one will be any the wiser," Bradford suggested.

"I—I wrote a letter," said the other troubled, "to my wife, you know. Penitence. Brute. Set her free. Watery grave." He relapsed into vague mutterings.

Bradford whistled his perplexity. "By Jove," he murmured, "you have put your foot in it."

"Yes," said the stranger, pleased with Bradford's sympathy and the complete blackness of his own outlook, "I think I have."

Then ensued a silence which lasted until Bradford's brow ached with the ornamental frown which he thought betrayed the proper amount of sympathetic interest in the other's worries. Then arrived Fate in the shape of a large and excited woman, who gave expression to unrestrained relief when she beheld the stranger.

"Kate!" cried the latter, with nothing now of the melodramatic in his voice.

And then and there before Bradford's eyes they embraced heartily.

The woman remembered first.

"Come away," she cried. "And don't be silly."

And the man followed her humbly enough without saying anything to Bradford in farewell. That one watched them go and wondered if he was really awake.

"How absurd!" he murmured, and tried to laugh.

But somehow he couldn't.

A Railway Journey

I suppose that when little boys made their journeys by coach with David Copperfield or Tom Brown and his pea-shooting comrades they did in truth find adventure easier to achieve than we who were born in an age of railways. But though the rarer joys of far travel by road were denied us, it did not need Mr. Rudyard Kipling in a didactic mood to convince us that there was plenty of romance in railway journeys if you approached them in the right spirit. We were as fond of playing at trains as most small boys, and a stationary engine with the light of the furnace glowing on the grim face of the driver was a disquieting feature of all my nightmares. So, when the grown-up people announced that one of us was to make a long journey young Ulysses became for the moment an envied and enchanted figure.

Our periodical excursions to London were well enough in their way; noisy, jolly parties in reserved carriages to pantomimes and the Lord Mayor's Show, or matter-of-fact visits to the dentist or the shops. But we all knew the features of the landscape on the way to London by heart, and it was the thought of voyaging through the unknown that fired our lively blood, our hazy sense of geography enabling us to believe that all manner of marvels were to be seen by young eyes from English railway-carriages. Also, we did not feel that we were real travellers until we had left all our own grown-ups behind, though in such circumstances we had to put up with the indignity of being confided to the care of the guard. Until children have votes they will continue to suffer from such slights as this!

One morning in early spring I left London for the north. The adult who saw me off performed his task on the whole very well. True, he introduced me to the guard, a bearded and sinister man; but, on the other hand, he realised the importance of my having a corner seat, and only once or twice committed the error of treating me as if I were a parcel. For my part, I was at pains to conceal my excitement beneath the mannerisms of an experienced traveller. I put the window up and down several times and read aloud all the notices concerning luncheon-baskets and danger-signals. Then my companion shook hands with me in a sensible, manly fashion, and the train started.

I sat back and examined my fellow-travellers, and found them rather disappointing. There were three ladies, manifestly of the aunt kind, and a stiff, well-behaved little girl who might have stepped out of one of my sister's storybooks. She was reading a book without pictures, and when I turned over the pages of my magazines, she displayed no interest in them whatever. I could never read in the train, so, with a tentative effort at good manners, I pushed them towards her, but she shook her head; to show her that I did not think this was a snub I pulled out my packet of sandwiches and had my lunch. After that I played with the blind, which worked with a spring, until one of the aunts told me not to fidget, although she was no aunt of mine. Then I looked out of the window, a prey to voiceless wrath.

By now we had left London far behind, and when I had finished composing imaginary retorts to the unscrupulous aunt, I was quite content to see the wonders of the world flit by. There were hills and valleys decked with romantic woods and set with fascinating and secretive ponds. To my eyes the hills were mountains and the valleys perilous hollows, the accustomed lairs of tremendous dragons. I saw little thatched houses wherein swart witches awaited the coming of Hansel and Gretel, and fairy children waved to me from cottage gardens and the gates of level-crossings, greetings which I dutifully returned until the aunt made me pull up the window.

After a while a change came over the scenery. The placid greens and browns of the countryside blossomed to gold and purple and crimson. I saw a roc float across the arching sky on sluggish wings, and my eyes were delighted with visions of deserts and mosques and palm-trees. That my fellow-passengers would not raise their heads to behold these marvels did not trouble me; I beat on the window with delight, until, like little Billee in Thackeray's ballad, I saw Jerusalem and Madagascar and North and South Amerikee.

Then something surprising happened. I saw the earth leap up and invade the sky and the sky drop down and blot out the earth, and I felt as though my wings were broken. Then the sides of the carriage closed in and squeezed out the door like a pip out of an orange, until there was only a three-cornered gap left. The air was full of dust, and I sneezed again and again, but could not find my pocket-handkerchief.

Presently a young man came and lifted me out through the hole, and seemed very surprised that I was not hurt. I realised that there had been an accident, for the train was broken into pieces and the permanent way was very untidy. Close at hand I saw the little girl sitting on a bank, and a man kneeling at her feet taking her boots off. I would have liked to speak to her, but I remembered how she had refused the offer of my magazines, and was afraid she would snub me again. The place was very noisy, for people were calling out, and there was a great sound of steam. I noticed that everybody's face was very white, especially the guard's, which made his beard seem as black as soot. The young man took me by the hand and led me along the uneven ground, and there was so much to see that my feet kept stumbling over things, and he had to hold me up.

On the way we passed the body of a man lying with a rug over his head. I knew that he was dead; but I had seen drunken men in the streets lie like that, and I could not help looking about for the policeman. Soon we came to a little station, and the platform was crowded with people who would not stand still, but walked round and round making noises. When I climbed up on the platform a woman caught hold of me and cried over me. One of her tears fell on my ear and tickled me; but she held me so tightly that I could not put up my hand to rub it. Her breath was hot on my head.

Then I heard a detested voice say, "Poor little boy, so tired!" and I shuddered back into consciousness of the world that was least interesting of all the worlds I knew. I need not have opened my eyes to be sure that the aunts were at their fell work again, and that the little girl's snub nose was tilted to a patronising angle. Had I awakened a minute later she, too, would have joined in the auntish chorus of compassion for my weakness. As it was, I looked at her with drowsy pity, finding that she was one of those luckless infants who might as well stay at home for all the fun they get out of travelling. She knew no better than to scream when the train ran into a tunnel; what would she have done if she had seen my roc?

The train ran on and on, and still I throned it in my corner, awake or dreaming, indisputably master of all the things that counted. The three aunts faded into antimacassars; the little girl endured her uninteresting life and became an aunt and an antimacassar in her turn, and still I swung my legs in my corner seat, a boy-errant in the strange places of the world. I do not remember the name of the station at which the bearded guard ultimately brought me out of my dreams. I do remember standing stiffly on the platform and deciding that I had been travelling night and day for three hundred years. When I communicated this fact to the relatives who met me, they were strangely unimpressed; but I knew that when I returned home to my brothers, they would display a decent interest in the story of my wanderings. After all, you can't expect grown-up people to understand everything!

A Tragedy in Little

1

Jack, the postmaster's little son, stood in the bow-window of the parlour and watched his mother watering the nasturtiums in the front garden. A certain intensity of purpose was expressed by the manner in which she handled the water-pot. For though it was a fine afternoon the carrier's man had called over the hedge to say that there would be a thunderstorm during the night, and everyone knew that he never made a mistake about the weather.

Nevertheless, Jack's mother watered the plants as if he had not spoken, for it seemed to her that this meteorological gift smacked a little of sorcery and black magic; but in spite of herself she felt sure that there would be a thunderstorm and that her labour was therefore vain, save perhaps as a protest against idle superstition. It was in the same spirit that she carried an umbrella on the brightest summer day.

Jack had been sent indoors because he would get his legs in the way of the watering-pot in order to cool them, so now he had to be content to look on, with his nose pressed so tightly against the pane that from outside it looked like the base of a sea-anemone growing in a glass tank. He could no longer hear the glad chuckle of the watering-pot when the water ran out, but, on the other hand, he could write his name on the window with his tongue, which he could not have done if he had been in the garden. Also, he had some sweets in his pocket, bought with a halfpenny stolen from his own money-box, and as the window did not taste very nice, he slipped one into his mouth and sucked it with enjoyment

He did not like being in the parlour, because he had to sit there with his best clothes on every Sunday afternoon and read the parish magazine to his sleepy parents. But the front window was lovely, like a picture, and, indeed, he thought that his mother, with the flowers all about her and the red sky overhead, was like a lady on one of the

51

beautiful calendars that the grocer gave away at Christmas. He finished his sweet and started another; he always meant to suck them right through to make them last longer, but when the sweet was half finished be invariably crunched it up. His father had done the same thing as a boy.

The room behind him was getting dark, but outside the sky seemed to be growing lighter, and mother still stooped from bed to bed, moving placidly, like a cow. Sometimes she put the watering-pot down on the gravel path, and bent to uproot a microscopic weed or to pull the head off a dead flower. Sometimes she went to the well to get some more water, and then Jack was sorry that he had been shut indoors, for he liked letting the pail down with a run and hearing it bump against the brick sides. Once he tapped upon the window for permission to come out, but mother shook her head vigorously without turning round; and yet his stockings were hardly wet at all.

Suddenly mother straightened herself, and Jack looked up and saw his father leaning over the gate. He seemed to be making grimaces, and Jack made haste to laugh aloud in the empty room, because he knew that he was good at seeing his father's jokes. Indeed, it was a funny thing that father should come home early from work and make faces at mother from the road. Mother, too, was willing to join in the fun, for she knelt down among the wet flowers, and as her head drooped lower and lower it looked, for one ecstatic moment, as though she were going to turn head over heels. But she lay quite still on the ground, and father came half-way through the gate, and then turned and ran off down the hill towards the station. Jack stood in the window, clapping his hands and laughing; it was a strange game, but not much harder to understand than most of the amusements of the grown-up people.

And then as nothing happened, as mother did not move and father did not come back. Jack grew frightened. The garden was queer and the room was full of darkness, so he beat on the window to change the game. Then, since mother did not shake her head, he ran out into the garden, smiling carefully in case he was being silly. First, he went to the gate, but father was quite small far down the road, so he turned back and pulled the sleeve of his mother's dress, to wake her. After a dreadful while mother got up off the ground with her skirt all covered with wet earth.

Jack tried to brush it off with his hands and made a mess of it, but she did not seem to notice, looking across the garden with such a desolate face that when he saw it he burst into tears. For once mother let him cry himself out without seeking to comfort him; when he sniffed dolefully, his nostrils were full of the scent of crushed marigolds. He could not help watching her hands through his tears; it seemed as though they were playing together at cat's-cradle; they were not still for a moment. But it was her face that at once frightened and interested him. One minute it looked smooth and white as if she was very cross, and the next minute it was gathered up in little folds as if she was going to sneeze.

Deep down in him something chuckled, and he jumped for fear that the cross part of her had heard it. At intervals during the evening, while mother was getting him his supper, this chuckle returned to him, between unnoticed fits of crying. Once she stood holding a plate in the middle of the room for quite five minutes, and he found it hard to control his mirth. If father had been there, they would have had good fun together, teasing mother, but by himself he was not sure of his ground. And father did not come back, and mother did not seem to hear his questions.

He had some tomatoes and rice-pudding for his supper, and as mother left him to help himself to brown sugar he enjoyed it very much, carefully leaving the skin of the rice-pudding to the last, because that was the part he liked best After supper he sat nodding at the open window, looking out over the plum-trees to the sky beyond, where the black clouds were putting out the stars one by one. The garden smelt stuffy, but it was nice to be allowed to sit up when you felt really sleepy. On the whole he felt that it had been a pleasant, exciting sort of day, though once or twice mother had frightened him by looking so strange.

There had been other mysterious days in his life, however; perhaps he was going to have another little dead sister. Presently he discovered that it was delightful to shut your eyes and nod your head and pretend that you were going to sleep; it was like being in a swing that went up and up and never came down again. It was like being in a rowing-boat on the river after a steamer had gone by. It was like lying in a cradle under a lamplit ceiling, a cradle that rocked gently to and fro while mother sang far-away songs.

He was still a baby when he woke up, and he slipped off his chair and staggered blindly across the room to his mother, with his knuckles in his eyes like a little, little boy. He climbed into her lap and settled himself down with a grunt of contentment. There was a mutter of thunder in his ears, and he felt great warm drops of rain falling on his face. And into his dreams he carried the dim consciousness that the thunderstorm had begun.

2

The next morning at breakfast-time father had not come back, and mother said a lot of things that made Jack feel very uncomfortable. She herself had taught him that anyone who said bad things about his father was wicked, but now it seemed that she was trying to tell him something about father that was not nice. She spoke so slowly that he hardly understood a word she said, though he gathered that father had stolen something, and would be put in prison if he was caught. With a guilty pang he remembered his own dealings with his money-box, and he determined to throw away the rest of the sweets when nobody was looking.

Then mother made the astounding statement that he was not to go to school that day, but his sudden joy was checked a little when she said he was not to go out at all, except into the back garden. It seemed to Jack that he must be ill, but when he made this suggestion to mother, she gave up her explanations with a sigh. Afterwards she kept on saying aloud, "I must think, I must think!" She said it so often that Jack started keeping count on his fingers.

The day went slowly enough, for the garden was wet after the thunderstorm, and mother would not play any games. Just before tea-time two gentlemen called and talked to mother in the parlour, and after a while they sent for Jack to answer some questions about father, though mother was there all the time. They seemed nice gentlemen, but mother did not ask them to stop to tea, as Jack expected. He thought that perhaps she was sorry that she had not done so, for she was very sad all tea-time, and let him spread his own bread and jam. When tea was over things were very dull, and at last Jack started crying because there was nothing else to do.

Presently he heard a little noise and found that mother was crying as well. This seemed to him so extraordinary that he stopped crying to watch her; the tears ran down her cheeks very quickly, and she kept on wiping them away with her handkerchief, but if she held her handkerchief to her eyes perhaps, they would not be able to come out at all. It occurred to him that possibly she was sorry she had said wicked things about father, and to comfort her, for it made him feel fidgety to see her cry, he whispered to her that he would not tell. But she stared at him hopelessly through her red eyelids, and he felt that he had not said the right thing. She called him her poor boy, and yet it appeared that he was not ill. It was all very mysterious and uncomfortable, and it would be a good thing when father came back and everything went on as before, even though he had to go back to school

Later on, the woman from the mill came in to sit with mother. She brought Jack some sweets, but instead of playing with him she burst into tears. She made more noise when she cried than mother; in fact, he was afraid that in a minute he would have to laugh at her snortings, so he went into the parlour and sat there in the dark, eating his sweets, and knitting his brow over the complexities of life. He could see five stars, and there was a light behind the red curtain of the front bedroom at Arber's farm. It was about twelve times as large as a star, and a much prettier colour. By nearly closing his eyes he could see everything double, so that there were ten stars and two red lights; he was trying to make everything come treble when the gate clicked and he saw his father's shadow. He was delighted with this happy end to a tiresome day, and as he ran through the passage, he called out to mother to say that father was back. Mother did not answer, but he heard a bit of noise in the kitchen as he opened the front door.

He said "Good evening" in the grown-up voice that father encouraged, but father slipped in and shut the door without saying a word. Every night when he came back from the post-office he brought Jack the gummed edgings off the sheets of stamps, and Jack held out his hand for them as a matter of course. Automatically father felt in his overcoat pocket and pulled out a great handful. "Take care of them, they're the last you'll get," he said; but when Jack asked why, his father looked at him with the same hopeless expression that he had found in his mother's eyes a short while before. Jack felt a little cross that everyone should be so stupid.

When they went into the kitchen everybody looked very strange, and Jack sat down in the comer and listened for an explanation. As a rule, the conversation of the grown-up people did not amuse him, but tonight he felt that something had happened, and that if he kept quiet, he might find out what it was. He had noticed before that when the grown-ups talked, they always said the same things over and over again, and now they were worse than usual.

Father said, "It's no good, I've got to go through it;" the mill-woman said, "Whatever made you do it, George?"

And mother said, "Nothing will ever happen to me again!"

They all went on saying these things till Jack grew tired of listening, and started plaiting his stamp-paper into a mat. If you did it very neatly it was almost as good as an ordinary sheet of paper by the time you had finished. By and by, while he was still at work, the mill-woman brought him his supper on a plate, and raising his head he saw that father and mother were sitting close together, looking at each other, and saying nothing at all. He was very disappointed that although father had come home, they had not had any jokes all the evening, and as they were all so dull, he did not very much mind being sent to bed when he had finished his supper.

When he said goodnight to father, he noticed that his boots were very muddy, as if he had walked a long way like a common postman. He made a joke about this, but they all looked at him as if he had said something wrong, so he hurried out of the room, glad to get away from these people whose looks had no reasonable significance, and whose words had no discoverable meaning. It had been a bad day, and he hoped mother would let him go back to school the next morning.

And yet though he took off his clothes and got into bed, the day was not quite over. He had only dozed for a few minutes when he was roused by a noise down below, and slipping out on to the staircase he heard the mill-woman saying goodnight in the passage. When she had gone and the door had banged behind her, he listened still, and heard his mother crying and his father talking on and on in a strange, hoarse voice. Somehow these incomprehensible sounds made him feel lonely and he would have liked to have gone downstairs and sat on his mother's lap and blinked drowsily in his father's face, as he had done often enough before.

But he was always shy in the presence of strangers, and he felt that he did not know this woman who wept and this man who did not laugh. His father was his play-friend, the sharer of all his fun; his mother was a quiet woman who sat and sewed, and sometimes told than not to be silly, which was the best joke of all. It was not right for people to alter. But the thought of his bedroom made him desolate, and at last he plucked up his courage, and crept downstairs on bare feet.

Father and mother had gone back into the kitchen, and he peeped through the crack of the door to see what they were doing. Mother was still crying, always crying, but he had to change his position before he could see father. Then he turned on his heels and ran upstairs trembling with fear and disgust. For father, the man of all the faces, the man of whom burglars was afraid and compared with whom all other little boys' fathers were as dirt, was crying like a little girl.

He jumped into bed and pulled the bedclothes over his face to shut out the ugliness of the world.

3

When Jack woke up the next morning, he found that the room was full of sunshine, and that father was standing at the end of the bed. The moment Jack opened his eyes, he began telling him something in a serious voice, which was alone sufficient to prevent Jack from understanding what he said. Besides, he used a lot of long words, and Jack thought that it was silly to use long words before breakfast, when nobody could be expected to remember what they meant. Father's body neatly fitted the square of the window, and the sunbeams shone in all round it and made it look splendid; and if Jack had not already forgotten the unfortunate impression of the night before, this would have enabled him to overcome it.

Every now and then father stopped to ask him if he understood, and he said he did, hoping to find out what it was all about later on. It seemed, however, that father was not going to the post-office any-more, and this caused Jack to picture a series of delightfully amusing days. When father had finished talking, he appeared to expect Jack to say something, but Jack contented himself with trying to look inter-ested, for he knew that it was always very stupid of little boys not to understand things they didn't understand. In reality he felt as if he had been listening while his father argued aloud with himself, talking up and down like an earthquake map.

At breakfast they were still subdued, but afterwards, as the morning wore on, father became livelier and helped Jack to build a hut in the back garden. They built it of bean-sticks against the wall at the end, and father broke up a packing-case to get planks for the roof. Only mother still had a sad face, and it made Jack angry with her, that she should be such a spoil-fun. After dinner, while Jack was playing in the hut, Mr. Simmons, of the police-station, and another gentleman called to take father for a walk, and Jack went down to the front to see them off.

Jack knew Mr. Simmons very well; he had been to tea with his little boy, but though he thought him a fine sort of man he could not help feeling proud of his father when he saw them side by side. Mr. Simmons looked as if he were ashamed of himself, while father walked along with square shoulders and a high head as if he had just done something splendid. The other gentleman looked like nothing at all beside father.

When they were out of sight Jack went into the house and found mother crying in the kitchen. As he felt more tolerant in his after-dinner mood, he tried to cheer her up by telling her how fine father had looked beside the other two men. Mother raised her face, all swollen and spoilt with weeping, and gazed at her son in astonishment. "They are taking him to prison," she wailed, "and God knows what will become of us."

For a moment Jack felt alarmed. Then a thought came to him and he smiled, like a little boy who has just found a new and delightful game. "Never mind, mother," he said, "we'll help him to escape."

But mother would not stop crying.

And Who Shall Say—?

It was a dull November day, and the windows were heavily curtained, so that the room was very dark. In front of the fire was a large armchair, which shut whatever light there might be from the two children, a boy of eleven and a girl about two years younger, who sat on the floor at the back of the room.

The boy was the better looking, but the girl had the better face. They were both gazing at the armchair with the utmost excitement,

"It's all right. He's asleep," said the boy.

"Oh, do be careful! You'll wake him," whispered the girl

"Are you afraid?"

"No, why should I be afraid of my father, stupid?"

"I tell you he's not father anymore. He's a murderer," the boy said hotly. "He told me, I tell you. He said, 'I have killed your mother, Ray,' and I went and looked, and mother was all red. I simply shouted, and she wouldn't answer. That means she's dead. His hand was all red, too."

"Was it paint?"

"No, of course it wasn't paint. It was blood. And then he came down here and went to sleep."

"Poor father, so tired."

"He's not poor father, he's not father at all; he's a murderer, and it is very wicked of you to call him father," said the boy.

"Father," muttered the girl rebelliously.

"You know the sixth commandment says 'Thou shalt do no murder,' and he has done murder; so, he'll go to hell. And you'll go to hell too if you call him father. It's all in the Bible."

The boy ended vaguely, but the little girl was quite overcome by the thought of her badness.

"Oh, I am wicked!" she cried, "And I do so want to go to heaven."

She had a stout and materialistic belief in it as a place of sheeted angels and harps, where it was easy to be good.

59

"You must do as I tell you, then," he said. "Because I know. I've learnt all about it at school."

"And you never told me," said she reproachfully.

"Ah, there's lots of things I know," he replied, nodding his head.

"What must we do?" said the girl meekly. "Shall I go and ask mother?"

The boy was sick at her obstinacy.

"Mother's dead, I tell you; that means she can't hear anything. It's no use talking to her; but I know. You must stop here, and if father wakes you run out of the house and call 'Police!' and I will go now and tell a policeman I know."

"And what happens then?" she asked, with round eyes at her brother's wisdom.

"Oh, they come and take him away to prison. And then they put a rope round his neck and hang him like Haman, and he goes to hell."

"Wha-at! Do they kill him?"

"Because he's a murderer. They always do."

"Oh, don't let's tell them! Don't let's tell them!" she screamed.

"Shut up!" said the boy, "or he'll wake up. We must tell them, or we go to hell—both of us."

But his sister did not collapse at this awful threat, as he expected, though the tears were rolling down her face. "Don't let's tell them," she sobbed.

"You're a horrid girl, and you'll go to hell," said the boy, in disgust. But the silence was only broken by her sobbing. "I tell you he killed mother dead. You didn't cry a bit for mother; I did."

"Oh, let's ask mother! Let's ask mother! I know she won't want father to go to hell. Let's ask mother!"

"Mother's dead, and can't hear, you stupid," said the boy. "I keep on telling you. Come up and look."

They were both a little awed in mother's room. It was so quiet, and mother looked so funny. And first the girl shouted, and then the boy, and then they shouted both together, but nothing happened. The echoes made them frightened.

"Perhaps she's asleep," the girl said; so, her brother pinched one of mother's hands—the white one, not the red one—but nothing happened, so mother was dead.

"Has she gone to hell?" whispered the girl.

"No! she's gone to heaven, because she's good. Only wicked people go to hell. And now I must go and tell the policeman. Don't you tell father where I've gone if he wakes up, or hell run away before the policeman comes."

"Why?"

"So as not to go to hell," said the boy, with certainty; and they went downstairs together, the little mind of the girl being much perturbed because she was so wicked. What would mother say tomorrow if she had done wrong?

The boy put on his sailor hat in the hall. "You must go in there and watch," he said, nodding in the direction of the sitting-room. "I shall run all the way."

The door banged, and she heard his steps down the path, and then everything was quiet

She tiptoed into the room, and sat down on the floor, and looked at the back of the chair in utter distress. She could see her father's elbow projecting on one side, but nothing more. For an instant she hoped that he wasn't there—hoped that he had gone—but then, terrified, she knew that this was a piece of extreme wickedness.

So, she lay on the rough carpet, sobbing hopelessly, and seeing real and vicious devils of her brother's imagining in all the corners of the room.

Presently, in her misery, she remembered a packet of acid-drops that lay in her pocket, and drew them forth in a sticky mass, which parted from its paper with regret. So, she choked and sucked her sweets at the same time, and found them salt and tasteless,

Ray was gone a long time, and she was a wicked girl who would go to hell if she didn't do what he told her. Those were her prevailing ideas.

And presently there came a third. Ray had said that if her father woke up, he would run away, and not go to hell at all. Now if she woke him up—.

She knew this was dreadfully naughty; but her mind clung to the idea obstinately. You see, father had always been so fond of mother, and he would not like to be in a different place. Mother wouldn't like it either. She was always so sorry when father did not come home or anything. And hell is a dreadful place, full of things. She half convinced herself, and started up, but then there came an awful thought.

If she did this she would go to hell for ever and ever, and all the others would be in heaven.

She hung there in suspense, sucking ha sweet and puzzling it over with knit brows.

How can one be good?

She swung round and looked in the dark corner by the piano; but the Devil was not there.

And then she ran across the room to her father, and shaking his arm, shouted, tremulously—

"Wake up, father! Wake up! The police are coming!"

And when the police came ten minutes later, accompanied by a very proud and virtuous little boy, they heard a small shrill voice crying, despairingly—

"The police, father! The police!"

But father would not wake.

Blue Blood

He sat in the middle of the great *café*, with his head supported on his hands, miserable even to bitterness. Inwardly he cursed the ancestors who had left him little but a great name and a small and ridiculous body. He thought of his father, whose expensive eccentricities had amused his fellow-countrymen at the cost of his fortune; his mother, for whom death had been a blessing; his grandparents and his uncles, in whom no man had found any good. But most of all he cursed himself, for whose follies even heredity might not wholly account. He recalled the school where he had made no friends, the university where he had taken no degree.

Since he had left Oxford, his aimless, hopeless life, profligate, but dishonourable, perhaps, only by accident, had deprived even his title of any social value, and one by one his very acquaintances had left him to the society of broken men and the women who are anything but light. And these, and here perhaps the root of his bitterness lay, even these recognised him only as a victim for their mockery, a thing more poor them themselves, whereon they could satisfy the anger of their tortured souls.

And his last misery lay in this: that he himself could find no day in his life to admire, no one past dream to cherish, no inmost corner of his heart to love. The lowest tramp, the least-heeded waif of the night, might have some ultimate pride, but be himself had nothing, nothing whatever. He was a dream-pauper, an emotional bankrupt.

With a choked sob he drained his brandy and told the waiter to bring him another. There had been a period in his life when he had been able to find some measure of sentimental satisfaction in the stupor of drunkenness. In those days, through the veil of illusion which alcohol had flung across his brain, he had been able to regard the contempt of the men as the intimacy of friendship, the scorn of the women as the laughter of light love. But now drink gave him nothing but the mordant insight of morbidity, which cut through his rotten soul like cheese.

Yet night after night he came to this place, to be tortured afresh by the ridicule of the sordid frequenters, and by the careless music of the orchestra which told him of a flowerless spring and of a morning which held for him no hope. For his last emotion rested in this self-inflicted pain; he could only breathe freely under the lash of his own contempt.

Idly he let his dull eyes stray about the room, from table to table, from face to face. Many there he knew by sight; from none could he hope for sympathy or even companionship. In his bitterness he envied the courage of the cowards who were brave enough to seek oblivion or punishment in death. Dropping his eyes to his soft, unlovely hands, he marvelled that anything so useless should throb with life, and yet he realised that he was afraid of physical pain, terrified at the thought of death. There were dim ancestors of his whose valour had thrilled the songs of minstrels and made his name lovely in the glowing folly of battles. But now he knew that he was a coward, and even in the knowledge he could find no comfort It is not given to every man to hate himself gladly.

The music and the laughter beat on his sullen brain with a mocking insistence, and he trembled with impotent auger at the apparent happiness of humanity. Why should these people be merry when he was miserable, what right had the orchestra to play a chorus of triumph over the stinging emblems of his defeat? He drank brandy after brandy, vainly seeking to dull the nausea of disgust which had stricken his worn nerves; but the adulterated spirit merely maddened his brain with the vision of new depths of horror, while his body lay below, a mean, detestable thing. Had he known how to pray he would have begged that something might snap. But no man may win to faith by means of hatred alone, and his heart was cold as the marble table against which he leant. There was no more hope in the world. . . .

When he came out of the *café*, the air of the night was so pure and cool on his face, and the lights of the square were so tender to his eyes, that for a moment his harsh mood was softened. And in that moment, he seemed to see among the crowd that flocked by a beautiful face, a face touched with pearls, and the inner leaves of pink rosebuds. He leant forward eagerly. "Christine!" he cried, "Christine!"

Then the illusion passed, and, smitten by the anger of the pitiless stars, he saw that he was looking upon a mere woman, a woman of the earth. He fled from her smile with a shudder.

As he went it seemed to him that the swaying houses buffeted him about as a child might play with a ball. Sometimes they threw him against men, who cursed him and bruised his soft body with their fists. Sometimes they tripped him up and hurled him upon the stones of the pavement. Still, he held on, till the embankment broke before him with the sudden peace of space, and he leant against the parapet, panting and sick with pain, but free from the tyranny of the houses.

Beneath him the river rolled towards the sea, reticent but more alive, it seemed, than the deeply painful thing which fate had attached to his brain. He pictured himself tangled in the dark perplexity of its waters, he fancied them falling upon his face like a girl's hair, till they darkened his eyes and choked the mouth which, even now, could not breathe fast enough to satisfy him. The thought displeased him, and he turned away from the place that held peace for other men but not for him. From the shadow of one of the seats a woman's voice reached him, begging peevishly for money.

"I have none," he said automatically. Then he remembered and flung coins, all the money he had, into her lap. "I give it to you because I hate you!" he shrieked, and hurried on lest her thanks should spoil his spite.

Then the black houses and the warped streets had him in their grip once more, and sported with him till his consciousness waxed to one white-hot point of pain. Overhead the stars were laughing quietly in the fields of space, and sometimes a policeman or a chance passer-by looked curiously at his lurching figure, but he only knew that life was hurting him beyond endurance, and that he yet endured. Up and down the ice-cold corridors of his brain, thought, formless and timeless, passed like a rodent flame. Now he was the universe, a vast thing loathsome with agony, now he was a speck of dust, an atom whose infinite torment was imperceptible even to God. Always there was something—something conscious of the intolerable evil called life, something that cried bitterly to be uncreated. Always, while his soul beat against the bars, his body staggered along the streets, a thing helpless, unguided.

There is an hour before dawn when tired men and women die, and with the coming of this hour his spirit found a strange release from pain. Once more he realised that he was a man, and, bruised and weary as he was, he tried to collect the lost threads of reason, which the night had torn from him. Facing him he saw a vast building dimly outlined against the darkness, and in some way, it served to touch a faint memory in his dying brain.

For a while he wandered amongst the shadows, and then he knew that it was the keep of a castle, his castle, and that high up where a window shone upon the night a girl was waiting for him, a girl with a face of pearls and roses. Presently she came to the window and looked out, dressed all in white for her love's sake. He stood up in his armour and flashed his sword towards the envying stars.

"It is I, my love!" he cried. "I am here."

And there, before the dawn had made the shadows of the Law Courts grey, they found him; bruised and muddy and daubed with blood, without the sword and spurs of his honour, lacking the scented token of his love. A thing in no way tragic, for here was no misfortune, but merely the conclusion of Nature's remorseless logic. For century after century those of his name had lived, sheltered by the prowess of their ancestors from the trivial hardships and afflictions that make us men. And now he lay on the pavement, stiff and cold, a babe that had cried itself to sleep because it could not understand, silent until the morning.

A Drama of Youth

For some days school had seemed to me even more tedious than usual The long train journey in the morning, the walk through Farringdon Meat Market, which aesthetic butchers made hideous with mosaics of the intestines of animals, as if the horror of suety pavements and bloody sawdust did not suffice, the weariness of inventing lies that no one believed to account for my lateness and neglected homework, and the monotonous lessons that held me from my dreams without ever for a single instant capturing my interest—all these things made me ill with repulsion. Worst of all was the society of my cheerful, contented comrades, to avoid which I was compelled to mope in deserted corridors, the prey of a sorrow that could not be enjoyed, a hatred that was in no way stimulating.

At the best of times the atmosphere of the place disgusted me. Desks, windows, and floors, and even the grass in the quadrangle, were greasy with London soot, and there was nowhere any clean air to breathe or smell. I hated the gritty asphalt that gave no peace to my feet and cut my knees when my clumsiness made me fall. I hated the long stone corridors whose echoes seemed to me to mock my hesitating footsteps when I passed from one dull class to another.

I hated the stuffy malodorous classrooms, with their whistling gasjets and noise of inharmonious life. I would have hated the yellow fogs had they not sometimes shortened the hours of my bondage. That five hundred boys shared this horrible environment with me did not abate my sufferings a jot; for it was clear that they did not find it distasteful, and they therefore became as unsympathetic for me as the smell and noise and rotting stones of the school itself.

The masters moved as it were in another world, and, as the classes were large, they understood me as little as I understood them. They knew that I was idle and untruthful, and they could not know that

I was as full of nerves as a girl, and that the mere task of getting to school every morning made me physically sick. They punished me repeatedly and in vain, for I found every hour I passed within the walls of the school an overwhelming punishment in itself, and nothing made any difference to me. I lied to them because they expected it, and because I had no words in which to express the truth if I knew it, which is doubtful. For some reason I could not tell them at home why I got on so badly at school, or no doubt they would have taken me away and sent me to a country school, as they did afterwards.

Nearly all the real sorrows of childhood are due to this dumbness of the emotions; we teach children to convey facts by means of words, but we do not teach them how to make their feelings intelligible. Unfortunately, perhaps, I was very happy at night with my storybooks and my dreams, so that the real misery of my days escaped the attention of the grown-up people. Of course, I never even thought of doing my homework, and the labour of inventing new lies every day to account for my negligence became so wearisome that once or twice I told the truth and simply said I had not done it; but the masters held that this frankness aggravated the offence, and I had to take up anew my tiresome tale of improbable calamities. Sometimes my stories were so wild that the whole class would laugh, and I would have to laugh myself; yet on the strength of this elaborate politeness to authority I came to believe myself that I was untruthful by nature.

The boys disliked me because I was not sociable, but after a time they grew tired of bullying me and left me alone. I detested them because they were all so much alike that their numbers filled me with horror. I remember that the first day I went to school I walked round and round the quadrangle in the luncheon-hour, and every boy who passed stopped me and asked me my name and what my father was. When I said he was an engineer every one of the boys replied, "Oh! the man who drives the engine." The reiteration of this childish joke made me hate them from the first, and afterwards I discovered that they were equally unimaginative in everything they did.

Sometimes I would stand in the midst of them, and wonder what was the matter with me that I should be so different from all the rest. When they teased me, repeating the same questions over and over again, I cried easily, like a girl, without quite knowing why, for their stupidities could not hurt my reason; but when they bullied me, I did not cry, because the pain made me forget the sadness of my heart Perhaps it was because of this that they thought I was a little mad.

Grey day followed grey day, and I might in time have abandoned all efforts to be faithful to my dreams, and achieved a kind of beastlike submission that was all the authorities expected of notorious dunces. I might have taught my senses to accept the evil conditions of life in that unclean place; I might even have succeeded in making myself one with the army of shadows that thronged in the quadrangle and filled the air with meaningless noise.

But one evening when I reached home, I saw by the faces of the grown-up people that something had upset their elaborate precautions for an ordered life, and I discovered that my brother, who had stayed at home with a cold, was ill in bed with the measles. For a while the significance of the news escaped me; then, with a sudden movement of my heart, which made me feel ill, I realised that probably I would have to stay away from school because of the infection. My feet tapped on the floor with joy, though I tried to appear unconcerned. Then, as I nursed my sudden hope of freedom, a little fearfully lest it should prove an illusion, a new and enchanting idea came to me.

I slipped from the room, ran upstairs to my bedroom and, standing by the side of my bed, tore open my waistcoat and shirt with clumsy, trembling fingers. One, two, three, four, five! I counted the spots in a triumphant voice, and then with a sudden revulsion sat down on the bed to give the world an opportunity to settle back in its place. I had the measles, and therefore I should not have to go back to school! I shut my eyes for a minute and opened them again, but still I had the measles. The cup of happiness was at my lips, but I sipped delicately because it was full to the brim, and I would not spill a drop.

This mood did not last long. I had to run down the house and tell the world the good news. The grown-up people rebuked my joyousness, while admitting that it might be as well that I should have the measles then as later on. In spite of their air of resignation I could hardly sit still for excitement. I wanted to go into the kitchen and show my measles to the servants, but I was told to stay where I was in front of the fire while my bed was moved into my brother's room.

So, I stared at the glowing coals till my eyes watered, and dreamed long dreams. I would be in bed for days, all warm from head to foot, and no one would interrupt my pleasant excursions in the world I preferred to this. If I had heard of the beneficent microbe to which I owed my happiness, I would have mentioned it in my prayers.

Late that night I called over to my brother to ask how long measles lasted. He told me to go to sleep, so that I knew he did not know the answer to my question. I lay at ease tranquilly turning the problem over in my mind. Four weeks, six weeks, eight weeks; why, if I was lucky, it would carry me through to the holidays! At all events, school was already very far away, like a nightmare remembered at noon. I said goodnight to my brother, and received an irritated grunt in reply. I did not mind his surliness; tomorrow when I woke up, I would begin my dreams.

2

When I found myself in bed in the morning, already sick at heart because even while I slept, I could not forget the long torment of my life at school, I would lie still for a minute or two and toy to concentrate my shuddering mind on something pleasant, some little detail of the moment that seemed to justify hope. Perhaps I had some money to spend or a holiday to look forward to; though often enough I would find nothing to save me from realising with childish intensity the greyness of the world in which it was my fate to move. I did not want to go out into life; it was dull and cruel and greasy with soot. I only wanted to stop at home in any little quiet corner out of everybody's way and think my long, heroic thoughts. But even while I mumbled my hasty breakfast and ran to the station to catch my train the atmosphere of the school was all about me, and my dreamer's courage trembled and vanished.

When I woke from sleep the morning after my good fortune, I did not at first realise the extent of my happiness; I only knew that deep in my heart I was conscious of some great cause for joy. Then my eyes, still dim with sleep, discovered that I was in my brother's bedroom, and in a flash the joyful truth was revealed to me. I sat up and hastily examined my body to make sure that the rash had not disappeared, and then my spirit sang a song of thanksgiving of which the refrain was, "I have the measles!" I lay back in bed and enjoyed the exquisite luxury of thinking of the evils that I had escaped.

For once my morbid sense of atmosphere was a desirable possession and helpful to my happiness. It was delightful to pull the bedclothes over my shoulders and conceive the feelings of a small boy who should ride to town in a jolting train, walk through a hundred kinds of dirt and a hundred disgusting smells to win to prison at last, where he should perform meaningless tasks in the distressing society of five hundred mocking apes. It was pleasant to see the morning sun and feel no sickness in my stomach, no sense of depression in my tired brain. Across the room my brother gulled and choked in his sleep, and in some subtle way contributed to my ecstasy of tranquillity. I was no longer concerned for the duration of my happiness. I felt that this peace that I had desired so long must surely last for ever.

To the grown-up folk who came to see us during the day—the doctor, certain germproof unmarried aunts, truculently maternal, and the family itself—my brother's case was far more interesting than mine because he had caught the measles really badly. I just had them comfortably; enough to be infectious, but not enough to feel ill, so I was left in pleasant solitude while the women competed for the honour of smoothing my brothers' pillow and tiptoeing in a fidgeting manner round his bed. I lay on my back and looked with placid interest at the cracks in the ceiling. They were like the main roads in a map, and I amused myself by building little houses beside them—houses full of books and warm hearthrugs, and with a nice pond lively with tadpoles in the garden of each.

From the windows of the houses, you could watch all the traffic that went along the road, men and women and horses, and best of all, the boys going to school in the morning—boys who had not done their homework and who would be late for prayers. When I talked about the cracks to my brother, he said that perhaps the ceiling would give way and fall on our heads. I thought about this too, and found it quite easy to picture myself lying in the bed with a smashed head, and blood all over the pillow. Then it occurred to me that the plaster might smash me all over, and my impressions of Farringdon Meat Market added a gruesome vividness to my conception of the consequences. I always found it pleasant to imagine horrible things; it was only the reality that made me sick.

Towards nightfall I became a little feverish, and I heard the grown-ups say that they would give me some medicine later on. Medicine for me signified the nauseous powders of Dr. Gregory, so I pretended to be asleep every time any one came into the room, in order to escape my destiny, until at last someone stood by my bedside so long that I became cramped and had to pretend to wake up. Then I was given the medicine, and found to my surprise that it was delicious and tasted of oranges. I felt that there had been a mistake somewhere, but my head sat a little heavily on my shoulders, and I would not trouble to fix the responsibility.

This time I fell asleep in earnest, and woke in the middle of the night to find my brother standing by my bed, making noises with his mouth. I thought that he had gone mad, and would kill me perhaps, but after a time he went back to bed saying all the bad words he knew. The excitement had made me wide awake, and I tossed about thinking of the cracked ceiling above my head. The room was quite dark, and I could see nothing, so that it might be bulging over me without my knowing it. I stood up in bed and stretched up my arm, but I could not reach the ceiling; yet when I lay down again, I felt as though it had sunk so far that it was touching my hair, and I found it difficult to breathe in such a small space.

I was afraid to move for fear of bringing it down upon me, and in a short while the pressure upon my body became unbearable, and I shrieked out for help. Someone came in and lit the gas, and found me looking very foolish and my brother delirious. I fell asleep almost immediately, but was conscious through my dreams that the gas was still alight and that they were watching by my brother's bedside. In the morning he was very ill and I was no longer feverish, so it was decided to move me back into my own bedroom. I was wrapped up in the bedclothes and told to sit still while the bed was moved.

I sat in an armchair, feeling like a bundle of old clothes, and looking at the cracks in the ceiling which seemed to me like roads. I knew that I had already lost all importance as an invalid, but I was very happy nevertheless. For from the window of one of my little houses I was watching the boys going to school, and my heart was warm with the knowledge of my own emancipation. As my legs hung down from the chair, I found it hard to keep my slippers on my stockingless feet.

3

There followed for me a period of deep and unbroken satisfaction. I was soon considered well enough to get up, and I lived pleasantly between the sofa and the fireside waiting on my brother's convalescence, for it had been settled that I should go away with him to the country for a change of air. I read Dickens and Dumas in English, and made-up long stories in which I myself played important but not always heroic parts. By means of intellectual exercises of this kind I achieved a tranquillity like that of an old man, fearing nothing, desiring nothing, regretting nothing. I no longer reckoned the days or the hours, content to enjoy a passionless condition of being that asked no questions and sought none of me, nor did I trouble to number my journeys in the world of infinite shadows.

But in that long hour of peace, I realised that in some inexplicable way I was interested in the body of a little boy, whose hands obeyed my unspoken wishes, whose legs sprawled before me on the sofa. I knew that before I met him, this boy, whose littleness surprised me, had suffered ill dreams in a nameless world, and now, worn out with tears and humiliation and dread of life, he slept, and while he slept, I watched him dispassionately, as I would have looked at a crippled dad-dy-long-legs. To have felt compassion for him would have disturbed the tranquillity that was a necessary condition of my existence, so I contented myself with noticing his presence and giving him a small part in the pageant of my dreams.

He was not so beautiful as I wished all my comrades to be, and he was besides very small; but shadows are amiable play-friends, and they did not blame him because he cried when he was teased and did not cry when he was beaten, or because the wild unreason of his sorrow made him find cause for tears in the very fullness of his rare enjoy-ment. For the first time in my life, it seems to me I saw this little boy as he was, squat-bodied, big-headed, thick-lipped, and with a face swept clean of all emotions save where his two great eyes glowed with a sulky fire under exaggerated eyebrows.

I noticed his grimy nails, his soiled collar, his unbrushed clothes, the patent signs of defeat changing to utter rout, and from the heights of my great peace I was not sorry for him. He was like that, other boys were different, that was all. And then on a day fear returned to my heart, and my newly discovered Utopia was no more. I do not know what chance word of the grown-up people or what random thought of mine did the mischief; but of a sudden I realised that for all my dreaming I was only separated by a measurable number of days from the horror of school. Already I was sick with fear, and in place of my dreams I distressed myself by visualising the scenes of the life I dreaded—the Meat Market, the dusty shadows of the gymnasium, the sombre reticence of the great hall.

All that my lost tranquillity had given me was a keener sense of my own being; my smallness, my ugliness, my helplessness in the face of the great cruel world. Before I had sometimes been able to dull my emotions in unpleasant circumstances and thus achieve a dogged calm; now I was horribly conscious of my physical sensations, and, above all, of that deadly sinking in my stomach called fear. I clenched my hands, telling myself that I was happy, and trying to force my mind to pleas-ant thoughts; but though my head swam with the effort, I continued to be conscious that I was afraid.

In the midst of my mental struggles, I discovered that even if I succeeded in thinking happy things I should still have to go back to school after all, and the knowledge that thought could not avert calamity was like a bruise on my mind. I pinched my arms and legs, with the idea that immediate pain would make me forget my fears for the future; but I was not brave enough to pinch them really hard, and I could not forget the motive for my action. I lay back on the sofa and kicked the cushions with my feet in a kind of forlorn anger. Thought was no use, nothing was any use, and my stomach was sick, sick with fear.

And suddenly I became aware of an immense fatigue that overwhelmed my mind and my body, and made me feel as helpless as a little child. The tears that were always near my eyes streamed down my face, making my cheek sore against the wet cushion, and my breath came in painful, ridiculous gulps. For a moment I made an effort to control my grief; and then I gave way utterly, crying with my whole body like a little child, until, like a little child, I fell asleep.

When I awoke the room was grey with dusk, and I sat up with a swaying head, glad to hide the shame of my foolish swollen face amongst the shadows. My mouth was still salt with tears, and I was very thirsty, but I was always anxious to hide my weakness from other people, and I was afraid that if I asked for something to drink, they would see that I had been crying. The fire had gone out while I slept, and I felt cold and stiff, but my abandonment of restraint had relieved me, and my fear was now no more than a vague unrest. My mind thought slowly but very clearly. I saw that it was a pity that I had not been more ill than I was, for then, like my brother, I should have gone away for a month instead of a fortnight.

As it was, everybody laughed at me because I looked so well, and said they did not believe that I had been ill at all. If I had thought of it earlier, I might have been able to make myself worse somehow or other, but now it was too late. When the maid came in and lit the gas for tea, she blamed me for letting the fire out, and told me that I had a dirty face. I was glad of the chance to slip away and wash my burning cheeks in cold water. When I had finished and dried my face on the rough towel, I looked at myself in the glass. I looked as if I had been to the seaside for a holiday, my cheeks were so red!

That night as I lay sleepless in my bed, seeking for a cool place between the sheets in which to rest my hot feet, the sickness of fear returned to me, and I knew that I was lost I shut my eyes tightly, but I could not shut out the vivid pictures of school life that my memory had stored up for my torment; I beat my head against the pillow, but I could not change my thoughts. I recalled all the possible events that might interfere with my return to school, a new illness, a railway accident, even suicide, but my reason would not accept these romantic issues. I was helpless before my destiny, and my destiny made me afraid.

And then, perhaps I was half asleep or fond with fear, I leapt out of bed and stood in the middle of the room to meet life and fight it. The hem of my nightshirt tickled my shin and my feet grew cold on the carpet; but though I stood ready with my fists clenched I could see no adversary among the friendly shadows, I could hear no sound but the drumming of the blood against the walls of my head. I got back into bed and pulled the bedclothes about my chilled body. It seemed that life would not fight fair, and being only a little boy and not wise like the grown-up people, I could find no way in which to outwit it.

4

My growing panic in the face of my imminent return to school spoilt my holiday, and I watched my brother's careless delight in the Surrey pine-woods with keen envy. It seemed to me that it was easy for him to enjoy himself with his month to squander; and in any case he was a healthy, cheerful boy who liked school well enough when he was there, though of course he liked holidays better. He had scant patience with my moods, and secretly I too thought they were wicked. We had been taught to believe that we alone were responsible for our sins, and it did not occur to me that the causes of my wickedness might lie beyond my control.

The beauty of the scented pines and the new green of the bracken took my breath and filled my heart with a joy that changed immediately to overwhelming grief; for I could not help contrasting this glorious kind of life with the squalid existence to which I must return so soon. I realised so fiercely the force of the contrast that I was afraid to make friends with the pines and admire the palm-like beauty of the bracken lest I should increase my subsequent anguish; and I hid myself in dark corners of the woods to fight the growing sickness of my body with the feeble weapons of my panic-stricken mind. There followed moments of bitter sorrow, when I blamed myself for not taking advantage of my hours of freedom, and I hurried along the sandy lanes in a desolate effort to enjoy myself before it was too late.

In spite of the miserable manner in which I spent my days, the fortnight seemed to pass with extraordinary rapidity. As the end approached, the people around me made it difficult for me to conceal my emotions, the grown-ups deducing from my melancholy that I was tired of holidays and would be glad to get back to school, and my brother burdening me with idle messages to the other boys—messages that shattered my hardly formed hope that school did not really exist.

I stood ever on the verge of tears, and I dreaded mealtimes, when I had to leave my solitude, lest some turn of the conversation should set me weeping before them all, and I should hear once more what I knew very well myself, that it was a shameful thing for a boy of my age to cry like a little girl. Yet the tears were there and the hard lump in my throat, and I could not master them, though I stood in the woods while the sun set with a splendour that chilled my heart, and tried to drain my eyes dry of their rebellious, bitter waters. I would choke over my tea and be rebuked for bad manners.

When the last day came that I had feared most of all, I succeeded in saying goodbye to the people at the house where I had stopped, and in making the mournful train journey home without disgracing myself. It seemed as though a merciful stupor had dulled my senses to a mute acceptance of my purgatory. I slept in the train, and arrived home so sleepy that I was allowed to go straight to bed without comment. For once my body dominated my mind, and I slipped between the sheets in an ecstasy of fatigue and fell asleep immediately.

Something of this rare mood lingered with me in the morning, and it was not until I reached the Meat Market that I realised the extent of my misfortune. I saw the greasy, red-faced men with their hands and aprons stained with blood. I saw the hideous carcases of animals, the masses of entrails, the heaps of repulsive hides; but most clearly of all I saw an ugly sad little boy with a satchel of books on his back set down in the midst of an enormous and hostile world.

The windows and stones of the houses were black with soot, and before me, there lay school, the place that had never brought me anything but sorrow and humiliation. I went on, but as I slid on the cobbles, my mind caught an echo of peace, the peace of pine-woods and heather, the peace of the library at home, and, my body trembling with revulsion, I leant against a lamp-post, deadly sick. Then I turned on my heels and walked away from the Meat Market and the school for ever. As I went, I cried, sometimes openly before all men, sometimes furtively before shop-windows, dabbing my eyes with a wet pocket-handkerchief, and gasping for breath. I did not care where my feet led me, I would go back to school no more.

I had played truant for three days before the grown-ups discovered that I had not returned to school. They treated me with that extraordinary consideration that they always extended to our great crimes and never to our little sins of thoughtlessness or high spirits. The doctor saw me. I was told that I would be sent to a country school after the next holidays, and meanwhile I was allowed to return to my sofa and my dreams. I lay there and read Dickens and was very happy. As a rule, the cat kept me company, and I was pleased with his placid society, though he made my legs cramped. I thought that I too would like to be a cat.

Children of the Moon

The boy stood at the place where the park trees stopped and the smooth lawns slid away gently to the great house. He was dressed only in a pair of ragged knickerbockers and a gaping buttonless shirt, so that his legs and neck and chest shone silver bare in the moonlight. By day he had a mass of rough golden hair, but now it seemed to brood above his head like a black cloud that made his face deathly white by comparison. On his arms there lay a great heap of gleaming dew-wet roses and lilies, spoil of the park flower-beds. Their cool petals touched his cheek, and filled his nostrils with aching scent. He felt his arms smarting here and there, where the thorns of the roses had torn them in the dark, but these delicate caresses of pain only served to deepen to him the wonder of the night that wrapped him about like a cloak.

Behind him there dreamed the black woods, and over his head multitudinous stars quivered and balanced in space; but these things were nothing to him, for far across the lawn that was spread knee-deep with a web of mist there gleamed for his eager eyes the splendour of a fairy palace. Red and orange and gold, the lights of the fairy revels shone from a hundred windows and filled him with wonder that he should see with wakeful eyes the jewels that he had desired so long in sleep.

He could only gaze and gaze until his straining eyes filled with tears, and set the enchanted lights dancing in the dark. On his ears, that heard no more the crying of the night-birds and the quick stir of the rabbits in the brake, there fell the strains of far music. The flowers in his arms seemed to sway to it, and his heart beat to the deep pulse of the night

So enraptured were his senses that he did not notice the coming of the girl, and she was able to examine him closely before she called to him softly through the moonlight.

"Boy! Boy!"

At the sound of her voice, he swung round and looked at her with startled eyes.

He saw her excited little face and her white dress.

"Are you a fairy?" he asked hoarsely, for the night-mist was in his voice.

"No," she said, "I'm a little girl. You're a wood-boy, I suppose?"

He stayed silent, regarding her with a puzzled face. Who was this little white creature with the tender voice that had slipped so suddenly out of the night?

"As a matter of fact," the girl continued, "I've come out to have a look at the fairies. There's a ring down in the wood. You can come with me if you like, wood-boy."

He nodded his head silently, for he was afraid to speak to her, and set off through the wood by her side, still clasping the flowers to his breast.

"What were you looking at when I found you?" she asked.

"The palace—the fairy palace," the boy muttered.

"The palace?" the girl repeated. "Why, that's not a palace; that's where I live."

The boy looked at her with new awe; if she were a fairy—But the girl had noticed that his feet made no sound beside her shoes.

"Don't the thorns prick your feet, wood-boy?" she asked; but the boy said nothing, and they were both silent for a while, the girl looking about her keenly as she walked, and the boy watching her face. Presently they came to a wide pool where a little tinkling fountain threw bubbles to the hidden fish.

"Can you swim?" she said to the boy.

He shook his head.

"It's a pity," said the girl; "we might have had a bathe. It would be rather fun in the dark, but it's pretty deep there. We'd better get on to the fairy ring."

The moon had flung queer shadows across the glade in which the ring lay, and when they stood on the edge listening intently the wood seemed to speak to them with a hundred voices.

"You can take hold of my hand, if you like," said the girl, in a whisper.

The boy dropped his flowers about his white feet and felt for the girl's hand in the dark. Soon it lay in his own, a warm live thing, that stirred a little with excitement.

"I'm not afraid," the girl said; and so, they waited.

80

The man came upon them suddenly from among the silver birches. He had a knapsack on his back and his hair was as long as a tramp's. At sight of him the girl almost screamed, and her hand trembled in the boy's; some instinct made him hold it tighter.

"What do you want?" he muttered, in his hoarse voice.

The man was no less astonished than the children.

"What on earth are you doing here?" he cried. His voice was mild and reassuring, and the girl answered him promptly.

"I came out to look for fairies."

"Oh, that's right enough," commented the man; "and you," he said, turning to the boy, "are you after fairies, too? Oh, I see; picking flowers. Do you mean to sell them?"

The boy shook his head.

"For my sister," he said, and stopped abruptly.

"Is your sister fond of flowers?"

"Yes; she's dead."

The man looked at him gravely.

"That's a phrase," he said, "and phrases are the devil. Who told you that dead people like flowers?"

"They always have them," said the boy, blushing for shame of his pretty thought.

"And what are *you* looking for?" the girl interrupted.

The man made a mocking grimace, and glanced around the glade as if he were afraid of being overheard.

"Dreams," he said bluntly.

The girl pondered this for a moment.

"And your knapsack?" she began.

"Yes," said the man, "it's full of them."

The children looked at the knapsack with interest, the girl's fingers tingling to undo the straps of it.

"What are they like?" she asked.

The man gave a short laugh.

"Very like yours and his, I expect; when you grow older, young woman, you'll find there's really only one dream possible for a sensible person. But you don't want to hear about my troubles. This is more in your line." He put his hand in his pocket and pulled out a flageolet, which he put to his lips. "Listen!" he said.

To the girl it seemed as though the little tune had leapt from the pipe, and was dancing round the ring like a real fairy, while echo came tripping through the trees to join it. The boy gaped and said nothing.

At last, when the fairy was beginning to falter and echo was quite out of breath, the man took the flageolet from his lips.

"Well," he said, with a smile.

"Thank you very much," said the girl politely. "I think that was very nice indeed. Oh, boy!" she broke off, "you're hurting my hand!"

The boy's eyes were shining strangely, and he was waving his arms in dismay.

"All the wasted moonlight!" he cried; the grass is quite wet with it."

The girl turned to him in surprise.

"Why, boy, you've found your voice."

"After that," said the man gravely, as he put his flageolet back in his pocket, "I think I will show you the inside of my knapsack."

The girl bent down eagerly, while he loosened the straps, but gave a cry of disappointment when she saw the contents.

"Pictures!" she said.

"Pictures," echoed the man drily—"pictures of dreams. I don't know how you're going to see them. Perhaps the moon will do her best."

The girl looked at them nicely, and passed them on one by one to the boy. Presently she made a discovery.

"Oh, boy!" she cried, "your tears are spoiling all the pictures."

"I'm sorry," said the boy huskily; "I can't help it."

"I know," the man said quickly; "it doesn't matter a bit. I expect you've seen these pictures before."

"I know them all," said the boy, "but I have never seen them."

The man frowned.

"It's the devil," he said to himself, "when boys speak English." He turned suddenly to the girl, who was puzzling over the boy's tears. "It's time you went back to bed," he said; "there won't be any fairies tonight. It's too cold for them."

The girl yawned.

"I shall get into a row when I get back if they've found it out. I don't care."

"The moon is fading," said the boy suddenly; "there are no more shadows."

"We will see you through the wood," the man continued, "and say goodnight."

He put his pictures back in his knapsack and then walked silently through the murmuring wood. At the edge of the wood the girl stopped.

"You are a wood-boy," she said to the boy, "and you mustn't come any farther. You can give me a kiss if you like."

The boy did not move, but stayed regarding her awkwardly.

"I think you are a very silly boy," said the girl, with a toss of her head, and she stalked away proudly into the mist.

"Why didn't you kiss her?" asked the man.

"Her lips would burn me," said the boy.

The man and the boy walked slowly across the park.

"Now, boy," said the man, "since civilisation has gone to bed the time has come for you to hear your destiny."

"I am only a poor boy," the boy replied simply. "I don't think I have any destiny."

"Paradox," said the man, "is meant to conceal the insincerity of the aged, not to express the simplicity of youth. But I wander. You have made phrases tonight."

"What are phrases?"

"What are dreams? What are roses? What, in fine, is the moon? Boy, I take you for a moon-child. You hold her pale flowers in your arms, her white beams have caressed your limbs, you prefer the kisses of her cool lips to those of that earth-child; all this is very well. But, above all, you have the music of her great silence; above all, you have her tears. When I played to you on my pipe you recognised the voice of your mother. When I showed you my pictures you recalled the tales with which she hushed you to sleep. And so, I knew that you were her son and my little brother."

"The moon has always been my friend," said the boy; "but I did not know that she was my mother."

"Perhaps your sister knows it; the happy dead are glad to seek her for a mother; that is why they are so fond of white flowers."

"We have a mother at home. She works very hard for us."

"But it is your mother among the clouds who makes your life beautiful, and the beauty of your life is the measure of your days."

While the boy reflected on these things, they had reached the gates of the park, and they stole past the silent lodge on to the high road. A man was waiting there in the shadows, and when he saw the boy's companion he rushed out and seized him by the arm.

"So, I've got you," he said; "I don't think I'll let you go again in a hurry."

The son of the moon gave a queer little laugh.

"Why, it's Taylor!" he said pleasantly; "but, Taylor, you know you're making a great mistake."

"Very possibly," said the keeper, with a laugh.

"You see this boy here, Taylor; I assure you he is much madder than I am."

Taylor looked at the boy kindly.

"Time you were in bed. Tommy," he said.

"Taylor," said the man earnestly, "this boy has made three phrases. "If you don't lock him up, he will certainly become a poet. He will set your precious world of sanity ablaze with the fire of his mother, the moon. Your palaces will totter, Taylor, and your kingdoms become as dust I have warned you."

"That's right sir; and now you must come with me."

"Boy," said the man generously, "keep your liberty. By grace of Providence, all men in authority are fools. We shall meet again under the light of the moon."

With dreamy eyes the boy watched the departure of his companion. He had become almost invisible along the road when, miraculously as it seemed, the light of the moon broke through the trees by the wayside and lit up his figure. For a moment it fell upon his head like a halo, and touched the knapsack of dreams with glory. Then all was lost in the blackness of night

As he turned homeward the boy felt a cold wind upon his cheek. It was the first breath of dawn.

Fate and the Artist

The workmen's dwellings stood in the northwest of London, in quaint rivalry with the comfortable ugliness of the Maida Vale blocks of flats. They were fairly new and very well built, with wide stone staircases that echoed all day to the impatient footsteps of children, and with a flat roof that served at once as a playground for them and a drying-ground for their mothers' washing. In hot weather it was pleasant enough to play hide-and-seek or follow-my-leader up and down the long alleys of cool white linen, and if a sudden gust of wind or some unexpected turn of the game set the wet sheets flapping in the children's faces, their senses were rather tickled than annoyed.

To George, mooning in a corner of the railings that seemed to keep all London in a cage, these games were hardly more important than the shoutings and whistlings that rose from the street below. It seemed to him that all his life—he had lived eleven years—he had been standing in a corner watching other people engaging in meaningless ploys and antics. The sun was hot, and yet the children ran about and made themselves hotter, and he wondered, as when he had been in bed with one of his frequent illnesses, he had wondered at the grown-up folk who came and went, moving their arms and legs and speaking with their mouths, when it was possible to lie still and quiet and feel the moments ticking themselves off in one's forehead.

As he rested in his corner, he was conscious of the sharp edge of the narrow stone ledge on which he was sitting and the thin iron railings that pressed into his back; he smelt the evil smell of hot London, and the soapy odour of the washing; he saw the glitter of the dust, and the noises of the place beat harshly upon his ears, but he could find no meaning in it all. Life spoke to him with a hundred tongues, and all the while he was longing for silence.

To the older inhabitants of the tenements, he seemed a morbid little boy, unhappily too delicate for sense to be safely knocked into him; his fellow-children would have ignored him completely if he had not had strange fancies that made interesting stories and sometimes inspired games. On the whole, George was lonely without knowing what loneliness meant.

All day long the voice of London throbbed up beyond the bars, and George would regard the chimneys and the housetops and the section of lively street that fell within his range with his small, keen eyes, and wonder why the world did not forthwith crumble into silent, peaceful dust, instead of groaning and quivering in continual unrest. But when twilight fell and the children were tired of playing, they would gather round him in his corner by the tank and ask him to tell them stories.

This tank was large and open and held rain water for the use of the tenants, and originally it had been cut off from the rest of the roof by some special railings of its own; but two of the railings had been broken, and now the children could creep through and sit round the tank at dusk, like Eastern villagers round the village well.

And George would tell them stories—queer stories with twisted faces and broken backs, that danced and capered merrily enough as a rule, but sometimes stood quite still and made horrible grimaces. The children liked the cheerful moral stories better, such as Arthur's Boots.

"Once upon a time," George would begin, "there was a boy called Arthur, who lived in a house like this, and always tied his bootlaces with knots instead of bows. One night he stood on the roof and wished he had wings like a sparrow, so that he could fly away over the houses. And a great wind began, so that everybody said there was a storm, and suddenly Arthur found he had a little pair of wings, and he flew away with the wind over the houses. And presently he got beyond the storm to a quiet place in the sky, and Arthur looked up and saw all the stars tied to heaven with little bits of string, and all the strings were tied in bows.

"And this was done so that God could pull the string quite easily when He wanted to, and let the stars fall. On fine nights you can see them dropping. Arthur thought that the angels must have very neat fingers to tie so many bows, but suddenly, while he was looking, his feet began to feel heavy, and he stooped down to take off his boots; but he could not untie the knots quick enough, and soon he started falling very fast. And while he was falling, he heard the wind in the telegraph wires, and the shouts of the boys who sell papers in the street, and then he fell on the top of a house. And they took him to the hospital, and cut off his legs, and gave him wooden ones instead. But he could not fly anymore because they were too heavy."

For days afterwards all the children would tie their bootlaces in bows.

Sometimes they would all look into the dark tank, and George would tell them about the splendid fish that lived in its depths. If the tank was only half full, he would whisper to the fish, and the children would hear its indistinct reply. But when the tank was full to the brim, he said that the fish was too happy to talk, and he would describe the beauty of its appearance so vividly that all the children would lean over the tank and strain their eyes in a desperate effort to see the wonderful fish. But no one ever saw it clearly except George, though most of the children thought they had seen its tail disappearing in the shadows at one time or another.

It was doubtful how far the children believed his stories; probably, not having acquired the habit of examining evidence, they were content to accept ideas that threw a pleasant glamour on life. But the coming of Jimmy Simpson altered this agreeable condition of mind. Jimmy was one of those masterful stupid boys who excel at games and physical contests, and triumph over intellectual problems by sheer braggart ignorance. From the first he regarded George with contempt, and when he heard him telling his stories he did not conceal his disbelief.

"It's a lie," he said; "there ain't no fish in the tank."

"I have seen it, I tell you," said George.

Jimmy spat on the asphalt rudely.

"I bet no one else has," he said.

George looked round his audience, but their eyes did not meet his. They felt that they might have been mistaken in believing that they had seen the tail of the fish. And Jimmy was a very good man with his fists. "Liar!" said Jimmy at last triumphantly, and walked away. Being masterful, he led the others with him, and George brooded by the tank for the rest of the evening in solitude.

Next day George went up to Jimmy confidently. "I was right about the fish," he said. "I dreamed about it last night"

"Rot!" said Jimmy; "dreams are only made-up things; they don't mean anything."

George crept away sadly. How could he convince such a man? All day long he worried over the problem, and he woke up in the middle of the night with it throbbing in his brain. And suddenly, as he lay in his bed, doubt came to him. Supposing he had been wrong, supposing he had never seen the fish at all? This was not to be borne. He crept quietly out of the flat, and tiptoed upstairs to the roof. The stone was very cold to his feet.

There were so many things in the tank that at first George could not see the fish, but at last he saw it gleaming below the moon and the stars, larger and even more beautiful than he had said. "I knew I was right," he whispered, as he crept back to bed. In the morning he was very ill.

Meanwhile blue day succeeded blue day, and while the water grew lower in the tank, the children, with Jimmy for leader, had almost forgotten the boy who had told them stories. Now and again one or other of them would say that Gorge was very, very ill, and then they would go on with their game. No one looked in the tank now that they knew there was nothing in it, till it occurred one day to Jimmy that the dry weather should have brought final confirmation of his scepticism. Leaving his comrades at the long jump, he went to George's neglected corner and peeped into the tank. Sure enough, it was almost dry, and, he nearly shouted with surprise, in the shallow pool of sooty water there lay a large fish, dead, but still gleaming with rainbow colours.

Jimmy was strong and stupid, but not ill-natured, and, recalling George's illness, it occurred to him that it would be a decent thing to go and tell him he was right. He ran downstairs and knocked on the door of the flat where George lived, George's big sister opened it, but the boy was too excited to see that her eyes were wet.

"Oh, miss," he said breathlessly, "tell George he was right about the fish. I've seen it myself!"

"Georgy's dead," said the girl.

Harold

I suppose that everyone has made the acquaintance of the subject of this little biography at some time or other, though to others he may not have appeared as he has appeared to me, and, as I know, he has been called by many names. Indeed, when I consider that there have been men and women who have sought his society with a passionate eagerness, it is clear to me that his disguises must be extremely subtle, and that he employs them with a just regard for the personalities of his companions. For while some have found in his society the ultimate splendour of life, for me he has always been wearisome and ridiculously mean.

Of course, it may be that I have known him too long, for even as a child I was accustomed to find him at my side, an unwelcome guest who came and went by no law that my youthful mind could determine. Certainly, in those days he was more capricious, and the method of argument by repetition, which he still employs, was only too well calculated to weary and distress a child. But for the rest, the Harold whom I knew then was materially the Harold whom I know now.

Conceive a small man so severely afflicted with St. Vitus's dance that his features are hardly definable, endow him with a fondness for clothes of dull colours grievously decorated with spots, and a habit of asking meaningless questions over and over again in an utterly unemotional voice, and you will be able to form a not unfair estimate of the joys of Harold's society. There have been exceptions, however, to the detestable colourlessness of Harold's appearance. I have seen him on occasion dressed in flaming red, like Mephistopheles, and his shrill staccato voice has pierced my head like a corkscrew. But these manifestations have always been brief, and might even be considered enjoyable when compared with the unrestful monotony of Harold's society in general.

Who taught me to call him by the name of Harold I do not know, but in my youthful days the man's character was oddly associated with the idea of virtue as expounded in the books I read on Sunday afternoons. That I hated him was, I felt, merely a fitting attribute in one whose instincts were admittedly bad, but I did not allow the consideration to affect my rejoicings when I escaped from his company. Curiously, too, I perceived that the Olympians were with me in this, and since the moral soundness of those improving books was beyond question, I had grave doubts as to their ultimate welfare. But it was always an easy task to detect the Olympians tripping in their own moralities; they had so many.

As time went on, and I grew out of the Sunday books and all that they stood for, I came to believe that I was growing out of Harold too. His appearances became rare, and, from his point of view, a little ineffective. It pleased me to consider with a schoolboy's arrogance that he was little more than a child's nightmare, and that if a man turned to fight him Harold would vanish. For a while Harold, in his cunning, played up to this idea. He would seek my side timidly, and fly at a word. The long, sleepless nights of childhood and the weary days were forgotten, and I made of him a jest. Sometimes I wondered whether he really existed.

And then he came. At first, I was only mildly astonished when I found that nothing, I could say would make him leave me, but as the hours passed the old hatred asserted itself, and to fight the little man with the dull voice and the cruel spots on his clothes seemed all that there was in life to do. The hours passed into days and nights, and sometimes I was passive in the hope that he might weary, sometimes I shouted answers to his questions—the same answer to the same question—over and over again.

I felt, too, that if I could only see his features plainly for a moment he would disappear, and I would stare at him until the sky grew red as my eyes. But I could not see him clearly, and the world became a thing of dull colours, terrible with spots. By now I was fighting him with a sense of my own fatuity, for I felt that nothing would make this man fight fairly. His voice had fallen to a passionless whisper and the spots on his clothes swelled into obscene blotches and burst like over-ripe fruit. It was then that the chloroform clutched me by the throat. I have never known anything on earth more sweet.

Since then, it seems to me, Harold has never been quite the same. He comes to see me now and again, and sometimes even he lingers by my side. But there is a note of doubt about him that I do not remember to have noticed before—some of his former spirit would seem to be lacking, and I am forced to wonder sometimes whether Harold is not ageing. And, though it may appear strange, the thought inspires me with a certain regret. I do not like the man, and I should be mad to seek him of my own accord, but in fairness I must acknowledge that in a negative way he has contributed to all the pleasures I have enjoyed. Sunsets and roses and the white light of the stars—I owe my appreciation of them all to Harold; and I know that it is by aid of his keen realism that I have founded the city of my dreams. It will be a grey world when Harold is no more.

On the Brighton Road

Slowly the sun had climbed up the hard white downs, till it broke with little of the mysterious ritual of dawn upon a sparkling world of snow. There had been a hard frost during the night, and the birds, who hopped about here and there with scant tolerance of life, left no trace of their passage on the silver pavements. In places the sheltered caverns of the hedges broke the monotony of the whiteness that had fallen upon the coloured earth, and overhead the sky melted from orange to deep blue, from deep blue to a blue so pale that it suggested a thin paper screen rather than illimitable space.

Across the level fields there came a cold, silent wind which blew fine dust of snow from the trees, but hardly stirred the crested hedges. Once above the sky-line, the sun seemed to climb more quickly, and as it rose higher it began to give out a heat that blended with the keenness of the wind.

It may have been this strange alternation of heat and cold that disturbed the tramp in his dreams, for he struggled for a moment with the snow that covered him, like a man who finds himself twisted uncomfortably in the bedclothes, and then sat up with staring, questioning eyes. "Lord! I thought I was in bed," he said to himself as he took in the vacant landscape, "and all the while I was out here." He stretched his limbs, and, rising carefully to his feet, shook the snow off his body. As he did so the wind set him shivering, and he knew that his bed had been warm.

"Come, I feel pretty fit," he thought "I suppose I am lucky to wake at all in this. Or unlucky—it isn't much of a business to come back to." He looked up and saw the downs shining against the blue like the Alps on a picture-postcard. "That means another forty miles or so, I suppose," he continued grimly. "Lord knows what I did yesterday. Walked till I was done, and now I'm only about twelve miles from Brighton. Damn the snow, damn Brighton, damn everything!" The sun crept up higher and higher, and he started walking patiently along the road with his back turned to the hills.

"Am I glad or sorry that it was only sleep that took me, glad or sorry, glad or sorry?" His thoughts seemed to arrange themselves in a metrical accompaniment to the steady thud of his footsteps, and he hardly sought an answer to his question. It was good enough to walk to.

Presently, when three milestones had loitered past, he overtook a boy who was stooping to light a cigarette. He wore no overcoat, and looked unspeakably fragile against the snow. "Are you on the road, guv'nor?" asked the boy huskily as he passed.

"I think I am," the tramp said.

"Oh! then I'll come a bit of the way with you if you don't walk too fast. It's a bit lonesome walking this time of day." The tramp nodded his head, and the boy started limping along by his side.

"I'm eighteen," he said casually. "I bet you thought I was younger."

"Fifteen, I'd have said."

"You'd have backed a loser. Eighteen last August, and I've been on the road six years. I ran away from home five times when I was a little 'un, and the police took me back each time. Very good to me, the police was. Now I haven't got a home to run away from."

"Nor have I," the tramp said calmly.

"Oh, I can see what you are," the boy panted; "you're a gentleman come down. It's harder for you than for me." The tramp glanced at the limping, feeble figure and lessened his pace.

"I haven't been at it as long as you have," he admitted.

"No, I could tell that by the way you walk. You haven't got tired yet. Perhaps you expect something the other end!"

The tramp reflected for a moment. "I don't know," he said bitterly, "I'm always expecting things."

"You'll grow out of that," the boy commented. "It's warmer in London, but it's harder to come by grub. There isn't much in it really."

"Still, there's the choice of meeting somebody there who will understand—"

"Country people are better," the boy interrupted. "Last night I took a lease of a barn for nothing and slept with the cows, and this morning the farmer routed me out and gave me tea and toke because I was little. Of course, I score there; but in London, soup on the Embankment at night, and all the rest of the time coppers moving you on."

"I dropped by the roadside last night and slept where I fell. It's a wonder I didn't die," the tramp said. The boy looked at him sharply.

"How do you know you didn't?" he said.

"I don't see it," the tramp said, after a pause.

"I tell you," the boy said hoarsely, "people like us can't get away from this sort of thing if we want to. Always hungry and thirsty and dog-tired and walking all the time. And yet if anyone offers me a nice home and work my stomach feels sick. Do I look strong? I know I'm little for my age, but I've been knocking about like this for six years, and do you think I'm not dead? I was drowned bathing at Margate, and I was killed by a gipsy with a spike—he knocked my head right in; and twice I was froze like you last night; and a motor cut me down on this very road, and yet I'm walking along here now, walking to London to walk away from it again, because I can't help it Dead! I tell you we can't get away if we want to."

The boy broke off in a fit of coughing, and the tramp paused while he recovered.

"You'd better borrow my coat for a bit, Tommy," he said, "your cough's pretty bad."

"You go to hell!" the boy said fiercely, puffing at his cigarette; "I'm all right I was telling you about the road. You haven't got down to it yet, but you'll find out presently. We're all dead, all of us who're on it, and we're all tired, yet somehow, we can't leave it. There's nice smells in the summer, dust and hay and the wind smack in your face on a hot day; and it's nice waking up in the wet grass on a fine morning. I don't know, I don't know—" he lurched forward suddenly, and the tramp caught him in his arms.

"I'm sick," the boy whispered—"sick."

The tramp looked up and down the road, but he could see no houses or any sign of help. Yet even as he supported the boy doubtfully in the middle of the road a motorcar suddenly flashed in the middle distance, and came smoothly through the snow.

"What's the trouble?" said the driver quietly as he pulled up. "I'm a doctor." He looked at the boy keenly and listened to his strained breathing.

"Pneumonia," he commented. "I'll give him a lift to the infirmary, and you, too, if you like."

The tramp thought of the workhouse and shook his head. "I'd rather walk," he said.

The boy winked faintly as they lifted him into the car.

"I'll meet you beyond Reigate," he murmured to the tramp. "You'll see." And the car vanished along the white road.

All the morning the tramp splashed through the thawing snow, but at midday he begged some bread at a cottage door and crept into a lonely barn to eat it. It was warm in there, and after his meal he fell asleep among the hay. It was dark when he woke, and started trudging once more through the slushy roads.

Two miles beyond Reigate a figure, a fragile figure, slipped out of the darkness to meet him.

"On the road, guv'nor?" said a husky voice. "Then I'll come a bit of the way with you if you don't walk too fast It's a bit lonesome walking this time of day."

"But the pneumonia!" cried the tramp aghast.

"I died at Crawley this morning," said the boy.

Shepherd's Boy

The path climbed up and up and threatened to carry me over the highest point of the downs till it faltered before a sudden outcrop of chalk and swerved round the hill on the level. I was grateful for the respite, for I had been waking all day and my knapsack was growing heavy. Above me in the blue pastures of the skies the cloud-sheep were grazing, with the sun on their snowy backs, and all about me the grey sheep of earth were cropping the wild pansies that grew wherever the chalk had won a covering of soil

Presently I came upon the shepherd standing erect by the path, a tall, spare man with a face that the sun and the wind had robbed of all expression. The dog at his feet looked more intelligent than he. "You've come up from the valley," he said as I passed; "perhaps you'll have seen my boy?"

"I'm sorry, I haven't," I said, pausing.

"Sorrow breaks no bones," he muttered, and strode away with his dog at his heels. It seemed to me that the dog was apologetic for his master's rudeness.

I walked on to the little hill-girt village, where I had made up my mind to pass the night. The man at the village shop said he would put me up, so I took off my knapsack and sat down on a sackful of cattle cake while the bacon was cooking.

"If you came over the hill, you'll have met shepherd," said the man, " and he'll have asked you for his boy."

"Yes, but I hadn't seen him."

The shopman nodded. "There are clever folk who say you can see him, and clever folk who say you can't. The simple ones like you and me, we say nothing, but we don't see him. Shepherd hasn't got no boy."

"What! is it a joke?"

"Well, of course it may be," said the shopman guardedly, "though I

97

can't say I've heard many people laughing at it yet. You see, shepherd's boy he broke his neck. . . .

"That was in the days before they built the fence above the big chalk-pit that you passed on your left coming down. A dangerous place it used to be for the sheep, so shepherd's boy he used to lie along there to stop them dropping into it, while shepherd's dog he stopped them from going too far. And shepherd he used to come down here and have his glass, for he took it then like you or me. He's blue ribbon now.

"It was one night when the mists were out on the hills, and maybe shepherd had had a glass too much, or maybe he got a bit lost in the smoke. But when he went up there to bring them home, he starts driving them into the pit as straight as could be. Shepherd's boy he hollered out and ran to stop them, but four-and-twenty of them went over, and the lad he went with them. You mayn't believe me, but five of them weren't so much as scratched, though it's a sixty feet drop. Likely they fell soft on top of the others. But shepherd's boy he was done.

"Shepherd he's a bit spotty now, and most times he thinks the boy's still with him. And there are clever folk who'll tell you that they've seen the boy helping shepherd's dog with the sheep. That would be a ghost now, I shouldn't wonder. I've never seen it, but then I'm simple, as you might say.

"But I've had two boys myself, and it seems to me that a boy like that, who didn't eat and didn't get into mischief, and did his work, would be the handiest kind of boy to have about the place."

The Bird in the Garden

The room in which the Burchell family lived in Love Street, S.E., was underground and depended for light and air on a grating let into the pavement above.

Uncle John, who was a queer one, had filled the area with green plants and creepers in boxes and tins hanging from the grating, so that the room itself obtained very little light indeed, but there was always a nice bright green place for the people sitting in it to look at. Toby, who had peeped into the areas of other little boys, knew that his was of quite exceptional beauty, and it was with a certain awe that he helped Uncle John to tend the plants in the morning, watering them and taking the pieces of paper and straws that had been through the grating from their hair.

"It is a great mistake to have straws in one's hair," Uncle John would say gravely; and Toby knew that it was true.

It was in the morning after they had just been watered that the plants looked and smelt best, and when the sun shone through the grating and the diamonds were shining and falling through the forest, Toby would tell the baby about the great bird who would one day come flying through the trees—a bird of all colours, ugly and beautiful, with a harsh sweet voice. "And that will be the end of everything," said Toby, though of course he was only repeating a story his Uncle John had told him.

There were other people in the big, dark room besides Toby and Uncle John and the baby; dark people who flitted to and fro about secret matters, people called father and mother and Mr. Hearn, who were apt to kick if they found you in their way, and who never laughed except at nights, and then they laughed too loudly.

"They will frighten the bird," thought Toby; but they were kind to Uncle John because he had a pension. Toby slept in a corner on the ground beside the baby, and when father and Mr. Hearn fought at nights he would wake up and watch and shiver; but when this happened it seemed to him that the baby was laughing at him, and he would pinch her to make her stop. One night, when the men were fighting very fiercely and mother had been asleep on the table, Uncle John rose from his bed and began singing in a great voice. It was a song Toby knew very well about Trafalgar's Bay, but it frightened the two men a great deal because they thought Uncle John would be too mad to fetch the pension any more. Next day he was quite well, however, and he and Toby found a large green caterpillar in the garden among the plants.

"This is a fact of great importance," said Uncle John, stroking it with a little stick. "It is a sign!"

Toby used to lie awake at nights after that and listen for the bird, but he only heard the clatter of feet on the pavement and the screaming of engines far away.

Later there came a new young woman to live in the cellar—not a dark person, but a person you could see and speak to. She patted Toby on the head; but when she saw the baby, she caught it to her breast and cried over it, calling it pretty names.

At first father and Mr. Hearn were both very kind to her, and mother used to sit all day in the corner with burning eyes, but after a time the three used to laugh together at nights as before, and the woman would sit with her wet face and wait for the coming of the bird, with Toby and the baby and Uncle John, who was a queer one.

"All we have to do," Uncle John would say, "is to keep the garden clean and tidy, and to water the plants every morning so that they may be very green." And Toby would go and whisper this to the baby, and she would stare at the ceiling with large, stupid eyes.

There came a time when Toby was very sick, and he lay all day in his corner wondering about wonder. Sometimes the room in which he lay became so small that he was choked for lack of air, sometimes it was so large that he screamed out because he felt lonely. He could not see the dark people then at all, but only Uncle John and the woman, who told him in whispers that her name was "Mummie." She called him Sonny, which is a very pretty name, and when Toby heard it he felt a tickling in his sides which he knew to be gladness. Mummie's face was wet and warm and soft, and she was very fond of kissing.

Every morning Uncle John would lift Toby up and show him the garden, and Toby would slip out of his arms and walk among the trees and plants. And the place would grow bigger and bigger until it was all the world, and Toby would lose himself amongst the tangle of trees and flowers and creepers. He would see butterflies there and tame animals, and the sky was full of birds of all colours, ugly and beautiful; but he knew that none of these was the bird, because their voices were only sweet. Sometimes he showed these wonders to a little boy called Toby, who held his hand and called him Uncle John, sometimes he showed them to his mummie and he himself was Toby; but always when he came back, he found himself lying in Uncle John's arms, and, weary from his walk, would fall into a pleasant dreamless sleep.

It seemed to Toby at this time that a veil hung about him which, dim and unreal in itself, served to make all things dim and unreal. He did not know whether he was asleep or awake, so strange was life, so vivid were his dreams, Mummie, Uncle John, the baby, Toby himself came with a flicker of the veil and disappeared vaguely without cause. It would happen that Toby would be speaking to Uncle John, and suddenly he would find himself looking into the large eyes of the baby, turned stupidly towards the ceiling, and again the baby would be Toby himself, a hot, dry little body without legs or arms, that swayed suspended as if by magic a foot above the bed.

Then there was the vision of two small feet that moved a long way off", and Toby would watch them curiously as kittens do their tails, without knowing the cause of their motion.

It was all very wonderful and very strange, and day by day the veil grew thicker; there was no need to wake when the sleep-time was so pleasant; there were no dark people to kick you in that dreamy place.

And yet Toby woke—woke to a life and in a place which he had never known before.

He found himself on a heap of rags in a large cellar which depended for its light on a grating let into the pavement of the street above. On the stone floor of the area and swinging from the grating were a few sickly, grimy plants in pots. There must have been a fine sunset up above, for a faint red glow came through the bars and touched the leaves of the plants.

There was a lighted candle standing in a bottle on the table, and the cellar seemed full of people. At the table itself two men and a woman were drinking, though they were already drunk, and beyond in a corner Toby could see the head and shoulders of a tall old man. Beside him there crouched a woman with a faded, pretty face, and between Toby and the rest of the room there stood a box in which lay a baby with large, wakeful eyes.

Toby's body tingled with excitement, for this was a new thing; he had never seen it before, he had never seen anything before.

The voice of the woman at the table rose and fell steadily without a pause; she was abusing the other woman, and the two drunken men were laughing at her and shouting her on; Toby thought the other woman lacked spirit because she stayed crouching on the floor and said nothing.

At last, the woman stopped her abuse, and one of the men turned and shouted an order to the woman on the floor. She stood up and came towards him, hesitating; this annoyed the man and he swore at her brutally; when she came near enough, he knocked her down with his fist, and all the three burst out laughing.

Toby was so excited that he knelt up in his corner and clapped his hands, but the others did not notice because the old man was up and swaying wildly over the woman. He seemed to be threatening the man who had struck her, and that one was evidently afraid of him, for he rose unsteadily and lifted the chair on which he had been sitting above his head to use as a weapon.

The old man raised his fist and the chair fell heavily on to his wrinkled forehead and he dropped to the ground.

The woman at the table cried out, "The pension!" in her shrill voice, and then they were all quiet, looking.

Then it seemed to Toby that through the forest there came flying, with a harsh sweet voice and a tumult of wings, a bird of all colours, ugly and beautiful, and he knew, though later there might be people to tell him otherwise, that that was the end of everything.

The Clerk

He was a paper-cuffed clerk, old and weary and forty-five years of age, and he left his office at quarter past four like a man who has been too long in prison and cared not whether he goes or stays.

But he passed down along Cheapside and Fleet Street and the Strand and on and on till he came to the purple mountains stained by a mad sun of crushed whortleberries.

There he stopped and wrung his hands a little and cried to the sun.

"Oh, sun, if you could speak you would join me in my song to my beloved, you would say to me, 'Oh, most miserable, how quiet she is and how cool, there is the softness of new snow on her cheeks!' And I should say, 'Truly there is a magic of cold stars wandering in her hair!' Now though you are dumb you are more fortunate than I, for you can smile on her and touch her, but I, I, woe is me, can only pass by trembling—"

And he went on to the garden of dull red walls and peach trees and roses and there was a moon there very lovely.

And he cried to the moon in his bitter sorrow:

"My beautiful is very young as you know, having kissed her in the night, oh fortunate moon, and her lips are like a new bud. But you are as old as the hills and I, I am forty-five. Weep with me a little."

And he passed on to the field of stars, but to these he said nothing, because they were part of her.

Now he was mad, and things happening, it fell that he was at home in his own bedroom, and she whom he loved lay in his bed, wakeful and wondering, but he sat apart in the room.

And outside the window the moon smiled and the sun lightened the east in his joy, but the stars trembled because they were part of her.

In the house a clock ticked off the seconds in the darkness and sung the hours on a little bell, and the hours were very short yet the clerk sat there marvelling that he had done this thing—that he had stolen her whom he might not speak to, and that she should rest in his bed.

And his blood that had grown weary of longing for the hills and the song of the glistening sea, and his mind that had known too long the yellow desk and electric fires and faces of unloved companions, was stirred by the bitter old desire, not as of old in sorrow to break her, but now in joy to kiss her and make her his.

And he heard her breathing and stirring in her sleep with a rustle of wings, and the tears of fire wove in his eyes and wandered down his cheeks.

For he knew how long it had been and how lonely ere yet he had taken the sun and moon for his friends and won her too; for all the old and bitter longing now that she was his, she was no more than a dream. Even her breath that sweetened all the room was only a thing thought of long ago. Even her hair that gleamed wonderfully on the white pillow was only a memory of the sunshine of a boy's spring.

Surely if he touched her, she would vanish as had all the others.

She was all he had longed for, all he had desired. His lost ideal. He would not have her perish with the rest, so he sat apart in his chair and watched her with filial wakeful eyes.

And the sun came up over the houses and through the window and kissing her, made her very sweet. And the birds sang at the panes, and her lips moving a little seemed to echo the song, and when her lips parted, they were like the breaking of all the rosebuds.

The clerk drew his chair nearer to the bed and leant forward to listen.

Surely there was a singing not of birds. A voice that was not new singing an old song of the spring.

And then bending forward he felt her cool breath beating on his cheek and wrapping round his face. Roses and thyme and lilies.

And the song swelled in his ears and he knew it for his own. The song he had never been able to sing.

And he saw her lips parting—

It was better to lose her, better to take the risk. If it might be one kiss—

He stood up with a great cry and fell forward on to the bed, dead.

The Coffin Merchant

1

London on a November Sunday inspired Eustace Reynolds with a melancholy too insistent to be ignored and too causeless to be enjoyed. The grey sky overhead between the house-tops, the cold wind round every streetcorner, the sad faces of the men and women on the pavements, combined to create an atmosphere of ineloquent misery. Eustace was sensitive to impressions, and in spite of a half-conscious effort to remain a dispassionate spectator of the world's melancholy, he felt the chill of the aimless day creeping over his spirit.

Why was there no sun, no warmth, no laughter on the earth? What had become of all the children who keep laughter like a mask on the faces of disillusioned men? The wind blew down Southampton Street, and chilled Eustace to a shiver that passed away in a shudder of disgust at the sombre colour of life. A windy Sunday in London before the lamps are lit, tempts a man to believe in the nobility of work.

At the corner by Charing Cross Telegraph Office a man thrust a handbill under his eyes, but he shook his head impatiently. The blueness of the fingers that offered him the paper was alone sufficient to make him disinclined to remove his hands from his pockets even for an instant. But the man would not be dismissed so lightly.

"Excuse me, sir," he said, following him, "you have not looked to see what my bills are."

"Whatever they are I do not want them."

"That's where you are wrong, sir," the man said earnestly. "You will never find life interesting if you do not lie in wait for the unexpected. As a matter of fact, I believe that my bill contains exactly what you do want."

Eustace looked at the man with quick curiosity. His clothes were ragged, and the visible parts of his flesh were blue with cold, but his eyes were bright with intelligence and his speech was that of an educated man. It seemed to Eustace that he was being regarded with a keen expectancy, as though his decision on the trivial point was of real importance.

"I don't know what you are driving at," he said, "but if it will give you any pleasure, I will take one of your bills; though if you argue with all your clients as you have with me, it must take you a long time to get rid of them."

"I only offer them to suitable persons," the man said, folding up one of the handbills while he spoke, "and I'm sure you will not regret taking it," and he slipped the paper into Eustace's hand and walked rapidly away.

Eustace looked after him curiously for a moment, and then opened the paper in his hand. When his eyes comprehended its significance, he gave a low whistle of astonishment. "You will soon be wanting a coffin!" it read. "At 606, Gray's Inn Road, your order will be attended to with civility and despatch. Call and see us!!"

Eustace swung round quickly to look for the man, but he was out of sight The wind was growing colder, and the lamps were beginning to shine out in the greying streets.

Eustace crumpled the paper into his overcoat pocket, and turned homewards.

"How silly!" he said to himself, in conscious amusement. The sound of his footsteps on the pavement rang like an echo to his laugh.

2

Eustace was impressionable but not temperamentally morbid, and he was troubled a little by the fact that the gruesomely bizarre hand-bill continued to recur to his mind. The thing was so manifestly absurd, he told himself with conviction, that it was not worth a second thought, but this did not prevent him from thinking of it again and again. What manner of undertaker could hope to obtain business by giving away foolish handbills in the street?

Really, the whole thing had the air of a brainless practical joke, yet his intellectual fairness forced him to admit that as far as the man who had given him the bill was concerned, brainlessness was out of the question, and joking improbable. There had been depths in those little bright eyes which his glance had not been able to sound, and the man's manner in making him accept the handbill had given the whole transaction a kind of ludicrous significance.

"You will soon be wanting a coffin—!"

Eustace found himself turning the words over and over in his mind. If he had had any near relations, he might have construed the thing as an elaborate threat, but he was practically alone in the world, and it seemed to him that he was not likely to want a coffin for anyone but himself.

"Oh, damn the thing!" he said impatiently, as he opened the door of his flat, "it isn't worth worrying about I mustn't let the whim of some mad tradesman get on my nerves. I've got no one to bury, anyhow."

Nevertheless, the thing lingered with him all the evening, and when his neighbour the doctor came in for a chat at ten o'clock, Eustace was glad to show him the strange handbill. The doctor, who had experienced the queer magics that are practised to this day on the West Coast of Africa, and who, therefore, had no nerves, was delighted with so striking an example of British commercial enterprise.

"Though, mind you," he added gravely, smoothing the crumpled paper on his knee, "this sort of thing might do a lot of harm if it fell into the hands of a nervous subject. I should be inclined to punch the head of the ass who perpetrated it. Have you turned that address up in the Post Office Directory?"

Eustace shook his head, and rose and fetched the fat red book which makes London an English city. Together they found the Gray's Inn Road, and ran their eyes down to No. 606.

"'Harding, G. J., Coffin Merchant and Undertaker.' Not much information there," muttered the doctor.

"Coffin merchant's a bit unusual, isn't it?" queried Eustace.

"I suppose he manufactures coffins wholesale for the trade. Still, I didn't know they called themselves that. Anyhow, it seems as though that handbill is a genuine piece of downright foolishness. The idiot ought to be stopped advertising in that way."

"I'll go and see him myself tomorrow," stud Eustace bluntly.

"Well, he's given you an invitation," said the doctor, "so it's only polite of you to go. I'll drop in here in the evening to hear what he's like. I expect that you'll find him as mad as a hatter."

"Something like that," said Eustace, "or he wouldn't give handbills to people like me. I have no one to bury except myself."

"No," said the doctor in the hall, "I suppose you haven't. Don't let him measure you for a coffin, Reynolds!"

Eustace laughed.

"We never know," he said sententiously.

Next day was one of those gorgeous blue days of which November gives but few, and Eustace was glad to run out to Wimbledon for a game of golf, or rather for two. It was therefore dusk before he made his way to the Gray's Inn Road in search of the unexpected. His attitude towards his errand despite the doctor's laughter and the prosaic entry in the directory, was a little confused. He could not help reflecting that after all the doctor had not seen the man with the little wise eyes, nor could he forget that Mr. G. J. Harding's description of himself as a coffin merchant, to say the least of it, approached the unusual. Yet he felt that it would be intolerable to chop the whole business without finding out what it all meant. On the whole he would have preferred not to have discovered the riddle at all; but having found it, he could not rest without an answer.

No, 606, Gray's Inn Road, was not like an ordinary undertaker's shop. The window was heavily draped with black cloth, but was otherwise unadorned. There were no letters from grateful mourners, no little model coffins, no photographs of marble memorials. Even more surprising was the absence of any name over the shop-door, so that the uninformed stranger could not possibly tell what trade was carried on within, or who was responsible for the management of the business. This uncommercial modesty did not tend to remove Eustace's doubts as to the sanity of Mr. G. J. Harding; but he opened the shop-door which started a large bell swinging noisily, and stepped over the threshold.

The shop was hardly more expressive inside than out A broad counter ran across it, cutting it in two, and in the partial gloom overhead a naked gas-burner whistled a noisy song. Beyond this the shop contained no furniture whatever, and no stock-in-trade except a few planks leaning against the wall in one corner. There was a large ink-stand on the counter. Eustace waited patiently for a minute or two, and then as no one came he began stamping on the floor with his foot. This proved efficacious, for soon he heard the sound of footsteps ascending wooden stairs, the door behind the counter opened and a man came into the shop.

He was dressed quite neatly now, and his hands were no longer blue with cold, but Eustace knew at once that it was the man who had given him the handbill. Nevertheless, he looked at Eustace without a sign of recognition.

"What can I do for you, sir?" he asked pleasantly.

Eustace laid the handbill down on the counter.

"I want to know about this," he said. "It strikes me as being in pretty bad taste, and if a nervous person got hold of it, it might be dangerous."

"You think so, sir? Yet our representative," he lingered affectionately on the words, "our representative told you, I believe, that the handbill was only distributed to suitable cases."

"That's where you are wrong," said Eustace sharply, "for I have no one to bury."

"Except yourself," said the coffin merchant suavely.

Eustace looked at him keenly. "I don't see—" he began. But the coffin merchant interrupted him.

"You must know, sir," he said, "that this is no ordinary undertaker's business. We possess information that enables us to defy competition in our special class of trade."

"Information!"

"Well, if you prefer it, you may say intuitions. If our representative handed you that advertisement, it was because he knew you would need it."

"Excuse me," said Eustace, "you appear to be sane, but your words do not convey to me any reasonable significance. You gave me that foolish advertisement yourself, and now you say that you did so because you knew I would need it. I ask you why?"

The coffin merchant shrugged his shoulders. "Ours is a sentimental trade," he said, "I do not know why dead men want coffins, but they do. For my part I would wish to be cremated."

"Dead men?"

"Ah, I was coming to that. You see Mr. ——?"

"Reynolds."

"Thank you, my name is Harding—G. J. Harding. You see, Mr. Reynolds, our intuitions are of a very special character, and if we say that you will need a coffin, it is—probable that you will need one."

"You mean to say that I—"

"Precisely. In twenty-four hours or less, Mr. Reynolds, you will need our services."

The revelation of the coffin merchant's insanity came to Eustace with a certain relief. For the first time in the interview, he had a sense of the dark empty shop and the whistling gas-jet over his head.

"Why, it sounds like a threat, Mr. Harding!" he said gaily.

The coffin merchant looked at him oddly, and produced a printed form from his pocket "If you would fill this up," he said.

Eustace picked it up off the counter and laughed aloud. It was an order for a hundred-guinea funeral.

"I don't know what your game is," he said, "but this has gone on long enough."

"Perhaps it has, Mr. Reynolds," said the coffin merchant, and he leant across the counter and looked Eustace straight in the face.

For a moment Eustace was amused; then he was suddenly afraid. "I think it's time I—" he began slowly, and then he was silent, his whole will intent on fighting the eyes of the coffin merchant. The song of the gas-jet waned to a point in his ears, and then rose steadily till it was like the beating of the world's heart. The eyes of the coffin merchant grew larger and larger, till they blended in one great circle of fire. Then Eustace picked a pen off the counter and filled in the form.

"Thank you very much, Mr. Reynolds," said the coffin merchant, shaking hands with him politely. "I can promise you every civility and despatch. Good-day, sir."

Outside on the pavement Eustace stood for a while trying to recall exactly what had happened. There was a slight scratch on his hand, and when he automatically touched it with his lips, it made them burn. The lit lamps in the Gray's Inn Road seemed to him a little unsteady, and the passers-by showed a disposition to blunder into him.

"Queer business," he said to himself dimly; "I'd better have a cab."

He reached home in a dream.

It was nearly ten o'clock before the doctor remembered his promise, and went upstairs to Eustace's flat. The outer door was half-open so that he thought he was expected, and he switched on the light in the little hall, and shut the door behind him with the simplicity of habit. But when he swung round from the door, he gave a cry of astonishment. Eustace was lying asleep in a chair before him with his face flushed and drooping on his shoulder, and his breath hissing noisily through his parted lips. The doctor looked at him quizzically, "If I did not know you, my young friend," he remarked, "I should say that you were as drunk as a lord."

And he went up to Eustace and shook him by the shoulder; but Eustace did not wake.

"Queer!" the doctor muttered, sniffing at Eustace's lips; "he hasn't been drinking."

The Conjurer

Certainly, the audience was restive. In the first place it felt that it had been defrauded, seeing that Cissie Bradford, whose smiling face adorned the bills outside, had failed to appear, and secondly, it considered that the deputy for that famous lady was more than inadequate. To the little man who sweated in the glare of the limelight and juggled desperately with glass balls in a vain effort to steady his nerve it was apparent that his turn was a failure. And as he worked, he could have cried with disappointment, for his was a trial performance, and a year's engagement in the Hennings' group of music-halls would have rewarded success. Yet his tricks, things that he had done with the utmost ease a thousand times, had been a succession of blunders, rather mirth-provoking than mystifying to the audience. Presently one of the glass balls fell crashing on the stage, and amidst the jeers of the gallery he turned to his wife, who served as his assistant.

"I've lost my chance," he said, with a sob; "I can't do it!"

"Never mind, dear," she whispered. "There's a nice steak and onions at home for supper."

"It's no use," he said despairingly. "I'll try the disappearing trick and then get off. I'm done here." He turned back to the audience.

"Ladies and gentlemen," he said to the mockers in a wavering voice, "I will now present to you the concluding item of my entertainment. I will cause this lady to disappear under your very eyes, without the aid of any mechanical contrivance or artificial device." This was the merest showman's patter, for, as a matter of fact, it was not a very wonderful illusion. But as he led his wife forward to present her to the audience the conjurer was wondering whether the mishaps that had ruined his chance would meet him even here. If something should go wrong—he felt his wife's hand tremble in his, and he pressed it tightly to reassure her. He must make an effort, an effort of will, and then no mistakes would happen. For a second the lights danced before his eyes, then he pulled himself together. If an earthquake should disturb the curtains and show Molly creeping ignominiously away behind, he would still meet his fate like a man. He turned round to conduct his wife to the little alcove from which she should vanish. She was not on the stage!

For a minute he did not guess the greatness of the disaster. Then he realised that the theatre was intensely quiet, and that he would have to explain that the last item of his programme was even more of a fiasco than the rest. Owing to a sudden indisposition—his skin tingled at the thought of the hooting. His tongue rasped upon cracking lips as he braced himself and bowed to the audience.

Then came the applause. Again and again, it broke out from all over the house, while the curtain rose and fell, and the conjurer stood on the stage, mute, uncomprehending. What had happened? At first, he had thought they were mocking him, but it was impossible to misjudge the nature of the applause. Besides, the stage-manager was allowing him call after call, as if he were a star. When at length the curtain remained down, and the orchestra struck up the opening bars of the next song, he staggered off into the wings as if he were drunk. There he met Mr. James Hennings himself.

"You'll do," said the great man; "that last trick was neat. You ought to polish up the others though. I suppose you don't want to tell me how you did it? Well, well, come in the morning and we'll fix up a contract." And so, without having said a word, the conjurer found himself hustled off by the Vaudeville Napoleon. Mr. Hennings had something more to say to his manager.

"Bit rum," he said. "Did you see it?"

"Queerest thing we've struck."

"How was it done do you think?"

"Can't imagine. There one minute on his arm, gone the next, no trap, or curtain, or anything."

"Money in it, eh?"

"Biggest hit of the century, I should think."

"I'll go and fix up a contract and get him to sign it tonight Get on with it." And Mr. James Hennings fled to his office.

Meanwhile the conjurer was wandering in the wings with the drooping heart of a lost child. What had happened? Why was he a success, and why did people stare so oddly, and what had become of his wife? When he asked them the stage hands laughed, and said they had not seen her. Why should they laugh? He wanted her to explain things, and hear their good luck. But she was not in her dressing-room, she was not anywhere. For a moment he felt like crying.

Then, for the second time that night, he pulled himself together. After all, there was no reason to be upset. He ought to feel very pleased about the contract, however it had happened. It seemed that his wife had left the stage in some queer way without being seen. Probably to increase the mystery she had gone straight home in her stage dress, and had succeeded in dodging the stage-door keeper. It was all very strange; but, of course, there must be some simple explanation like that. He would take a cab home and find her there already. There was a steak and onions for supper.

As he drove along in the cab, he became convinced that this theory was right. Molly had always been clever, and this time she had certain-ly succeeded in surprising everybody. At the door of his house, he gave the cabman a shilling for himself with a light heart. He could afford it now. He ran up the steps cheerfully and opened the door. The passage was quite dark, and he wondered why his wife hadn't lit the gas.

"Molly!" he cried, "Molly!"

The small, weary-eyed servant came out of the kitchen on a sa-voury wind of onions.

"Hasn't missus come home with you, sir?" she said.

The conjurer thrust his hand against the wall to steady himself, and the pattern of the wallpaper seemed to burn his fingertips.

"Not here!" he gasped at the frightened girl. "Then where is she? Where is she?"

"I don't know, sir," she began stuttering; but the conjurer turned quickly and ran out of the house. Of course, his wife must be at the theatre. It was absurd ever to have supposed that she could leave the theatre in her stage dress unnoticed; and now she was probably wor-rying because he had not waited for her. How foolish he had been.

It was a quarter of an hour before he found a cab, and the theatre was dark and empty when he got back to it. He knocked at the stage door, and the night watchman opened it

"My wife?" he cried.

"There's no one here now, sir," the man answered respectfully, for he knew that a new star had risen that night.

The conjurer leant against the doorpost faintly,

"Take me up to the dressing-rooms," he said. "I want to see wheth-er she has been there while I was away."

The watchman led the way along the dark passages. "I shouldn't worry if I were you, sir," he said. "She can't have gone far." He did not know anything about it, but he wanted to be sympathetic.

"God knows," the conjurer muttered, "I can't understand this at all."

In the dressing-room Molly's clothes still lay neatly folded as she had left them when they went on the stage that night, and when he saw them his last hope left the conjurer, and a strange thought came into his mind.

"I should like to go down on the stage," he said, "and see if there is anything to tell me of her."

The night watchman looked at the conjurer as if he thought he was mad, but he followed him down to the stage in silence. When he was there the conjurer leaned forward suddenly, and his face was filled with a wistful eagerness.

"Molly!" he called, "Molly!"

But the empty theatre gave him nothing but echoes in reply.

The Inheritor

Arthur Bradford pushed away his plate of tepid bacon and eggs and looked at the letter with swimming eyes. His Aunt Geraldine, whom he had only seen as a stern vision that disapproved of his mother, had died intestate, leaving property to the value of twelve thousand pounds.

And he was the only heir, he, Arthur Bradford, clerk in the employment of the Commonwealth Insurance Co., on a salary of £115 a year.

Over twelve thousand pounds—at four *per cent*, that would be nearly five hundred a year, perhaps he would get five *per cent*, he knew people in the City who were wise in such matters, six hundred pounds a year—the bed-sitting-room with the faded, silly furniture grew dim and uncertain to his sight; the white tablecloth seemed to move beneath his fingers; it was all so strange.

Once, three years before, when he had first met Molly, he had applied ambitiously for a vacant post, and had narrowly missed getting it. The salary would have been £150 a year, and it was pleasant to recall the old bitterness now that he need work no more, now that he was rich.

He walked to the window and opened it with fumbling fingers. The sky was grey and threatened rain, and at any other time the outlook would have depressed him; but today he felt that he had at last inherited London, its streets and shops and horses were in a manner his; he could ride in its carriages if he wished.

He thought of Molly in that little dull shop across the water, the shop that sold penny packets of notepaper and gorgeous penholders and ill-printed classics bound in cloth for eightpence halfpenny, and at the thought he smiled. For they could marry now, they for whom marriage had always been an impactable ideal, they for whom love had been perforce little but a series of Sunday afternoon walks in the park; they could marry and live where they pleased, even in the green country of which folk wrote in books.

Other men, he reflected, in the face of so great an inheritance would make haste to forget the little shop assistant whom they had loved when they were poor. But that was not his way. No! She should share his fortune and serve at a counter no more. He felt that he was not a mean man.

He looked at his watch and saw that he was too late to be in time for his office; and he did not care. He would send them a cheque for a month's salary in lieu of notice, and he found a certain pleasure in the thought that his sudden resignation at balancing time would inconvenience them. Perhaps they would see that his services were worth more than the paltry sum they had been paying him, perhaps even they would offer him an increase in order to tempt him back. He pictured himself declining with a certain courteous dignity; after all, they were a decent enough lot of fellows, he bore them no ill-will.

The rain still held off, and he found the room close and too small for his new aspirations and put on his hat and coat to go into the streets; he would walk across to the shop in Lambeth and tell Molly of his good luck, of their good luck, rather; that would be the graceful way to put it, and then how glad she would be! Of course, he was only doing the decent thing, yet he could not help feeling that there were a good many men who would fail to do it in similar circumstances, for although Molly was a quite exceptional girl, she was not, of course, of the same social rank as—

He checked himself with a certain shame and glanced in the faces of the people who were passing to see if they had detected a thought that seemed to him treacherous; then he laughed aloud at his fear and the thing that had caused it.

Why, he was on his way now to tell her of his good fortune. Over twelve thousand pounds, say, if he invested it carefully, some six hundred and fifty a year; how happy she would be! He was going to tell her immediately, the very hour he had heard of it himself. Surely that was what a good man would do.

Now he would be able to buy her new dresses in place of the old drab blouses and skirts and the soiled aprons. And they would forget that she had ever worn such things and served in a cheap stationer's shop, or if they did recall them, it would be with pleasure, because they belonged to a grey past and would come again no more.

How mean the shop was, he thought, as approached it, and how grey and soiled the street in which it stood. Dirty babes too young for school scrambled in the gutters while their mothers, unkempt and ragged, breathed gin and profanity from the doors of the decaying houses. The few shops with their muddy fronts and unclean windows appeared to be on the verge of failure; the one in which Molly worked might well be, he thought, for who in such a neighbourhood would want notepaper or gaudy penholders or cheap ill-printed copies of Ainsworth's novels?

He stopped before the shop and looked through the window past the sheets of verses by talented author of *The Fireman's Wedding*, and saw that Molly was standing behind the counter; so, he slipped quietly through the open door to take her by surprise.

She was fixing picture postcards of the most fatuously vulgar character in melancholy rows by means of paper fasteners, and hanging these rows by means of paper fasteners, and hanging these rows as they were completed from the long gas bracket that was suspended from the ceiling. The dust from the swinging bracket had made her face dirty, there were smudges on her blouse and on her apron, she did not look so pretty as she did on Sunday afternoon in the park. When she looked up and saw him there was mingled with her surprise that he should come to visit her during office hours, obvious annoyance that he should find her in such an untidy condition; but he had news, wonderful news for her.

"Over twelve thousand pounds, Molly, over twelve thousand pounds!"

When he had finished his story and displayed the letter she burst into tears.

So, this was the end of his fine thinking and of his generosity, this was the manner in which she received the news of his good fortune, of their good fortune. Arthur Bradford tapped his fingers on the counter in his annoyance. He did not know that she was crying because her face was dirty and she was drab and old—because the shop was dark and the postcards vulgar and the boxes on the upper shelves so covered with dust that to move them was torment—because the little boys of the street were wont to run into the shop and mock her across the counter.

Still, she cried; Arthur could see two women looking curiously through the window and a third approaching to see what they were looking at, and he saw, as if he were a neutral observer, himself the rich man standing in the dark, low shop pleading desperately with a dirty, ill-dressed girl, who receiving his entreaties with sobs and chokings; he felt a wild anger rise in him that anything should have happened to mar his happiness on such a day of good fortune.

Then the horror overcame him; he saw himself and his business laid before a scornful, grinning crowd, he felt that he had allowed himself to be bound to a world of muss and vulgarity and grimy tears at the moment when fortune had given him wings to rise; he saw love as a thing that choked and sniffled.

The crowd had lapsed across the door when he burst out of the shop.

Still the rain held off. Folk passed along the twilit streets with their lips parted as if they were thirsty. There would be no peace until the yellow clouds broke and washed the heavy air.

So, this was the end and he was a bad man after all. And yet he felt that he had tried to do the decent thing. Why had she cried and made him look ridiculous? Why had everything been so dusty and grey? It was true that it was not too late to go back, but he knew he would never do it. He was free, and even the thought of the untidy little figure crying as though its heart would break in the dark empty shop would not make him retrace his steps to a grey street and a grey business. Was he not rich? And after all, she—she would forget him and marry someone of her own class. Oh, he was a hound and a blackguard, but still he had meant well. A good many men would have dropped her without telling her of their good luck, but he had told her at once, and now he was free and would forget all about it.

Over twelve thousand pounds. What might he not do?

On his table at home, he found another letter from the lawyers. Perhaps they were sending a cheque on account.

As he opened it, the storm burst and the rain dashed against the windowpanes with a muffled roar, like the tapping of many fingers on a counter. So, the old woman who had disliked his mother had made a will; there was a matter of twelve thousand pounds for three charities, and he, Arthur Bradford, who had lost Molly, would be a clerk for evermore. He dropped his face in his hands and cried like a child.

The Magic Pool

Being born in a sceptical age, heirs of a world that certainly took its Darwin too seriously, we children did not readily enlarge the circle of our supernatural acquaintances. There was the old witch who lived in the two-storied house beyond the hill, in whom less discriminate eyes recognised only the very respectable widow of an officer in the Indian Army. There was the ghost of the murdered shepherd-lad that haunted the ruined hut high up on the windy downs; on gusty nights we heard him piping shrilly to his phantom flocks, and sometimes their little bells seemed to greet us from the chorus of the storm.

There was a little drowned kitten who mewed to us from the shadows of the rain-water cistern, and a small boy who cried about the garden in the autumn because he could not find his ball among the dead leaves. We had all heard the three last, and most of us had seen them at twilight-time, when ghosts pluck up their poor thin courage and take their walks abroad. As for the witch, we relied on our intuitions and gave her house a wide berth.

The credentials of these four unquiet spirits having been examined and found satisfactory, schoolroom opinion was against any addition to their number. We would not accept my younger brother's murderer carrying a sack or my little sister's procession of special tortoises, though we acknowledged that there was merit in them, regarded merely as artistic conceptions. Perhaps, subconsciously, we realised that to make the supernatural commonplace is also to make it ineffective, and that there is no dignity in a life jostled by spooks. At all events, we relied for our periodical panics on those which had received the official sanction, and on the terrifying monsters our imaginations had drawn from real life—burglars, lunatics, and drunken men.

It was therefore noteworthy that as soon as we discovered the pool in Hayward's Wood, we were all agreed that it was no ordinary sheet of water, but one of those enchanted pools which draw their waters from magic sources and are capable of throwing spells over mortals who approach them unwarily. And yet, though we felt instinctively that there was something queer about it, the pool in itself was not unattractive. Held, as it were, in a cup in the heart of the wood, it still contrived to win its share of sunshine through the branches above. On its surface the water-boatmen were ferrying cheerfully to and fro, while overhead the dragon-flies drove their gaudy monoplanes in ceaseless competition.

All about the woods were gay with wild garlic and the little purple gloves that Nature provides for foxes, and through a natural alley we could see a golden meadow, where cups of cool butter were spread with lavish generosity to quench the parched tongues of bees. The mud that squelched under our feet as we stood on the brink seemed to be good, honest mud, and gave our boots the proper holiday finish. Nevertheless, we stared silently at the waters, half-expecting to see them thicken and part in brown foam, to allow some red-mouthed prehistoric monster to rise oozily from his resting-place in the mud— some such mammoth as we had seen carved in stone on the borders of the lake at the Crystal Palace. But no monster appeared; only a rabbit sprang up suddenly on the far side of the pool, and, seeing we had no gun and no dog, limped off in a leisurely manner to the warren.

After a while we grew weary of our doubts, and, tacitly agreeing to pretend that it was only an ordinary pond, fell to paddling in the shallows with a good heart. The mud slid warmly through our toes, and the water lay round our calves like a tight string, but we were not changed, as we had half anticipated, into tadpoles or water-lilies. It was apparent that the magic was of a subtler kind than this, and we splashed about cheerfully until the inevitable happened and one of us went in up to his waist. Then we sat on the bank nursing our wet feet, and laughing at the victim as he ruefully wrung out his clothes.

We were all of a nautical turn of mind, and we agreed that the pond would serve very well for minor naval engagements, though it was too sheltered to provide enough wind for sailing-ships. Still, here we should at all events be secure from such a disaster as had recently overtaken my troopship *Dauntless*, which was cruising in calm weather on Pickhurst Pond when all of a sudden "a land breeze shook the shrouds and she was overset," and four-and-twenty good soldiers sank to the bottom like lead, which they were. Regarded merely as an attractive piece of water, the pool could not fail to be of service in our adventurous lives.

But all the time we felt in our hearts that it was something more, though we would have found it hard to give reasons for our conviction, for the pool seemed very well able to keep the secret of its enchantment. We did not even know whether it was the instrument of black magic or of white, whether its influence on human beings was amiable or malevolent. We only knew that it was under a spell, that beneath its reticent surface, that showed nothing more than the reflection of our own inquiring faces, lay hidden some part of that especial magic that makes the dreams of young people as real as life, and contradicts the unlovely generalisations of disillusioned adults. All that was necessary was to find the key that would unlock the golden gates.

The brother who was nearest to me in terms of years found it two days later, and came to me breathlessly with the news. He had been reading a book of fairy stories, and had come upon the description of just such a magic pool as ours, even to the rabbit—who was, it seemed, a kind of advance-agent to the spirit of the pool. The rules were very clear. All you had to do was to go to the pool at midnight and wish aloud, and your wish would be granted. If you were greedy enough to wish more than once, you would be changed into a goldfish. My brother thought it would be rather jolly to be a goldfish, and so for a while did I; but on reflection we decided that if the one wish were carefully expended it might be more amusing to remain a boy.

It says something for our spirit of adventure that we did not even discuss the advisability of undertaking this lawless expedition. We were more engaged in rejoicing in anticipation over the discomfiture of our elder brothers and settling the difficult problem of what we should wish. My brother was all for seven-league boots and invisible caps and other conjuring tricks of a fairy character; I had set my heart on money, more sovereigns than we could carry, and I finally brought my brother round to my point of view. After all, he could always buy the other things if he had enough money. It was agreed that he should wind up his birthday watch and that we should only pretend to go to bed, as we should have to start at half-past eleven. When planned by daylight the whole thing seemed absurdly easy.

We had no difficulty in getting out of the house when the time came, simply because this was not the sort of thing that the grown-up people expected us to do, but we found the world strangely altered. The familiar lanes had become rivers of changing shadows, the hedgerows were ambuscades of robbers, the tall trees were affronted giants. Fortunately, we were on very good terms with the moon at the time, so when she made her periodical appearances from behind the scudding clouds she came as a friend. Nevertheless, when my hand accidentally touched my brother's in the dark it stayed there, and we were glad to walk along hand in hand, a situation which we would have thought deplorable for two fellows of our years by day.

It seemed to me that my brother was breathing shortly and noisily as if he were excited, but presently the surprising thought came to me that it might be my own breathing that I heard. As we drew near to Hayward's Wood the moon retired behind a cloud, and stayed there. This was hardly friendly of her, for the wood was terribly dark, and the noise of our own stumblings made us pause in alarm again and again. When we stood still and listened all the trees seemed to be saying "Hush!"

Somehow, we reached the pool at last, and stayed our steps on the bank expectantly. At first, we could see nothing but shadows, but, after a while, we discovered that it was full of drowned stars, a little pale as though the water had extinguished some of their fire. And then, as we wondered at this, the moon shone through the branches overhead and lit the wood with a cool and mysterious radiance that reminded me oddly of the transformation scene in our last pantomime. My brother pulled his watch out of his pocket, but his hand shook so that he could hardly tell the time. "Five minutes more," he whispered hoarsely. I tried to answer him, and found that I could not speak.

And then, as we waited breathlessly, we heard a noise among the undergrowth on the other side of the pool—a noise, it seemed, of footsteps, that grew louder and louder in our excited ears, till it was as if all the armies of the world were tramping through the wood. And then . . . and then . . .

When we stopped to get our breath halfway home, we first discovered that neither of us had had presence of mind enough to wish. But we knew that there was no going back. We had had our chance, and missed it. But, even now, I do not doubt that it was a magic pool.

The Passing of Edward

I found Dorothy sitting sedately on the beach, with a mass of black seaweed twined in her hands and her bare feet sparkling white in the sun. Even in the first glow of recognition I realised that she was paler than she had been the summer before, and yet I cannot blame myself for the tactlessness of my question.

"Where's Edward?" I said; and I looked about the sands for a sailor suit and a little pair of prancing legs.

While I looked, Dorothy's eyes watched mine inquiringly, as if she wondered what I might see.

"Edward's dead," she said simply. "He died last year, after you left."

For a moment I could only gaze at the child in silence, and ask myself what reason there was in the thing that had hurt her so.

Now that I knew that Edward played with her no more, I could see that there was a shadow upon her face too dark for her years, and that she had lost, to some extent, that exquisite carelessness of poise which makes children so young. Her voice was so calm that I might have thought her forgetful had I not seen an instant of patent pain in her wide eyes.

"I'm sorry," I said at length, "very, very, sorry indeed. I had brought down my car to take you for a drive, as I promised."

"Oh! Edward *would* have liked that," she answered thoughtfully; "he was so fond of motors."

She swung round suddenly and looked at the sands behind her with staring eyes.

"I thought I heard—" She broke off in confusion.

I, too, had believed for an instant that I had heard something that was not the wind or the distant children or the smooth sea hissing along the beach. During that golden summer which linked me with the dead, Edward had been wont, in moments of elation, to puff up and down the sands, in artistic representation of a nobby, noisy motorcar. But the dead may play no more, and there was nothing there but the sands and the hot sky and Dorothy.

"You had better let me take you for a run, Dorothy," I said. "The man will drive, and we can talk as we go along."

She nodded gravely, and began pulling on her sandy stockings.

"It did not hurt him," she said inconsequently.

The restraint in her voice pained me like a blow.

"Oh, don't, dear, don't!" I cried. "There is nothing to do but forget."

"I have forgotten, quite," she answered, pulling at her shoe-laces with calm fingers. "It was ten months ago."

We walked up to the front, where the car was waiting, and Dorothy settled herself among the cushions with a little sigh of contentment, the human quality of which brought me a certain relief. If only she would laugh or cry! I sat down by her side, but the man waited by the open door.

"What is it?" I asked.

"I'm sorry, sir," he answered, looking about him in concision, "I thought I saw a young gentleman with you."

He shut the door with a bang, and in a minute, we were running through the town. I knew that Dorothy was watching my face with her wounded eyes; but I did not look at her until the green fields leapt up on either side of the white road.

"It is only for a little while that we may not see him," I said; "all this is nothing."

"I have forgotten," she repeated. "I think this is a very nice motor."

I had not previously complained of the motor, but I was wishing then that it would cease its poignant imitation of a little dead boy, a boy who would play no more. By the touch of Dorothy's sleeve against mine I knew that she could hear it too. And the miles flew by, green and brown and golden, while I wondered what use I might be in the world, who could not help a child to forget. Possibly there was another way, I thought.

"Tell me how it happened," I said.

Dorothy looked at me with inscrutable eyes, and spoke in a voice without emotion.

"He caught a cold, and was very ill in bed. I went in to see him, and he was all white and faded. I said to him, 'How are you, Edward?' and he said, 'I shall get up early in the morning to catch beetles.' I didn't see him anymore."

"Poor little chap!" I murmured.

"I went to the funeral," she continued monotonously. "It was very rainy, and I threw a little bunch of flowers down into the hole. There was a whole lot of flowers there but I think Edward liked apples better than flowers."

"Did you cry?" I said cruelly.

She paused. "I don't know I suppose so. It was a long time ago; I think I have forgotten.

Even while she spoke, I heard Edward puffing along the sands: Edward who had been so fond of apples.

"I cannot stand this any longer," I said aloud. "Let's get out and walk in the woods for a change.

She agreed with a depth of comprehension that terrified me; and the motor pulled up with a jerk at a spot where hardly a post served to mark where the woods commenced and the wayside grass stopped. We took one of the dim paths which the rabbits had made and forced our way through the undergrowth into the peaceful twilight of the trees.

"You haven't got very sunburnt this year," I said as we walked.

"I don't know why. I've been out on the beach all the days. Sometimes I've played, too,"

I did not ask her what games she had played, or who had been her play-friend. Yet even there in the quiet woods I knew that Edward was holding her back from me. It is true that, in his boy's way, he had been fond of me; but I should not have dared to take her out without him in the days when his live lips had filled the beach with song, and his small brown body had danced among the surf. Now it seemed that I had been disloyal to him.

And presently we came to a clearing where the leaves of forgotten years lay brown and rotten beneath our feet, and the air was full of the dryness of death.

"Let's be going back. What do you think, Dorothy?" I said.

"I think," she said slowly—"I think that this would be a very good place to catch beetles."

A wood is full of secret noises, and that is why, I suppose, we heard a pair of small quick feet come with a dance of triumph through the rustling bracken. For a minute we listened deeply, and then Dorothy broke from my side with a piercing call on her lips.

"Oh, Edward, Edward!" she cried; "Edward!"

But the dead may play no more, and presently she came back to me with the tears that are the riches of childhood streaming down her face.

"I can hear him, I can hear him," she sobbed; "but I cannot see him. Never, never again."

And so, I led her back to the motor. But in her tears, I seemed to find a promise of peace that she had not known before.

Now Edward was no very wonderful little boy; it may be that he was jealous and vain and greedy; yet now, it seemed as he lay in his small grave with the memory of Dorothy's flowers about him, he had wrought this kindness for his sister. Yes, even though we heard no more than the birds in the branches and the wind swaying the scented bracken; even though he had passed with another summer, and the dead and the love of the dead may rise no more from the grave.

On Digging Holes

When all the world was young and we were young with it there was no occupation more pleasing to our infant minds than the digging of great holes in that placid and maternal earth that endured the trampling of our childish feet with patience, and betrayed no realisation of the extraordinary miracle of life that had set us dancing in the fields and valleys of the world. As repentant children trace with curious finger on their mother's foreheads the lines that they themselves have set there, so we followed the furrows on the forehead of our mother Earth with our little spades, smoothing here and deepening there, and not the less contented that our labours had but a vague and illusory aim.

Sometimes, perhaps, we had a half-formed ambition to dig to those dim and incredible Antipodes where children walk head downwards, clinging to the earth with their feet, like the flies on the playroom ceiling. Sometimes, perhaps, we dug for treasure, immense masses of golden coin, like those memorable hoards described in *Treasure Island* and the *Gold Bug*. Or, again, it might be that we planned vast caves and galleries wherein tawny pirates and swart smugglers might carouse, shocking the echoes with blood-curdling oaths, and drinking boiling rum like Quilp. We dug, in fine.

There seems to be some element in the human mind that is definitely attracted by the digging of holes, for it is not only children who are interested by the spectacle. The genial excavators whose duty it is to make havoc of the London streets never fail to draw an attentive and apparently appreciative audience, whether of loafers or philosophers the critic may not lightly determine. They gaze into the pit with countenances of abysmal profundity, that appear to see all, to understand all, and to express nothing in particular.

It is possible that they are placidly enjoying the reflection that beneath the complex contrivances of our civilisation, beneath London itself, the virgin earth lies unturned and unaffected. Perhaps, as each spadeful of earth reaches the surface, they perceive, like a child watching the sawdust trickle from the broken head of a doll, that here is the raw material of which worlds are made. Perhaps they do not think at all, but merely derive a mild satisfaction from watching other people work. Yet it is at least agreeable to believe that they are watchers for the unexpected, that they have discovered the great truth that if you dig long enough you will probably dig something up.

We children knew this very well, and we never dug without feeling the thrill proper to treasure-seekers. Even half a brick becomes eventful when found in these circumstances, and the earth had a hundred pleasant secrets in the shape of fragments of pottery, mysterious lumps of metal and excited insects for those who approached her reverently, trowel in hand. It was this variety of treasure that made us prefer inland digging to those more fashionable excavations that are carried on at the seaside. Sand is a friendly substance in which to dig, and it is very convenient to have a supply of water like the sea close at hand when it is necessary to fill a pond or add a touch of realism to a moat.

But the ease with which sand obeys the spade soon becomes monotonous, and the seaside in general suffers from an air of having been elaborately prepared for children to play there. Our delving operations in the garden had the charm of nominal illegality, and the brown earth had a hundred moods to thwart and help and enchant us continually. Sometimes we dug with scientific precision; sometimes we set to work with fury, flinging the earth to all sides in our eagerness to rob her of her secrets. A philosopher might have found in us a striking instance of the revolt of civilised man against Nature; a woman would have noticed that we were getting our pinafores dirty.

And though we liked digging for its own sake, we were not unmindful of the possibilities of a good big hole. From its cool depths we could obtain a new aspect of the sky; and, cunningly roofed over with branches and earth, it made a snug retreat for a harassed brigand and a surprising pitfall for the unwary gardener. In smaller cavities we concealed treasure of stones decked with the colours left behind by the painters at the last spring-cleaning, and if we could not wholly convince ourselves of their intrinsic value, they at least bore adequate resemblance to the treasures of Aladdin's cave, as revealed to us in pantomime. We kept the knowledge of the spots where these treasures were buried a close secret, even from each other, and it was etiquette for the finder of one of these repositories to remove its contents and conceal them elsewhere. The conflict between seeker and finder never languished, and men who rose up millionaires would go to bed paupers.

Like all sincere artists, we did not allow our own efforts to hinder a just appreciation of those of others, and we had the utmost admiration for rabbits, down whose enchanted burrows we would peer longingly, reflecting wisely how fine a home it must be that had so romantic and fascinating an entrance. For us half the charm of "Alice" lay in the natural and sensible means by which she reached her wonderland, though we could never bring ourselves to forgive the author for pretending that his clearly veracious narrative was only a dream. This, we recognised, was an obvious grown-up device for preventing the youthful from slipping away from governesses to wonderlands of their own, and true enough we found rabbit-holes oddly reluctant to admit our small bodies, even though we widened their mouths with our trowels.

Looking-glasses, it may be mentioned, proved no less refractory, and at this day, it is said, children find it impossible to emulate the flying feats of "Peter Pan," though they carefully follow the directions. It is clear that these grown-up authors are not wholly straightforward with their youthful readers, but guard the Olympian interests by concealing some essential part of the ritual in these matters. Sooner or later the children find them out, and expel them from all nurseries, playrooms, gardens, and places where youth and wisdom congregate.

But if we could not tread those long corridors into which the rabbits scuttled so featly on our approach, there was nothing to hinder us from digging a tunnel to fairyland of our own. The grand project formed, all the forces of the garden would unite, and we would dig seriously for an hour or so. At the end of that time somebody's foot would be hurt by a spade, or some bright spirit would suggest that we should fill the hole with water and call it a lake. Or, perhaps, it would be teatime—at all events, we never got to fairyland at all. Or did we? As we grow old our memories fade, but dimly I seem to remember a garden that was like no garden I have found in grown-up places. It is possible that we did reach fairyland, treading the same road that Alice and Cinderella and Aladdin had trod before us. Perhaps a grown-up writer may be pardoned for forgetting.

The Poet's Allegory

1

The boy came into the town at six o'clock in the morning, but the baker at the corner of the first street was up, as is the way of bakers, and when he saw the boy passing, he hailed him with a jolly shout.

"Hullo, boy! What are you after?"

"I'm going about my business," the boy said pertly.

"And what might that be, young fellow?"

"I might be a good tinker, and worship god Pan, or I might grind scissors as sharp as the noses of bakers. But, as a matter of fact, I'm a piper, not a rat-catcher, you understand, but just a simple singer of sad songs, and a mad singer of merry ones."

"Oh," said the baker dully, for he had. hoped the boy was in search of work. "Then I suppose you have a message."

"I sing songs," the boy said emphatically. "I don't run errands for anyone save it be for the fairies."

"Well, then, you have come to tell us that we are bad, that our lives are corrupt and our homes sordid. Nowadays there's money in that if you can do it well."

"Your wit gets up too early in the morning for me, baker," said the boy. "I tell you I sing songs."

"Aye, I know, but there's something in them, I hope. Perhaps you bring news. They're not so popular as the other sort, but still, as long as it's bad news—"

"Is it the flour that has changed his brains to dough, or the heat of the oven that has made them like dead grass?"

"But you must have some news—?"

"News! It's a fine morning of summer, and I saw a kingfisher across the water-meadows coming along. Oh, and there's a cuckoo back in the fir plantation, singing with a May voice. It must have been asleep all these months."

131

"But, my dear boy, these things happen every day. Are there no battles or earthquakes or Amines in the world? Has no man murdered his wife or robbed his neighbour? Is no one oppressed by tyrants or lied to by their officers."

The boy shrugged his shoulders.

"I hope not," he said. "But if it were so, and I knew, I should not tell you. I don't want to make you unhappy."

"But of what use are you then, if it be not to rouse in us the discontent that is alone divine? Would you have me go fat and happy, listening to your babble of kingfishers and cuckoos, while my brothers and sisters in the world are starving?"

The boy was silent for a moment

"I give my songs to the poor for nothing," he said slowly. "Certainly, they are not much use to empty bellies, but they are all I have to give. And I take it, since you speak so feelingly, that you, too, do your best. And these others, these people who must be reminded hourly to throw their crusts out of window for the poor—would you have me sing to them? They must be told that life is evil, and I find it good; that men and women are wretched, and I find them happy; that food and cleanliness, order and knowledge are the essence of content while I only ask for love. Would you have me lie to cheat mean folk out of their scraps?"

The baker scratched his head in astonishment.

"Certainly, you are very mad," he said. "But you won't get much money in this town with that sort of talk. You had better come in and have breakfast with me."

"But why do you ask me?" said the boy, in surprise.

"Well, you have a decent, honest sort of face, although your tongue is disordered."

"I had rather it had been because you liked my songs," said the boy, and he went in to breakfast with the baker.

2

Over his breakfast the boy talked wisely on art, as is the wont of young singers, and afterwards he went on his way down the street

"It's a great pity," said the baker; "he seems a decent young chap."

"He has nice eyes," said the baker's wife.

As the boy passed down the street, he frowned a little.

"What is the matter with them?" he wondered. "They're pleasant people enough, and yet they did not want to hear my songs."

Presently he came to the tailor's shop, and as the tailor had sharper eyes than the baker, he saw the pipe in the boy's pocket

"Hullo, piper!" he called. "My legs are stiff. Come and sing us a song!"

The boy looked up and saw the tailor sitting cross-legged in the open window of his shop.

"What sort of song would you like?" he asked.

"Oh! the latest," replied the tailor. "We don't want any old songs here." So, the boy sung his new song of the kingfisher in the water-meadow and the cuckoo who had overslept itself.

"And what do you call that?" asked the tailor angrily, when the boy had finished.

"It's my new song, but I don't think it's one of my best" But in his heart the boy believed it was, because he had only just made it.

"I should hope it's your worst," the tailor said rudely. "What sort of stuff is that to make a man happy?"

"To make a man happy?" echoed the boy, his heart sinking within him.

"If you have no news to give me, why should I pay for your songs? I want to hear about my neighbours, about their lives, and their wives and their sins. There's the fat baker up the street—they say he cheats the poor with light bread. Make me a song of that, and I'll give you some breakfast. Or there's the magistrate at the top of the hill who made the girl drown herself last week. That's a poetic subject."

"What's all this?" said the boy disdainfully. "Can't you make dirt enough for yourself?"

"You with your stuff about birds," shouted the tailor; "you're a rank impostor! That's what you are!"

"They say that you are the ninth part of a man, but I find that they have grossly exaggerated," cried the boy, in retort; but he had a heavy heart as he made off the street

By noon he had interviewed the butcher, the cobbler, the milk-man, and the maker of candlesticks, but they treated him no better than the tailor had done, and as he was feeling tired, he went and sat down under a tree.

"I begin to think that the baker is the best of the lot of them," he said to himself ruefully, as he rolled his empty wallet between his fingers.

Then, as the folly of singers provides them in some measure with a philosophy, he fell asleep.

When he woke it was late in the afternoon, and the children, fresh from school, had come out to play in the dusk. Far and near, across the town-square, the boy could hear their merry voices, but he felt sad, for his stomach had forgotten the baker's breakfast, and he did not see where he was likely to get any supper. So, he pulled out his pipe, and made a mournful song to himself of the dancing gnats and the bitter odour of the bonfires in the townsfolk's gardens. And the children drew near to hear him sing, for they thought his song was pretty, until their fathers drove them home, saying, "That stuff has no educational value."

"Why haven't you a message?" they asked the boy.

"I come to tell you that the grass is green beneath your feet and that the sky is blue over your heads."

"Oh! but we know all that," they answered.

"Do you! Do you!" screamed the boy. "Do you think you could stop over your absurd labours if you knew how blue the sky is? You would be out singing on the hills with me!"

"Then who would do our work?" they said, mocking him.

"Then who would want it done?" he retorted; but it's ill arguing on an empty stomach.

But when they had tired of telling him what a fool he was, and gone away, the tailor's little daughter crept out of the shadows and patted him on the shoulder.

"I say, boy!" she whispered. "I've brought you some supper. Father doesn't know." The boy blessed her and ate his supper while she watched him like his mother and when he had done she kissed him on the lips.

"There, boy!" she said.

"You have nice golden hair," the boy said. "See! it shines in the dusk. It strikes me it's the only gold I shall get in this town."

"Still, it's nice, don't you think?" the girl whispered in his ear. She had her arms round his neck.

"I love it," the boy said joyfully; "and you like my songs, don't you?"

"Oh, yes, I like them very much, but I like you better."

The boy put her off roughly.

"You're as bad as the rest of them," he said indignantly. "I tell you my songs are everything, I am nothing."

"But it was you who ate my supper, boy," said the girl.

The boy kissed her remorsefully. "But I wish you had liked me for my songs," he sighed.

"You are better than any silly old songs!"

"As bad as the rest of them," the boy said lazily, "but somehow pleasant"

The shadows flocked to their evening meeting in the square, and overhead the stars shone out in a sky that was certainly exceedingly blue.

4

Next morning, they arrested the boy as a rogue and a vagabond, and in the afternoon, they brought him before the magistrate.

"And what have you to say for yourself?" said the magistrate to the boy, after the second policeman, like a faithful echo, had finished reading his notes.

"Well," said the boy, "I may be a rogue and a vagabond. Indeed, I think that I probably am; but I would claim the license that has always been allowed to singers."

"Oh!" said the magistrate. "So, you are one of those, are you? And what is your message?"

"I think if I could sing you a song or two, I could explain myself better," said the boy.

"Well," replied the magistrate doubtfully, "you can try if you like, but I warn you that I wrote songs myself when I was a boy, so that I know something about it."

"Oh, I'm glad of that," said the boy, and he sang his famous song of the grass that is so green, and when he had finished the magistrate frowned.

"I knew that before," he said.

So, then the boy sang his wonderful song of the sky that is so blue. And when he had finished the magistrate scowled. "And what are we to learn from that?" he said.

So, then the boy lost his temper and sang some naughty doggerel he had made up in his cell that morning. He abused the town and townsmen, but especially the townsmen. He damned their morals, their customs, and their institutions. He said that they had ugly faces, raucous voices, and that their bodies were unclean. He said they were thieves and liars and murderers, that they had no ear for music and no sense of humour. Oh, he was bitter!

"Good God!" said the magistrate, "that's what I call real improving poetry. Why didn't you sing that first! There might have been a miscarriage of justice."

Then the baker, the tailor, the butcher, the cobbler, the milkman, and the maker of candlesticks rose in court and said—

"Ah, but we all knew there was something in him."

So, the magistrate gave the boy a certificate that showed that he was a real singer, and the tradesmen gave him a purse of gold, but the tailor's little daughter gave him one of her golden ringlets. "You won't forget, boy, will you?" she said.

"Oh, no," said the boy; "but I wish you had liked my songs."

Presently, when he had come a little way out of the town, he put his hand in his wallet and drew out the magistrate's certificate and tore it in two; and then he took out the gold pieces and threw them into the ditch, and they were not half as bright as the buttercups. But when he came to the ringlet, he smiled at it and put it back.

"Yet she was as bad as the rest of them," he thought with a sigh.

And he went across the world with his songs.

The Soul of a Policeman

1

Outside, above the uneasy din of the traffic, the sky was glorious
with the far peace of a fine summer evening. Through the upper pane
of the station window Police-Constable Bennett, who felt that his
senses at the moment were abnormally keen, recognised with a sinking heart such reds and yellows as bedecked the best patchwork quilt
at home. By contrast the lights of the superintendent's office were
subdued, so that within the walls of the police-station sounds seemed
of greater importance. Somewhere a drunkard, deprived of his boots,
was drumming his criticism of authority on the walls of his cell. From
the next room, where the men off duty were amusing themselves,
there came a steady clicking of billiard-balls and dominoes, broken
now and again by gruff bursts of laughter. And at his very elbow the
superintendent was speaking in that suave voice that reminded Bennett of grey velvet

"You see, Bennett, how matters stand. I have nothing at all against
your conduct. You are steady and punctual, and I have no doubt that
you are trying to do your duty. But it's very unfortunate that as far as
results go you have nothing to show for your efforts. During the last
three weeks you have not brought in a charge of any description, and
during the same period I find that your colleagues on the beat have
been exceptionally busy. I repeat that I do not accuse you of neglect-
ing your duty, but these things tell with the magistrates and convey a
general suggestion of slackness."

Bennett looked down at his brightly polished boots. His fingers
were sandy and there was soft felt beneath his feet.

"I have been afraid of this for some time, sir," he said, "very much
afraid."

The superintendent looked at him questioningly.

"You have nothing to say?" he said.

137

"I have always tried to do my duty, sir."

"I know, I know. But you must see that a certain number of charges, if not of convictions, is the mark of a smart officer."

"Surely you would not have me arrest innocent persons?"

"That is a most improper observation," said the superintendent severely. "I will say no more to you now. But I hope you will take what I have said as a warning. You must bustle along, Bennett, bustle along."

Outside in the street, Police-Constable Bennett was free to reflect on his unpleasant interview. The superintendent was ambitious and therefore pompous; he, himself, was unambitious and therefore modest. Left to himself he might have been content to triumph in the reflection that he had failed to say a number of foolish things, but the welfare of his wife and children bound him, tiresomely enough for a dreamer, tightly to the practical. It was clear that if he did not forthwith produce signs of his efficiency as a promoter of the peace that welfare would be imperilled.

Yet he did not condemn the chance that had made him a policeman or even the mischance that brought no guilty persons to his hands. Rather he looked with a gentle curiosity into the faces of the people who passed him, and wondered why he could not detect traces of the generally assumed wickedness of the neighbourhood. The unkempt men and women were thieves and even murderers, it appeared; but to him they shone as happy youths and maidens, joyous victims of love's tyranny.

As he drew near the street in which he lived this sense of universal love quickened in his blood and stirred him strangely. It did not escape his eyes that to the general his uniform was an unfriendly thing. Men and women paused in their animated chattering till he had passed, and even the children faltered in their games to watch him with doubtful eyes. And yet his heart was warm for them; he knew that he wished them well

Nevertheless, when he saw his house shining in a row of similar houses, he realised that their attitude was wiser than his. If he was to be a success as a breadwinner he must wage a sterner war against these happy, lovable people. It was easy, he had been long enough in the force to know how easy, to get cases. An intolerant manner, a little provocative harshness, and the thing was done. Yet with all his heart he admired the poor for their resentful independence of spirit. To him this had always been the supreme quality of the English character; how could he make use of it to fill English gaols?

He opened the door of his house, with a sigh on his lips. There came forth the merry shouting of his children.

2

Above the telephone wires the stars dipped at anchor in the cloudless sky. Down below, in one of the dark, empty streets, Police-Constable Bennett turned the handles of doors and tested the fastenings of windows, with a complete scepticism as to the value of his labours. Gradually, he was coming to see that he was not one of the few who are born to rule—to control—their simple neighbours, ambitious only for breath. Where, if he had possessed this mission, he would have been eager to punish, he now felt no more than a sympathy that charged him with some responsibility for the sins of others. He shared the uneasy conviction of the multitude that human justice, as interpreted by the inspired minority, is more than a little unjust.

The very unpopularity with which his uniform endowed him seemed to him to express a severe criticism of the system of which he was an unwilling supporter. He wished these people to regard him as a kind of official friend, to advise and settle differences; yet, shrewder than he, they considered him as an enemy, who lived on their mistakes and the collapse of their social relationships.

There remained his duty to his wife and children, and this rendered the problem infinitely perplexing.

Why should he punish others because of his love for his children; or, again, why should his children suffer for his scruples? Yet it was clear that, unless fortune permitted him to accomplish some notable yet honourable arrest, he would either have to cheat and tyrannise with his colleagues or leave the force. And what employment is available for a discharged policeman?

As he went systematically from house to house the consideration of these things marred the normal progress of his dreams. Conscious as he was of the stars and the great widths of heaven that made the world so small, he nevertheless felt that his love for his family and the wider love that determined his honour were somehow intimately connected with this greatness of the universe rather than with the world of little streets and little motives, and so were not lightly to be put aside. Yet, how can one measure one love against another when all are true?

When the door of Gurneys', the moneylenders, opened to his touch, and drew him abruptly from his speculations, his first emotion was a quick irritation that chance should interfere with his thoughts.

But when his lantern showed him that the lock had been tampered with, his annoyance changed to a thrill of hopeful excitement. What if this were the way out? What if fate had granted him compromise, the opportunity of pitting his official virtue against official crime, those shadowy forces in the existence of which he did not believe, but which lay on his life like clouds?

He was not a physical coward, and it seemed quite simple to him to creep quietly through the open door into the silent office without waiting for possible reinforcements. He knew that the safe, which would be the natural goal of the presumed burglars, was in Mr. Gurney's private office beyond, and while he stood listening intently, he seemed to hear dim sounds coming from the direction of that room. For a moment he paused, frowning slightly as a man does when he is trying to catalogue an impression.

When he achieved perception, it came oddly mingled with recollections of the little tragedies of his children at home. For someone was crying like a child in the little room where Mr. Gurney browbeat recalcitrant borrowers. Dangerous burglars do not weep, and Bennett hesitated no longer, but stepped past the open flaps of the counter, and threw open the door of the inner office.

The electric light had been switched on, and at the table there sat a slight young man with his face buried in his hands, crying bitterly. Behind him the safe stood open and empty, and the grate was filled with smouldering embers of burnt paper. Bennett went up to the young man and placed his hand on his shoulder. But the young man wept on and did not move.

Try as he might Bennett could not help relaxing the grip of outraged law, and patting the young man's shoulder soothingly as it rose and fell. He had no fit weapons of roughness and oppression with which to oppose this child-like grief; he could only fight tears with tears.

"Come," he said gently, "you must pull yourself together."

At the sound of his voice the young man gave a great sob and then was silent, shivering a little.

"That's better," said Bennett encouragingly, "much better."

"I have burnt everything," the young man said suddenly, "and now the place is empty. I was nearly sick just now."

Bennett looked at him sympathetically, as one dreamer may look at another, who is sad with action dreamed too often for scatheless accomplishment "I'm afraid you'll get into serious trouble," he said.

"I know," replied the young man, "but that blackguard Gurney—" His voice rose to a shrill scream and choked him for a moment. Then he went on quietly, "But it's all over now. Finished! Done with!"

"I suppose you owed him money?"

The young man nodded. "He lives on fools like me. But he threatened to tell my father, and now I've just about ruined him. Pah! Swine!"

"This won't be much better for your father," said Bennett gravely.

"No, it's worse; but perhaps it will help some of the others. He kept on threatening and I couldn't wait any longer. Can't you see?"

Over the young man's shoulder, the stars becked and nodded to Bennett through the blindless window.

"I see," he said; "I see."

"So now you can take me."

Bennett looked doubtfully at the outstretched wrists. "You are only a fool," he said, "a dreaming fool like me, and they will give you years for this. I don't see why they should give a man years for being a fool."

The young man looked up, taken with a sudden hope. "You will let me go?" he said, in astonishment. "I know I was an ass just now. I suppose I was a bit shaken. But you will let me go?"

"I wish to God, I had never seen you!" said Bennett simply. "You have your father, and I have a wife and three little children. Who shall judge between us!"

"My father is an old man."

"And my children are little. You had better go before I make up my mind."

Without another word the young man crept out of the room, and Bennett followed him slowly into the street This gallant criminal, whose capture would have been honourable, had dwindled to a hysterical foolish boy; and aided by his own strange impulse this boy had ruined him. The burglary had taken place on his beat; there would be an inquiry; it did not need that to secure his expulsion from the force. Once in the street he looked up hopefully to the heavens; but now the stars seemed unspeakably remote, though as he passed along his beat his wife and his three little children were walking by his side.

3

Bennett had developed mentally without realising the logical result of his development until it smote him with calamity. Of his betrayal of trust as a guardian of property he thought nothing; of the possibility of poverty for his family he thought a great deal—all the more that his dreamer's mind was little accustomed to gripping the practical It was strange, he thought, that his final declaration of war against his position should have been a little lacking in dignity. He had not taken the decisive step through any deep compassion of utter poverty bravely borne. His had been no more than trivial pity of a young man's folly; and this was a frail thing on which to make so great a sacrifice. Yet he regretted nothing. His task of moral guardian of men and women had become impossible to him, and sooner or later he must have given it up. And there was also his family. "I must come to some decision," he said to himself firmly.

And then the great scream fell upon his ears and echoed through his brain for ever and ever. It came from the house before which he was standing, and he expected the whole street to wake aghast with the horror of it. But there followed a silence that seemed to emphasise the ugliness of the sound. Far away an engine screamed as if in mocking imitation; and that was all. Bennett had counted up to a hundred and seventy before the door of the house opened, and a man came out on to the steps.

"Oh, constable," he said coolly, "come inside, will you? I have something to show you."

Bennett mounted the steps doubtfully. "There was a scream," he said.

The man looked at him quickly. "So, you heard it," he said. "It was not pretty."

"No, it was not," replied Bennett.

The man led him down the dim passage into the back sitting-room. The body of a man lay on the sofa; it was curled like a dry leaf.

"That is my brother," said the man, with a little emphatic nod; "I have killed him. He was my enemy."

Bennett stared dully at the body, without believing it to be really there.

"Dead!" he said mechanically.

"And anything I say will be used against me in evidence! As if you could compress my hatred into one little lying notebook."

"I don't care a damn about your hatred," said Bennett, with heat. "An hour ago, perhaps, I might have arrested you; now I only find you uninteresting."

The man gave a long, low whistle of surprise.

"A philosopher in uniform," he said, "God! sir, you have my sympathy."

"And you have my pity. You have stolen your ideas from cheap melodrama, and you make tragedy ridiculous. Were I a policeman, I would lock you up with pleasure. Were I a man, I should thrash you joyfully. As it is I can only share your infamy. I too, I suppose, am a murderer."

"You are in a low, nervous state," said the man; "and you are doing me some injustice. It is true that I am a poor murderer; but it appears to me that you are a worse policeman."

"I shall wear the uniform no more from tonight."

"I think you are wise, and I shall mar my philosophy with no more murders. If, indeed, I have killed him; for I assure you that beyond administering the poison to his wretched body I have done nothing. Perhaps he is not dead. Can you hear his heart beating?"

"I can hear the spoons of my children beating on their empty platters!"

"Is it like that with you? Poor devil! Oh, poor, poor devil! Philosophers should have no wives, no children, no homes, and no hearts."

Bennett turned from the man with unspeakable loathing.

"I hate you and such as you!" he cried weakly. "You justify the existence of the police. You make me despise myself because I realise that your crimes are no less mine than yours. I do not ask you to defend the deadness of that thing lying there. I shall stir no finger to have you hanged, for the thought of suicide repels me, and I cannot separate your blood and mine. We are common children of a noble mother, and for our mother's sake I say farewell."

And without waiting for the man's answer he passed from the house to the street.

4

Haggard and with rebellious limbs, Police-Constable Bennett staggered into the superintendent's office in the early morning.

"I have paid careful attention to your advice," he said to the superintendent, "and I have passed across the city in search of crime. In its place I have found but folly—such folly as you have, such folly as I have myself—the common heritage of our blood. It seems that in some way I have bound myself to bring criminals to justice. I have passed across the city, and I have found no man worse than myself. Do what you will with me."

The superintendent cleared his throat.

"There have been too many complaints concerning the conduct of the police," he said; "it is time that an example was made. You will be charged with being drunk and disorderly while on duty."

"I have a wife and three little children," said Bennett softly—"and three pretty little children." And he covered his tired face with his hands.

The Wrong Turning

It was a dark night, and the traveller shuddered as he strode along the white road. On each side of that sorely-made way lay the marshes, waiting for a chance slip to catch the blunderer by the heel and slowly suck him under, when nought but the will o' the-wisps would know the manner of his passing.

Had it been light he could have seen the dry land shake and tremble and melt into greasy waters, or muddy banks rise like the heads of great reptiles through the surface of pools, but the darkness hid these horrors, and he could only hear the choking of the falling mud, and the harsh cries of seabirds far away.

He clutched his bag closer to him and hurried on, keeping carefully to the middle of the road, and looking anxiously ahead at the surface of the way, for fear that a landslip might have turned the path of safety to a death-trap. So, it was he noticed far ahead amongst the dim stars and marsh flames a light, that burned with a steady glow, and neither flickered nor danced.

The traveller paused in some surprise at the sight. He had been told of no house to be passed on the way, while if it should be the light of a fellow-traveller, that one might well be a thief or worse; and where would lie his safety in so forsaken a spot?

But the light burned quite steadily, and the traveller continued on his way reassured. It was, without doubt, a house. As he drew near, and the light proved to come from an uncurtained window in a squat and miserable dwelling, his doubts recurred. What honest man would endure to live in such a place; and its ill-appearance was hardly redeemed by the sign that hung creaking across the sky—"The House of Woe." Who had ever heard of such a name for an inn as that? He had come to a standstill while he scanned the place, but the name decided him; and with his heart like a lump in his throat he began to steal past the place on tiptoe, praying that they might not keep a dog within.

Thus, he crept along by the black wall, and had just come to the end when he pulled himself up with a terrible shock.

The road went no farther, and the black waters lay muttering at his feet.

After the first sensation of panic, he found himself thinking with a curious calmness. Of course, the explanation was simple. He had mistaken the path to the inn for the road he should have followed; and all he had to do was to retrace his steps, and all would be well.

So, he set himself again to his tiptoeing, and once more passed the house without disturbing its inmates.

But now a new difficulty presented itself; round the inn the ground was dead white, so that it was hard to tell where the road might be. He struck out at a venture, hesitated, took a step, and felt his leg sink to the knee in a soft mass that closed on it like steel. With a frantic effort he flung his body backwards on to the firm ground, and fought silently with the mud in the darkness. At last, he rolled back free, but exhausted, with the air striking his panting lungs with the force of a blow.

After a while he pulled himself up and gazed fearfully around him. Behind lay "The House of Woe," dark and forbidding, while before lay the deadly marshes chuckling at the victim they had failed to keep. He felt he durst not venture towards them again while his leg was yet numb with the force of their grip.

He stepped slowly towards the house with the mud oozing in his torn boot, and as he went he comforted himself, as timid men do in lonely places, with the thought of great cities and their carefully regulated police. He could have stayed where he was all night, but he felt himself wrought on by a petulant desire for action, being, in truth, too fearful to remain passively between the known dangers of the marsh and that dark and repellent monster with the luminous eye.

The sound of his knuckles on the door set his heart fluttering again, and he would have given kingdoms for the moment, if only the sound might not have been made. Yet his knock was not answered, and so contradictory is the nature of man that after a few minutes he was banging lustily and impatiently on the door, and swearing to himself at the dilatoriness of those within.

The door opened at last, and a man appeared in the dim passage, who, without listening to the traveller's explanations, stood aside silently to let him pass.

That one hesitated, felt that he had gone too far to retreat, stepped trembling past he man, and heard with a heart of lead the door banged and fastened behind him.

At the end of the passage a slit of light showed the presence of a doorway, and with the man treading closely behind the traveller pushed this open, still with the same dread of something terrible within. But his fear seemed misplaced, the room might indeed have been the living-room of an old inn, with its oak panels, wide fireplace, sides of bacon, and strings of onions pendant from the high ceiling, and a bright enough fire burning on the hearth, with the additional light of the lamp in the window, which he had seen from without.

Seated by the fire was an elderly man engaged in stirring the contents of a pot, while in the further corner, with her back turned to the door, was a woman bending over the bed of a little child. Neither the man nor the woman looked up to see who had entered, and when his conductor, still without a word, motioned him to a chair by the table, the wanderer began to think the whole household was deaf and dumb. To walk into a room in the dead of night drenched with mud and water, and to escape practically unnoticed, was disconcerting, and it hardly reassured him to suspect that he was the object of scrutiny on the part of the two men.

But when he looked up sharply, he only saw the old man stirring his pot, and the other gazing stolidly at the fire.

Suddenly the girl got up and swung round to the room, and as he saw her face the traveller knew why his feet had wandered to that place, and why he was afraid.

"You, Lucy!" he cried.

"Me, Hubert," she said quietly. And a deep silence fell on the room.

He sat like one already dead, white and speechless. Lucy and the men and the sides of the bacon danced madly in his vision, and he was afraid they would know he was a coward by the loudness of his breathing, but there was such a weight on his chest that when he sought to close his lips he was nearly choked.

It was the silence he hated—the silence and the suspense. Why did not something happen? Anything rather than those mute and incurious figures.

"For God's sake," he cried, and the tears welled in his eyes at the sound of his voice, so sad and appealing.

There was a pause, and then suddenly the elder man, Lucy's father it would be, threw back his swart and bearded face in a hoarse cackle of laughter. Again and again, he renewed it, his dried lips pulled back

147

from the yellow teeth and the cruel red gums; even so might the Prince of darkness mock a lost soul.

Lucy had turned back to the child.

Anon the man grew tired of his laughing and fell more to stirring his broth, tasting it from time to time with his spoon and pursing his lips at the heat.

The cruelty of it. The traveller could endure it no longer. He staggered to his feet and clutched his hat to his head, his bag lying forgotten on the floor.

"I—I think I will go out," he said with an effort, and moved to the door.

The man by the fire spoke first.

"Put the gentleman on the right way, Lucy," he said, and there was a glint of malice in his voice.

Lucy left the bed and walked to the door. She had not always had that iron face. The wanderer followed her quietly and hopelessly down the passage and out into the night. He had only needed one glance at the grim face to know what was his fate.

As he trod behind her through the greying marshes, he heard the waters laughing cruelly each side, and the sound reminded him of the man he had left behind in "The House of Woe." And as he thought of that name, he knew many things.

"You liked me once, Lucy," he said, but his words ended in a gasp. With a rapid leap or two the woman had passed to a spot about twenty feet off and he knew not which way to tread.

"Your child. I am its father You cannot kill me."

Lucy did not seem to hear the words, but she began singing very softly, and with a thrill of horror Hubert recognised the words. It was a love song.

She sang without a tremor, but for the rest it was the same sweet voice that had charmed him so much before, and he had prided himself on his taste in such matters.

He heard her fascinated to the end of her song; and as he listened a wave of something like remorse broke on his self-centred mind.

"You know I meant to come back, Lucy," he cried when she had finished. "It was all a mistake."

She looked at him with hard and steady contempt. "I saw you go that morning," she said.

He bowed his head, for there are some things that even the worst man cannot think of without shame. There was no romance about that flight at dawn, that creeping down the stairs with his boots in his hand, that painful straining to hear if Lucy had wakened, all this had been sordid enough. And she had known all the time and let him go.

There was none of the fierce spirit distracted and led astray in this; he merely felt like a mean man, found out, and for the moment he was genuinely penitent, and so lost to externals that he did not even notice that the reason his feet were of lead was because he was slowly sinking, that the mud had risen above his boots.

"I'm sorry, Lucy," he said humbly.

This was a better way.

"Why did you say you loved me, Hubert?" she said sadly.

"I was a brute."

He was watching Lucy's face when he said this, and a sudden change, suggestive of fear, made him look down. The mud reached nearly to his knees.

For a minute he struggled, trying desperately to withdraw one leg, but he sank only deeper. At last, he desisted, and looked wistfully across at Lucy.

"I'm gone," he said.

Lucy stood irresolute, with her face half-turned away, and her fingers plucking at her gown.

"I can't!" she cried suddenly, and came running to his side, her trained eye choosing the spots which she knew to be comparatively safe.

He held out his arms to her, and she took his hands one in each of hers as if she would embrace him, but she made no effort to help him out.

"I'm sinking, Lucy," he said plaintively.

"Yes, Hubert," she said simply.

The mud had passed his waist, and she knew no effort of hers could release him.

"You are cruel," he cried, struggling feebly in the scarcely liquid mass.

Lucy dropped his hands, and placing hers on his shoulders thrust his body back with all her might. His arms flailed desperately in all directions, but the mud was sliding over his chest and over his chin and over his face.

When the surface had ceased to quiver and the bubbles had passed, Lucy drew forth her hands and straightened herself against the dawning sky.

"It was better," she said.
And then she turned back to her child.

An Enchanted Place

When elder brothers insisted on their rights with undue harshness, or when the grown-up people descended from Olympus with a tiresome tale of broken furniture and torn clothes, the groundlings of the schoolroom went into retreat. In summer-time this was an easy matter; once fairly escaped into the garden, any climbable tree or shady shrub provided us with a hermitage. There was a hollow tree-stump full of exciting insects and pleasant earthy smells that never failed us, or, for wet days, the tool-shed, with its armoury of weapons with which, in imagination, we would repel the attacks of hostile forces. But in the game that was our childhood, the garden was out of bounds in winter-time, and we had to seek other lairs. Behind the schoolroom piano there was a three-cornered refuge that served very well for momentary sulks or sudden alarms. It was possible to lie in ambush there, at peace with our grievances, until life took a turn for the better and tempted us forth again into the active world.

But when the hour was tragic and we felt the need for a hiding-place more remote, we took our troubles, not without a recurring thrill, to that enchanted place which our elders contemptuously called the "mouse-cupboard." This was a low cupboard that ran the whole length of the big attic under the slope of the roof, and here the aggrieved spirit of childhood could find solitude and darkness in which to scheme deeds of revenge and actions of a wonderful magnanimity turn by turn. Luckily our shelter did not appeal to the utilitarian minds of the grown-up folk or to those members of the younger generation who were beginning to trouble about their clothes.

You had to enter it on your hands and knees; it was dusty, and the mice obstinately disputed our possession. On the inner walls the plaster seemed to be oozing between the rough laths, and through little chinks and crannies in the tiles overhead our eyes could see the sky. But our imaginations soon altered these trivial blemishes. As a cave the

151

mouse-cupboard had a very interesting history. As soon as the smugglers had left it, it passed successively through the hands of Aladdin, Robinson Crusoe, Ben Gunn, and Tom Sawyer, and gave satisfaction to them all, and it would no doubt have had many other tenants if someone had not discovered that it was like the cabin of a ship. From that hour its position in our world was assured.

For sooner or later our dreams always returned to the sea—not, be it said, to the polite and civilised sea of the summer holidays, but to that sea on whose foam there open magic casements, and by whose crimson tide the ships of Captain Avery and Captain Bartholomew Roberts keep faithful tryst with the *Flying Dutchman*. It needed no very solid vessel to carry our hearts to those enchanted waters—a paper boat floating in a saucer served well enough if the wind was propitious—so the fact that our cabin lacked portholes and was of an unusual shape did not trouble us.

We could hear the water bubbling against the ship's side in a neighbouring cistern, and often enough the wind moaned and whistled overhead. We had our lockers, our sleeping-berths, and our cabin-table, and at one end of the cabin was hung a rusty old cutlass full of notches; we would have hated anyone who had sought to disturb our illusion that these notches had been made in battle. When we were stowaways even the mice were of service to us, for we gave them a full roving commission as savage rats, and trembled when we heard them scampering among the cargo.

But though we cut the figure of an old admiral out of a Christmas number, and chased slavers with Kingston very happily for a while, the vessel did not really come into her own until we turned pirates and hoisted the "Jolly Roger" off the coast of Malabar. Then, by the light of guttering candles, the mice witnessed some strange sights. If any of us had any money we would carouse terribly, drinking ginger-beer like water, and afterwards water out of the ginger-beer bottles, which still retained a faint magic. Jam has been eaten without bread on board the *Black Margaret*, and when we fell across a merchantman laden with a valuable consignment of dried apple-rings—tough fare but interesting—and the savoury sugar out of candied peel, there were boisterous times in her dim cabin. We would sing what we imagined to be sea chanties in a doleful voice, and prepare our boarding-pikes for the next adventure, though we had no clear idea what they really were.

And when we grew weary of draining rum-kegs and counting the pieces of eight, our life at sea knew quieter though no less enjoyable hours. It was pleasant to lie still after the fever of battle and watch the flickering candles with drowsy eyes. Surely the last word has not been said on the charm of candle-light; we liked little candles—dumpy sixteens they were perhaps—and as we lay they would spread among us their attendant shadows. Beneath us the water chuckled restlessly, and sometimes we heard the feet of the watch on deck overhead, and now and again the clanging of the great bell. In such an hour it was not difficult to picture the luminous tropic seas through which the *Black Margaret* was making her way. The skies of irradiant stars, the desert islands like baskets of glowing flowers, and the thousand marvels of the enchanted ocean—we saw them one and all.

It was strange to leave this place of shadows and silences and hour-long dreams to play a humble part in a noisy, gas-lit world that had not known these wonders; but there were consolations. Elder brothers might prevail in argument by methods that seemed unfair, but, beneath a baffled exterior, we could conceal a sublime pity for their unadventurous lives. Governesses might criticise our dusty clothes with wearisome eloquence, but the recollection that women were not allowed on board the *Black Margaret* helped us to remain conventionally polite. Like the gentleman in Mr. Wells's story, we knew that there were better dreams, and the knowledge raised us for a while above the trivial passions of our environment.

We were not the only children who had found the mouse-cupboard a place of enchantment, for when we explored it first, we discovered a handful of wooden beads carefully hidden in a cranny in the wall. These breathed of the nursery rather than of the schoolroom, and yet, perhaps, those forgotten children had known what we knew, and our songs of the sea stirred only familiar echoes. It is likely enough that today other children have inherited our dreams, and that other hands steer the *Black Margaret* under approving stars. If this indeed be so, they are in our debt, for in one of our hiding-places we left the "Count of Monte Cristo" in English, rare treasure-trove for any proper boy. If this should ever meet his eyes he will understand.

Children and the Sea

The sea, like all very large things, can only be intimately under-stood by children. If we can conceive a sensible grown-up person looking at the sea for the first time, we feel that he should either yawn or wish to drown himself. But a child would take a sample of it in a bucket, and consider that in all its aspects; and then it would know that the sea is a great many bucketfuls of water, and further that by an odd freak of destiny this water is not fit to drink. Storms and ships and sand-castles and lighthouses and all the other side-shows would follow later; but in the meantime, the child would have seen the sea in a bucket, as it had previously seen the moon in a looking-glass, so would know all about it. The moon is a variable and interesting kind of lamp; the sea is buckets and buckets and buckets full of water. I think the stars are holes in a sort of black curtain or ceiling, and the sun is a piece of brightness, except at sunset or in a mist, when it is a whole Dutch cheese. The world is streets and fields and the seaside and our house.

I doubt whether a child has any sense of what I may call the ap-peal of breadth. If it is confronted with a fine view, it will concentrate its interest on a windmill or a doll's house, and the seaside is no more than a place where one wears no shoes or stockings, and the manu-facture of mud pies becomes suddenly licit. The child does not share the torments of the adult Londoner, who feels that there is no room in the world to stretch his arms and legs, and therefore wins a pathetic sense of freedom in seeing the long yellow sands and the green wastes of the sea. Nor is it at all excited by the consideration that there is a lot more sea beyond the horizon; the extent of its interest in the water is the limit to which it may paddle.

Yet in some dim, strange way the child realises æsthetic values more here than elsewhere. I am quite sure it can see no real beauty in its normal surroundings. Sunsets and small houses lit for evening, the shining streets after rain, and even flowers and pictures and dolls, are never beautiful to a child in the sense that a story or an idea may be beautiful. But tacitly, for a child has no language to express such things, something of the blueness of the sea seems to seek expression in its eyes, something of the sparkle of the sand seems to be tangled in its hair, something of the sunshine burns in its rounded calves that glow like brown eggs.

A child is always a thing of wonder. But on the edge of the sea this wonder deepens until the artificial observer is abashed. A seaside child is no creature to be petted and laughed over; it were as easy to pet the tireless waters, and to laugh over the grave of a little cat; children whom one has known very well indeed in town will find new playing fields by the sea into which it is impossible to follow them. Dorothy weighs five stone four pounds at Maida Vale; at Littlehampton the sea wind blows her along like a feather; she is become a wispy, spiritual thing, a faint, fair creature a-dance on light feet that would make the fairy-girl of a poet's dream seem clumsy by comparison. She is nearer to us when she paddles.

The warm sand creeping up through her toes, the silver thread of coolness about her legs, these things are within our comprehension though they fall no more within our experience. But when she flings herself along the beach with the wild hair and loose limbs and the song of an innocent Bacchante, when she bids the gold sands heave up and support her body, tired with play, when she stoops to gather diamonds and pearls from the shore made wet and smooth by the retreating waves, she is as far from us and our human qualities as a new-awakened butterfly. There have been sea-washed moments when I should not have been astonished if she had flung out a pair of mother-of-pearl wings and stood in the blue sky, like a child saint in a stained-glass window.

There have been other moments when she has approached me with a number of impossible questions in wanton parody of her simple London self. Between these two extremes her moods vary from second to second, and she plays upon them as Pan upon his pipes, and to much the same tune. She loves the long tresses of seaweed and the pink shells like the nails of her own little hands; and her coloured pail, when she is not the architect of sea-girt palaces, is a treasury of salty wonders. To climb the rough rocks and call them mountains, to drive back the waves with a chiding foot, and to alter the face of Nature with a wooden spade, these were not tasks for the domesticated creature who shares the hearth-rug with the cat at home. But the spirit of the sea has changed Dorothy; she is now a little more and a little less than child; and she recognises no comrades but those other nymphs of the sea, who hold the beach with the sparkle of wet feet and careless petticoats, who run hither and thither in search of the big adventure, while their parents and guardians sleep in the sun.

It is hard that age should deprive us of so many privileges, and least of all can we spare the glamour of the sands of the sea. Yet to the adult mind Brighton beach, sprinkled with newspapers and washed by a sea whose surface is black with smuts, brings little but disgust. We insist on having our fairy-lands clean and end, too often, by finding no fairy-land at all. The sea, after all, is no more than water that may be caught in a bucket; the sand may glitter on a child's spade, and we who believe that the essential knowledge of the thing is ours are no wiser than the children. For me the sea is a restless and immeasurable waste of greens and blues and greys, and I know that its strength lies in its monotony. It is not the noisy turbulence of storms that moves me to fear, but the dull precision of the tides and the tireless succession of waves.

And my impression is no truer than the children's and lends itself less readily to a sympathetic manner of living. I feel that if I could once more hold the ocean in my bucket, if the whole earth might be uprooted by my spade, I should be nearer to a sense of the value of life than I am now. I see the children go trooping by with their calm eyes, not, as is sometimes said, curious, but rather tolerant of life, and I know that for them the universe is merely an aggregate of details, some agreeable and some stupid, while I must needs depress myself by regarding it as a whole. And this is the proved distinction between juvenile and adult philosophies, if we may be permitted to regard a child's very definite point of view as the effect of a philosophy. Life is a collection of little bits of experience; the seaside bits are pleasant, and there is nothing more to be said.

The Flute-Player

He used to play to me in the magic hour before bedtime, when, in the summer, the red sun threw long shadows across the lawn, and in winter the fire burned brighter and brighter in the hearth. This was the hour when all the interminable squabbles of the schoolroom were forgotten, and even the noisiest of us would hush his voice to listen drowsily to a fairy-tale, or to watch the palaces raise aloft their minarets, and crumble to dull red ash in the heart of the fire. It was then that I would see him sitting astride of the fireguard and puffing out his cheeks over his shining flute.

Even in the most thrilling moments of fairy stories, when Cinderella lost her crystal slipper or Sister Ann saw the cloud of dust from the summit of Bluebeard's tower, his shrill melodies would ring in my ears and quicken my sleepy senses with the desire to hear more of this enchanted music. I knew that it was real magic, but I did not find it strange, because as far as I knew I had heard it all my life. Perhaps he had played to me when I yet lay in my cradle, and watched the night-light winking on the nursery ceiling; but I did not try to remember whether this was so.

I was content to accept my strange musician as a fact of my existence, and to feel a sense of loss on the rare evenings when he failed me. I did not know how to dance, but sometimes I would tap my feet on the floor in time to the music, till someone would tell me not to fidget. For no one else would either see him or hear him, which proved that it was real magic, and flattered my sense of possession. It was evident that he came for me alone.

The years passed, and in due course the imaginative graces of my childhood were destroyed by the boys of my own age at school. They compelled me to exchange a hundred star-roofed palaces, three distinct kingdoms of dreams, and my enchanted flute-player for a threadbare habit of mimicry that left me cold and unprotected from the winds in the large places of life. There was something at once pathetic and ridiculous in our childish efforts to imitate our elders, but as it seemed that our masters and grown-up relatives were in the conspiracy to make us materialistically wise before our time, a boy would have needed a rare force of character to linger with his childhood and refuse to ape the man.

So, for a while, I saw my glad musician no more, though sometimes I thought I heard him playing far away, and the child within me was warmed and encouraged even while my new-found manhood was condemning the weakness. I knew now that no man worthy of the name was escorted through life by a fairy flute-player, and that dreamers and wool-gatherers invariably sank to be poets and musicians, persons who wear bowler-hats with frock-coats, have no crease in their trousers, and come to a bad end. Fortunately, all education that is repressive rather than stimulating is only skin-deep, and it was inevitable that sooner or later I should meet the flute-player again.

One Saturday afternoon in high summer I avoided cricket and went for a long walk in the woods, moved by a spirit of revolt against all the traditions and conventions of boy-life; and presently, in a mossy clearing, all splashed and wetted by little pools of sunlight, I found him playing to an audience of two squirrels and a redstart. When he saw me, he winked the eye that glittered over his parading fingers, as though he had left me only five minutes before, but I had not listened long before I realised that I must pay the price of my infidelity. It was the old music and the old magic, but try as I might I could not hear it so clearly as I had when I was a child.

The continuity of my faith had been broken, and though he was willing to forgive, I myself could not forget those dark years of doubt and denial; and while I often met him in the days that followed, I never won back to the old childish intimacy. I sought his company eagerly and listened passionately to his piping, but I was conscious now that this was a strange thing, and sometimes when he saw by my eyes that I was moved by wonder rather than by the love of beauty, he would put his flute in his pocket and disappear. The world is an enchanted place only to the incurious and tranquil-minded.

Nevertheless, though like all boys I had been forced to discard my childish dreams before I had really finished with them, the lovely melodies of the flute-player served to enrich my latter years at school with much of the old enchantment. Often enough he would play to me at night during preparation, and I would spend my time in trying to set words to his tunes instead of doing my lessons. It was then that I regretted the lost years that had dulled my ear and prevented me from winning the inmost magic of his song, compared with which my verses seemed but the shadow of a shadow.

Yet I saw that he was content with my efforts, and gradually made the discovery that while great achievement is granted to the fortunate, it is the fine effort that justifies a man to himself. What did it matter whether my songs were good or bad? They were the highest expression I could find for the rapture of beauty that had filled my heart as a child when I had been gifted to see life with clean and truthful eyes. For the songs the flute-player played to me were the great dreams of my childhood, the dreams that a wise man prolongs to the day of his death.

I do not hear him often now, for I have learnt my lesson, and though my hands tremble and my ear deceives me, I am by way of being a flute-player myself. This article, it is clear, is a child's dream, and so have been, and will be, I hope, all the articles I shall ever write. What else should we write about? We have learnt a few long words since we grew up, and a few crimes, but no new virtues. That is why I like to get back to the nursery floor, and play with the old toys and think the old thoughts. We knew intuitively then a number of beautiful truths that circumstance appears to deny now, and we grown men are the poorer in consequence. It is folly to find life ugly when the flute lies within our reach and we can pipe ourselves back to the world of beauty with a song made of an old dream.

As for the flute-player, if I see him no more with wakeful eyes, I know that he is never very far away. Likely enough one of these wintry evenings, in the hour before bedtime, when the fire burns brighter and brighter in the hearth, I shall look up and see him sitting astride of the fireguard and puffing out his cheeks over his shining flute. Not many nights ago I heard someone playing the flute out in the street, and I went down and found a poor fellow blowing his heart out for rare *sous*. There was not much enchantment about him—he had been dismissed from a music-hall orchestra for drinking red wine to excess—but he was a real flute-player, and I could well imagine that such a man might be driven to intemperance by the failure to achieve those "unheard melodies" not to be detected by the sensual ear.

To be a bad flute-player must be rather like being a bad poet, a joyous but sadly finite life. He was a sad dog, this earthly musician, and he frankly conceived the ideal state as a kind of communal Bodega where thirsty souls could find peace in satiety. I gave him fivepence to help him on his way, and left him to make doleful music in the night till he had enough money to supply his crimson dreams. But he ought not to have said that my flute-player was only an amateur.

The Peril of the Fairies

It is something to have heard once in a lifetime the ecstatic thrill that glorifies Essex Hall while that intellectual pirate Mr. Bernard Shaw sails out and scuttles a number of little merchant ships of thought that have never hurt anybody. The applause and admiring laughter that punctuate his periods really suggest that Fabianism makes people happy, while the continued prosperity of the group gives the lie to the cynic who reminded me how popular ping-pong was while the craze lasted, and how utterly forgotten it is today. But I had to rub my eyes while I stood in the overcrowded room, listening to Puck in Jaeger, more witty, perhaps, than the old Puck, but no less boyishly malicious, and ask myself whether, after all, this was only the old magic in a new form.

True, civilisation had perforce made him larger in order that human beings might appreciate his eloquence, and I saw no traces of wings or magic flowers. But beyond that I recognised the same pitying contempt for mortals, the same arrogant confession of his own faults, the same *naïve* cunning. And then (perhaps a turn of the voice did it, or some slight slurring of the words) the enchantment passed, the ears of his audience resumed their ordinary dimensions, and I offered mentally two teaspoonfuls of honey to the real Puck, for I saw that he had tricked me into recognising his qualities in the most serious man the twentieth century knows.

Yet, though I found Mr. Shaw to be only a prophet and his fellow-Fabians honest enthusiasts instead of bewitched weavers, I cannot say that the discovery left my mind at ease for the welfare of the fairy kingdom that is so important to everyone who has not forgotten it. What if this terrible seriousness were to spread? What if everyone were to turn prophet? What if a night should come when never a child in all the Duke of York's Theatre would clap its hands to keep Tinker Bell alive? At first, I wished to reject this frightful end of all our play and laughter and wonder as impossible. Yet sinister stories of children who preferred sewing-machines and working models to dolls and tin soldiers rose in my mind, and it is hardly more than a step from that degree of progress to the case of the child who may find the science of sanitation more interesting than tales of fairies.

The possibility should make even the extremists shudder, but it must be remembered that many honest people believe in technical education, and that for that matter practically the whole of the teaching in our schools takes the form of an attack on the stronghold of the imaginative child. It is our barbarous custom to supplant a child's really beautiful theories with the ugly crudities which we call facts, and it is impossible to realise how much humanity loses in the process. As for the fairies, frail little folk at best, how shall they prevail against the criticism of our sulphur and the cunning of our permanganate of potash? Shall we always be able to distinguish them from microbes?

It may be well to pause here and see whither the wise, serious men of today are taking us. I suppose they will abolish Will-o'-the-Wisp by draining all the marshes, and their extreme industry will render Puck's kindly household labours ludicrously unnecessary. They will turn their swords against all the bad barons, unjust kings, and spiteful magicians, whose punishment has been hitherto the fairies' special task; and this they will do in blackleg fashion, neither demanding nor receiving their just wages of beauty and immortality. They will scornfully set aside the law, so dear to the younger inhabitants of nurseries, by which it is always the youngest son or the youngest daughter whom the gods delight to honour. They will fill with porridge and deck with flannel underclothing the little flower-girls and crossing-sweepers, whose triumphs set faith in the eyes of babes. With their hard, cruel facts they will completely wreck the fairy civilisation which has taken centuries of dreaming and wondering children to construct. They will brush our fancies away like cobwebs.

A while ago, when I was a little boy, some enemy seeing me admire the stars thought it necessary to tell me exactly what they were; later, my natural interest in the extraordinary behaviour of the sea led another enemy to place a globe in my hands, and prick the bubble of the universe with ridiculous explanations. So it is that when I regard the heavens I see enormous balls of rotting chemicals, rendered contemptibly small by distance, floating in a thin fluid called space; so, it is that when I look at the sea my mind is occupied with stupid problems about the route of floating bamboos, when I ought to be exalted as one who peers out through the darkness towards the Unknown.

Where there were two then, there are today twenty kindly persons about every child, eager to prove the things it would like to believe in superstitions, and eager to explain away its miracles in terms of dustcarts and vegetable soup. Our babies are taught to hang out their stockings and to batter in their empty egg-shells, but are reminded at the same moment that these charming rituals are but follies, and that the capital of Scotland is Edinburgh. Youngsters babble Imperialism and Socialism when they ought to be standing on their heads to look at the Antipodes, and their parents commend their common sense. Already, I fear, the wings of many of the fairies are beginning to fade, and Puck capers but mournfully in his lonely haunts.

But fairies, goblins, elves, call them what you will, they are worth having, and that is why I would entreat the wise men who are arranging tomorrow for us to spare them, even though they have forgotten themselves all that the presence of fairies in the world is worth. By all means feed the children and give them Union Jacks, but let their faith in the beautiful be looked to as well. And, finally, to the serious person who says with raised eyebrows, "You can't honestly say you believe in fairies!" I would answer this: In a world which at present is fiercely antagonistic to the belief in any emotion less material than hunger, it is impossible to avoid occasional doubt concerning the existence of anything which it is not possible to eat. But when I am in the company of those who really do believe, I do not fail to hear the echoes of fairy laughter in their speech, and see the flicker of fairy wings reflected in their eyes, and with this knowledge I am content.

The Last Adventure

George Austin Faningford was a young man with a temperament and a handsome income. The former served to make him attractive to all save the very sedate, the latter, which the foresight of a shrewd father had caused to be paid quarterly, enabled him to allow his joyous nature full play, so that he took life as young poets take opium, in a series of magnificent quarterly carouses. The length of these periodical expressions of his youth was determined by fortune; sometimes when he was unlucky his money would last for a weary two months; once a gorgeous thirty six hours sufficed to land him in a Brighton lodging-house, penniless and with no more clothes than those on his back.

One feature, however, of these temperamental effervescences was common to them all. Always at their termination he would wake up like a man who had been dreaming a pleasant dream and could not quite remember what it was, and this romantic vagueness was only dispelled on the rare occasions when the troublesome curiosity of the police served to expose some part of his lurid adventures. In one sense, of course, his awakenings differed from those of a man who merely wakes from his sleep; for he often found himself involved in problems of no little complexity, and in the difficult situation of having to supply an answer without any knowledge of what the conundrum might be.

On a night of November, three weeks after his quarterly cheque had been paid into the bankers, George stepped back suddenly but without shock, as was his wont, into the material world. He was a man of nice taste, but he could find little to criticise in the decorative scheme of the charming room in which he found himself seated. The carpets were silky as the back of a Persian kitten, the curtains and tapestries were of subtly undecided colours, the furniture had that air of fragile discomfort which modern designers appear to have derived from a study of modern morals; in a word, it was a room that no one could live in—a delightful example of the attractive useless. Nor was it displeasing to George, who did not extend his defiance of convention to his clothes, to find that he was wearing evening dress; and though the clothes were not his own, it was reassuring to trace in their delicate lines the cunning hand of Dawson, the dreamer of sartorial masterpieces. And George was regarding the situation with expectant complacency, when the door opened and a woman, beautifully dressed and with a face that was more worthy of the creation she wore, walked blithely into the room.

"Now, George, dear," she said, "are you ready for supper?"

To a man of his varied experiences there was nothing extraordinary in being addressed in such terms of affection by a woman he had never seen before in his normal life. But that he should be invited to sup at an hour usually devoted to dinner, by one who was beyond doubt a member of the world which he himself adorned, appeared to George in the light of a miracle. And it did not escape his notice that beneath her pleasantly frivolous manner the lady was regarding him with a certain keenness as if she too had cause to wonder.

The true art of diplomacy is to proceed, and George hardly allowed himself in a pause in which to register his surprise before he rose and assented with the grace that had cost his parents four thousand pounds.

"I don't know what the servants will think," his companion said, prettily, as they passed along the ferny corridor. "I never do know what they think; possibly about sun-spots or the blind Celtic fish."

"My man is the eighteenth European authority on the chemist of the ancients," said George. "He writes monographs about it and sells my things to pay for having them printed."

"Of course, that isn't true."

They laughed together as they entered the supper-room, a vast chamber of the dimensions of a banqueting hall.

"No, I'm afraid it's only conversation," George admitted, while secretly admiring the curves of her throne. "But all the true things have been said so often."

She looked at him oddly. "I wonder whether they have. Some things are true enough, but——" She screwed her lips into a grotesque smile and they sat down at the table in such an offhand way that George felt that he must have supped with her before, in his dreams. The meal, though cold, was admirable, and the wines fit for an undergraduate in the first flush of his credit, but there was no sign of the servants who might wonder—what?

"This is an adventure," George said to himself, cheerfully; and then aloud: "I don't know about that, I'm sure,"—he wished that he knew her Christian name. "I myself am to some extent a student of the extraordinary, and, if I may say so, I have seen some unusual things and been in some out-of-the-way places. But really, the possible is soon exhausted and miracles are rare. Ninety-nine out of every hundred of my adventures are mere perversions of the obvious. In tabulating them I have divided them into ten groups——"

"And how many of the Commandments have you broken?" she asked, smiling quietly.

"All but one, I'm afraid," said George, wondering a little at her quickness.

She laughed aloud.

"Why, that's what you told my husband," she said. "You are not up to date."

Here was something to puzzle about, thought George. This pretty problem had a husband and he had told him—and what in thunder did she mean by her last remark?

"By the way, where is your husband now?" he said casually.

In itself this does not appear a very humorous question, but it certainly had a remarkable effect on the lady.

"Some people would call you grim," she murmured, between her shrill ripples of laughter. "Perhaps you'd like to have him down to sup with us; he's upstairs you know."

"Well, I don't mind, you know," said George, feeling his way towards an explanation, "so long as I do not lose the pleasure of supping with you."

The lady looked at him with bright lights of excitement in her eyes.

"It would be a thrill, wouldn't it?" she said rising, "if you'll help me to carry him."

So, her husband was an invalid, a madman, or a picture. "I hope it isn't leprosy," George thought to himself. "There's something about this woman—" But he dutifully followed her upstairs.

She stopped outside a door on the first floor, with her hand on the handle.

"Shall I knock?" she said flippantly.

George nodded, and her little knuckles set a playful echo trotting lightly down the passage like a child released from lessons. Then she opened the door and beckoned him in.

Thirty seconds later he reeled out of the room into the corridor with a white face and his body shaking.

"Good God! What have you done?" he cried.

The woman, who had followed him, was hardly less disturbed.

"Don't say you've got a conscience! Don't say you've repented! You've been splendid up to now."

He glared at her fiercely.

"What do you mean?" he stammered.

She stood looking at him in obvious amazement.

"It's not possible," she muttered to herself, frowning. Then she caught him by the arm and led him up to a mirror which was set upright in the wall. "Look!" she said, watching him.

On the white front of his shirt, just below his tie, George saw the imprint of four red fingers, and as he looked, he wavered and sickened, and thought of the dead thing in the room behind him.

"I thought it was bizarre of you to change everything but that," said the woman, in the tone of one who is disappointed.

George pulled himself up and turned his eyes on her pitifully. "What am I to do?" he cried.

"I should think we had better finish our supper."

He followed her down to the supper-room like a child, and like a child he marvelled that the bitterness of his regret should leave the fact unaltered. The woman seated herself and proceeded to eat with a good appetite, blinking at him over the flowers, while he sat miserably fingering his glass.

"You want about a magnum and a bottle," she said, critically. "It's no use wasting any regrets on him. He was really of very little use to me."

"What are you?" he said, suddenly, gulping a glass of wine.

"That's much better," she replied, with a nod of approval. "I? Well, I'm a widow, I suppose."

He looked at her speechlessly.

"You see," she went on, calmly, "melodrama isn't life, nor is it rational for people of education to fall back on crudities when they do have an excuse for self-expression. Now, what is the situation? I wanted my freedom without a bother, and I have got it. You have spent your life in a search for adventures, and here you ate. He—no, I'm not as bad as that. I won't say anything about him. But you can go away after supper and call it a dream if you like."

170

George drank another glass of wine.

"The body!" he said.

"Polymelus!" said the woman thoughtfully. "I never thought of that. What *does* one do with bodies? I suppose I've got a trunk somewhere, but I never was good at packing, and my maid is one of the new sort, you know, and objects to everything out of the beaten track. I shouldn't be surprised to hear that she was a novelist."

"Oh, I can't! I can't!" cried George. "Say it is a joke! Say it isn't true!"

She shook her head at him reproachfully.

"More of your Lyceum imaginings, George," she said, sadly. "It wouldn't go down at the court. Theatre, you know. As for this business of a murder, if I must use your sentimental terms, I can easily burn down the house, or something. Thompson, my late husband's valet, now is a very sensible man, and a thousand pounds, or perhaps two——"

George cut short her remarks, and surprised her by uttering a laugh like the bark of a startled collie.

"Do you know what I ought to do?" he queried.

"Nothing," she said promptly.

"No, it isn't that. I ought to take that pretty neck of yours and choke you. What difference would it make to anyone on earth?"

"Well, you're not going to do it or you wouldn't have mentioned it," she said, calmly. "Besides, it would be bathos. Now, if you'll be a good boy and go home and forget all about it, it will save a lot of bother. And I will give you a very sound piece of advice."

"Well?"

"Don't come out adventuring any more. You haven't got the temperament for it. You allow yourself to be turned from the pursuit of your ideals by trivialities. It is so silly."

George looked at her for a few seconds with leaden eyes.

"I think I shall go home," he said. "I suppose you can manage the body; for all I know you may have done this sort of thing a dozen times."

"No, it's the first time," she said. "But there's really no reason to make a fuss. You've only completed your set."

He walked out into the entrance hall, and the woman followed him. When he reached the door, he turned round and looked her in the face.

"If I gave myself up for this——" he said.

171

"I'm afraid I should laugh dreadfully; it would seem so noble of you."

He bit his lip and opened the door.

"This is my last adventure," he said, with a faint note of tragedy in his voice. "Goodnight!"

"At any rate, I think I should wear a hat if I were you," the lady remarked, sweetly.

And so, at last he went.

"The servants will be back tomorrow, and it is ten o'clock," thought the woman. "I'm going to be pretty busy, it seems; but anyhow, I spoilt his exit." And she went back to finish her supper.

The Boy in the Garden

There were two kinds of gardening to employ our sunny hours—the one concerned with the vast tracts of the Olympians, the other with the cultivation of those intimate patches of earth known as "the children's gardens," wherein was waged an endless contest between Nature and our views of what a garden should be. Of the joys of this nobler order of tillage I have written elsewhere, and I may not penetrate now into that mysterious world beyond the shrubbery, where plants assumed the proportions of mammoth trees, and beds of mustard-and-cress took the imaginative eye of youth as boundless prairies. But if the conventional aims of grown-up gardening set limits to our fancy, if their ideal of beauty in the garden—unfriendly as it was to cricket and the fiercer outbreaks of Indians—was none of ours, we found, nevertheless, certain details in the process by which they sought to attain their illusory ends stimulating and wholly delightful.

Flowers might inspire in us no more than a rare and short-lived curiosity, but the watering-pot (and even better the garden-hose) were our very good friends. Tidiness was no merit in the garden of our dreams, but our song of joy rose straight to heaven with the smoke of bonfires. Meadows were more to our taste than the prim culture of lawns, but in our hands the lawn-mower became a flaming chariot, and we who drove it as unscorched Phaetons praised for the zest with which we pursued our pleasure by all Olympus.

It was one of the charms of childhood that such praise would sometimes fall from the lips of our rulers as suddenly and as mysteriously as their censure. It was pleasant, after a gorgeous afternoon spent in extinguishing imaginary conflagrations with the garden hose to be congratulated on the industry with which we had watered the flowers. It was pleasant to be rewarded with chocolates from France for burning witches on the rubbish-heap behind the greenhouse. As a matter of fact, we never "helped" the gardener unless it suited us, and we would have hidden in the shrubbery a whole day rather than be entrapped into half an hour's weeding—an occupation which we regarded in the light of a severe punishment. And the odd confusion in the grown-up mind between right and wrong never ceased to intrigue us.

When my elder brother, in a sentimental hour, flung a wreath of roses on to the stately head of the aunt of the moment, we knew that it was a pretty thought, very happily translated into action; but the Olympians treated it as a crime. Yet it was not his fault that the thorns tore her hair; had there been any thornless roses he would probably have used them. And, being honest, we wondered no less when we were praised for playing with the garden-hose, that coiled about our legs like wet snakes, and made our stockings wet on the warmest summer day; for in our hearts, we knew that into any occupation so pleasant must surely enter the elements of crime. But the rulers of our destiny would bid us change our wet clothes with a calm brow, and would congratulate each other on our interest in the garden. We lived in a strange world.

The judgments of the gardener we could better understand, though, alas! we had to sum him up as unreliable. He was a twisted little man who had been to sea in his youth, and we knew that he had been a pirate because he had a red face, an enormous clasp-knife, and knew how to make every imaginable kind of knot. Moreover, there was a small barrel in the tool-house that had manifestly held gunpowder once upon a time. Such evidence as this was not to be refuted, but we had to conclude that he had been driven from the High Seas in disgrace, for he was pitifully lacking in the right pirate spirit. No pirate, we felt, would have taken the tale of our petty misdeeds to the Olympian courts for settlement, yet this is what Esau did under cover of a duplicity that aggravated the offence.

In one and the same hour he would expound to us the intricacies of the Chinese knot with many friendly and sensible observations, and tell the shocked Olympians that we had thrown his rose-sticks all over the garden in the manner of javelins. Captain Shark, of the barque *Rapacious*, would not have acted like this, if it was conceivable that that sinister hero could have turned gardener. Perhaps he would have smitten us sorely with the Dutch hoe, or scalped us with his pruning-knife by means of a neat twist learnt in Western America, but whatever form his revenge might have assumed he would have scorned to betray us to the people who had forgotten how to play.

Esau was a sad knave.

And, unlike the Olympians, he had no illusions as to the value of our labours in the garden, treating our generous assistance with the scantiest gratitude, and crediting our enthusiasm with the greater part of Nature's shortcomings. Whenever our horticultural efforts became at all spirited, he would start up suddenly from behind a hedge and admonish us as the boy in *Prunella* admonishes the birds. He would not allow us to irrigate the flowerbeds by means of a system of canals; he checked, or at least attempted to check, our consumption of fruit, deliciously unripe (has anyone noticed that an unripe greengage eaten fresh from the tree is a gladder thing than any ripe fruit?); he would not let us play at executions with the scythe, or at avalanches with the garden-roller. The man's soul was a cabbage, and I fear that he regarded us as a tiresome kind of vermin that he might not destroy.

Nevertheless, as the Olympians liked to see us employed in the garden, he could not wholly refuse our proffered aid, and he would watch our adventures with the garden-hose and the lawn-mower, with his piratical features incarnadined, as it were, by the light of his lurid past. Naturally, water being a good friend of children, to water the garden was the most popular task of all, and as I was the youngest brother it was but rarely that I was privileged to experience that rare delight. To feel the cool rush of the water through fingers hot with play and the comfortable trickle down one's sleeve, to smite a plant with muddy destruction and to hear the cheerful sound made by the torrent in falling on to the soaked lawn—these and their fellow-emotions may not be those of adult gardeners, but they are not to be despised. But as I have said, they were not for me, and usually I had to be content with mowing the lawn, an occupation from which I drew a full measure of placid enjoyment.

Age dims our realisation of the emotional significance of our own actions, and it is only by an effort of memory that I can arrive at the philosophy of the contented mower of lawns. I suppose that professional gardeners find the labour monotonous, lacking both the artistic interest of such work as pruning and the scientific subtleties of cucumber-growing; but youth has the precious faculty of finding the extraordinary in the commonplace, and I had only to drag the lawn-mower from its rugged bed among the forks and spades in the tool-house, to embark on a sea of intricate and diverse adventure.

The very appearance of the thing was cheery and companionable, with its hands outstretched to welcome mine, and its coat of green

175

more vivid than any lawn. To seize hold of its smooth handles was like shaking hands with an old friend, and as it rattled over the gravel path it chattered to me in the gruff tones of a genial uncle. Once on the smooth lawn its voice thrilled to song, tremulous and appealing, and filled with the throbbing of great wings. Even now I know no sound that cries of the summer so poignantly as the intermittent song of the lawn-mower heard far off through sunny gardens.

And cheered by that song I might drive my chariot, or it might be my plough, where I would. Not for me the stiff brocaded pattern beloved of Esau; I made curves, skirting the shadows of the tall poplars or cutting the lawn into islands and lagoons. Over the grass-box—or the nose-bag, as we called it—the grass danced like a mist of green flies, and I beheaded the daisies with the zest of a Caligula, pausing sometimes to marvel at those modest blossoms that survived my passage. I marvelled, too, with the cold inhumanity of youth, at the injudicious earthworms that tried to stay my progress, and perished for their pains. Sometimes a stray pebble would grate unpleasantly on the blades and waken my lulled senses with a jerk; sometimes I would drive too close to a flower-bed, and munched fragments of pansies and wallflowers would glow amongst the grass in the grass-box.

No doubt a part of my enjoyment lay in the feeding of that natural spirit of destructiveness that present-day Olympians satisfy with frequent gifts of clockwork toys, ingenious mechanisms very proper to be inquired into by young fingers. But there was more in it than that. I liked the smell of the newly cut grass, and I would run my fingers through it and press damp, warm handfuls of it to my face to win the full savour of it. I even liked the more pungent odour of the grass-heap where last week's grass lay drying in the sun. And the effort necessary to drive the worker of wonders across the lawn gave me a pleasant sense of my own sturdiness.

But the fact remains that, with all these reasons, I cannot wholly fathom the true philosophy of lawn-mowing with my adult mind. I have set down all the joys that I remember, but some significant fact, some essential note of enchantment, is missing. What did I think about as I pressed to and fro with my lawn-mower? Sometimes, perhaps, I was a ploughman, guiding vast horses along the crests of mountains, and pausing now and again to examine the treasures that my labour had revealed in the earth, leather bags of guineas and jewelled crowns that sparkled through their mask of clay. Sometimes I might be a charioteer driving a team of mad horses round the circus for Nero's pleasure, or a fireman driving a fire-engine scatheless through bewildered streets. But with all I believe that sometimes I was no more than a little boy, mowing the lawn of a sunny garden, loving the task for its own sake, and inspired by no subtler spirit than that which led Esau to cultivate cabbages with dogged enthusiasm.

It would not do to condemn that dishonoured pirate because he saw heaven as a kitchen-garden and regarded flowers as the fond toys of the Olympian dotage. He, too, had his illusions; he, too, while he sowed the seed had visions of an impossible harvest. His ultimate fate eludes my memory, but doubtless he has finished with his husbandry by now. I, too, no longer mow the lawn save when arrayed in fantastic knickerbockers and dream-shod as of yore I trim the grass-plats of sleep with a lawn-mower that sings as birds no longer sing. What the purpose of my youthful labours may have been I do not know. . . . *Parturiunt montes, nascetur ridiculus mus*. Perhaps I was already enrolled in the employment agency of destiny as a writer of idle articles.

The Magic Carpet

There were two rugs in the library, and for some time we used to dispute the vexed question of their relative merits. Æsthetically, there was something to be said for both of them. The rug that stood by the writing-desk from which father wrote to the newspapers was soft and furry; indeed, it was almost as pleasant a couch as the sofa with the soft cushions in the drawing-room, which was taboo. Moreover, it lent itself very readily to such fashionable winter sport as bear-hunting, providing as it did a trackless prairie, a dangerous marsh, or the quarry itself as the adventure required. The joys of the other rug were of a calmer kind, and were, perhaps, chiefly due to its advantageous position before the fire.

It was pleasant to toast oneself on a winter evening and trace with idle fingers the agreeable deviations of its pattern. Sometimes it might be the ground plan of a make-up city, with forts and sweet-shops and palaces for our friends; sometimes it would be a maze, and we would pursue, with bated breath, the vaulted passages that led to the dread lair of the Minotaur. But such plots as these were of passive, rather than active, interest. Reviewing the argument dispassionately, Fenimore Cooper may have had a slight advantage over Nathaniel Hawthorne; bear-hunting may have been a little more popular than the dim excitements of Greek myth.

But while the discussion was at its height, there dawned in the East the sun that was to prove fatal to Perseus and the Deerslayer alike. I do not know from which of our uncles *The Arabian Nights* first came to an enraptured audience; but I am sure that an uncle must have been responsible for its coming, for as a gift it was avuncular in its splendour. We quickly realised that the world had changed, and took the necessary steps to welcome our new guest. The old lamp in the hall that had graced the illicit doings of pirates and smugglers in the past was thenceforward the property of Aladdin; a strange bottle that had been Crusoe's served to confine the unfortunate genie; and with quickening pulses we discovered that in the fireside rug we possessed no less a treasure than the original magic carpet.

I must explain that we were not like those fortunate children of whom Miss Nesbit writes with such humorous charm. To us there fell no tremendous adventures; we might polish Aladdin's lamp till it shone like the moon without gaining a single concrete acid-drop for our pains. But the *Arabian Nights* gave us all that we ever thought of seeking either in books or toys in those uncritical days—a starting-point for our dreams. And this, I take it, is the best thing that a writer can give a child, and it was for lack of this that we considered the works of Lewis Carroll silly, while finding one of the books of Miss Molesworth—I wish I could recall its name—a masterpiece of fancy and erudition.

So, when the din of the schoolroom did not suit my mood, or the authorities were unduly didactic, I would slip away to the twilit library and guide the magic carpet through the delicate meadows of my dreams. The fire would blaze and crackle in the grate and fill my eyes with tears, so that it was easy to fancy myself in a sparkling world of sunshine. And from the shadows of the room little creatures would creep out to touch my glowing cheeks with cool, soft fingers, or to pluck timidly at the sleeve of my coat. I did not endeavour to give these shy companions of the dark any definite place in my universe.

Their sympathetic reticence was reassuring in that room of great leaping shadows, and I was glad that they should keep me company in the blackness, a thing so terrible when I woke up at night in my bed. Sometimes, perhaps, I wondered how they could bear to live in the place where nightmare was; but for the rest I accepted their society gladly and without question. There was plenty of room on the carpet for such quiet fellows, and if they liked to accompany me on my travels I, at least, would not prevent them.

It did not occur to me at the time, as it certainly does now, that I should never again be so near to fairyland as I was then. I was inclined to be sceptical concerning the actual existence of the supernatural, though I recognised that a judicious acceptance of its theories set a new kingdom beneath one's feet for play. And it is only now that I realise how wonderfully vivid my dreams were, with what zest of timid life the little shadow-folk thrilled and trembled round me. It is true that I remained conscious of my normal environment; the fire, the dark room, and the bookcases were all there, and even a kind of quiet sense of the World beyond the Door, the hall and the passages and my brothers and sisters at their quarrels.

But it was as if these things had become merely an idea in my mind, while my feet were set on the pleasant roads of a new world. The thing that I had hoped became true; and the truth that I had been taught lingered in my mind only as a familiar story, a business of second-hand emotions, neither very desirable nor very interesting. The little folk gathered and whispered round me in the dark, and there was full day in the world that was my own.

It was hard to leave that world for this other place, which even now I cannot understand; but when some errant Olympian or righteously indignant brother had dragged me from my lair, I did not attempt to defend myself from the charge of moodiness. I had no words to tell them what they had done, and I could only stand blinking beneath the light of the gas in the hall, and endeavour to recall their wholly tiresome rules and regulations for the life of youth.

Dimly I knew that my right place was before the fire in the library, and I wondered whether the little folk could use the Magic Carpet without me, or whether they stayed expectant in the shadows, like me, a little lonely, and a little chill. But in those days, moodiness was only a lesser crime than sulkiness, and I had perforce to fold up my fancies and pass, an emotional bankrupt, into the unsympathetic world of the playroom. Tomorrow, perhaps, the Magic Carpet might be mine again; meanwhile, I would exist.

Peter Pan has asked us a good many times whether we believe in fairies. It is, of course, a matter of faith, to be accepted or denied, but not to be discussed. For my part, I think of a little boy nodding on a rug before the fire on many a winter's evening, and I clap my hands. Gratitude could do no less.

The Story-Teller

He changed with the seasons, and, like the seasons, was welcome in every mood. In spring he was forlorn and passionate in turn; now fiercely eloquent, now tuneful with those little cheerful songs that seem in terms of human emotion to be the saddest of all. In summer he dreamed in sensuous and unambitious idleness, gladly conscious of the sunshine and warm winds and flower-smells, and using only languorous and gentle words. In autumn, with the dead leaves of the world about his feet, he became strangely hopeful and generous of glad promises of adventure and conquest. It seemed as though he found it easier to triumph when Nature had abdicated her jealous throne.

But it was in the winter-time when he came into his own kingdom, and mastered his environment and his passions to make the most joyful songs. Then he would lie at full length on the hearthrug, and we children, sitting in a rapt circle, fantastically lit by the fire, would listen to his stories, and know that they were the authentic wisdom.

It was in vain that the grown-ups warned us against the fascinations of his society, telling us that dreamers came to no good end in a practical world. As well might the townsfolk of Hamelin, in Brunswick, have ordered their children to turn a deaf ear to the tune of the Pied Piper. We had studied life from a practical point of view between our games, and found it unsatisfying; this man brought us something infinitely more desirable. He would come stepping with delicate feet, fearful of trampling on our own tender dreams, and he would tell us the enchanted stories that we had not heard since we were born. He told us the meaning of the stars and the significance of the sun and moon; and, listening to him, we remembered that we had known it all once before in another place.

Sometimes even we would remind him of some trivial incident that he had forgotten, and then he would look at us oddly and murmur sadly that he was getting very old. When the stories were over, and all the room was still ringing with beautiful echoes, he would stand erect and ask us fiercely whether we saw any straws in his hair. We would climb up him to look (for he was very tall), and when we told him that we could not find any he would say: "The day you see them there will be no more stories." We knew what the stories were worth to us, so we were always afraid of looking at his head for fear that we should see the straws and all our gladdest hours should be finished.

His voice was all the music extant, and it was only by recalling it that our young ears could find that there was beauty in fine singing and melodiousness in the chaunt of birds. Yet when his words were eloquent, we forgot the voice and the speaker, content to sacrifice our critical individualities to his inspiration till we were no more than dim and silent figures in the background of his tale. It was only in winter-time that he achieved this supreme illusion; perhaps the fire-light helped him, and the chill shadows of the world. In the summer his stories had the witchery of dreams; their realism startled us, and yet we knew that they were not real.

After listening to them through a hot afternoon we would stretch back into consciousness, as though we had been asleep; his drowsy fancies lulled our personalities, but did not conquer them. The winter magic was of a rarer kind. Then even his silences became significant, for he brought us to so close an intimacy with his mind that his very thoughts seemed like words.

It is idle to expect a child to believe that every grown-up person was a child once upon a time, for it is not credible that they could have forgotten so much. But this man was a child both in feeling and in un-derstanding. He knew the incidents that perplexed us in those nursery legends that have become classics, and sometimes it was his pleasure to tell them to us again, having regard to our wakeful sympathies.

He was the friend of all the poor, lost creatures of romance—the giants whose humiliating lot it was to be defeated by any stripling lad, the dragons whose flaming strength was a derision when opposed to virtue in armour. He shared our pity for Antæus and Caliban and Goliath of Gath, and even treated sorcerers and wicked kings with reasonable humanity. Somehow, though we felt that it was wicked, we could not help being sorry for people when they were punished very severely. The very ease with which giants could be outwitted suggested that the great simple fellows might prove amiable enough if they were kindly treated, while it was always possible that dragons might turn out to be bewitched princes, if only the beautiful princesses would kiss them instead of sending heroes to kill them unfairly, without giving them an opportunity of explaining their motives. Our story-teller understood our scruples and sympathised with them, and in his versions, everyone had a chance, whether they were heroes or no. Even the best children are sometimes cruel, but they are never half so pitiless as the writers of fairy-stories.

But better than any fairy-stories were the stories that he told us of our own lives, which under his touch became the wonderful adventures which they really were. He showed us that it was marvellous to get out of bed in the morning, and marvellous to get into bed at night. He made us realise the imaginative value of common things, and the fun that could be derived even from the performance of duties, by aid of a little make-believe. The grown-up folk would probably have derided his system, but he made us tolerate our lessons, and endure the pangs of toothache with some degree of fortitude. He had a short way with the ugly bogies with which thoughtless nurses and chance echoes from the horrors columns of newspapers had peopled the shadows of our life.

We were no longer afraid of the dark when he had told us how friendly it could be to the distressed. Hitherto we had vainly sought to find the colours and sounds of romance in life, and, failing, had been tempted to sum up the whole business as tedious. After he had shown us how to do it, it was easy to see that life itself was a story as romantic as we cared to make it. Our daily official walks became gallant expeditions, and we approached arithmetic with a flaming sword.

Can any childhood ever have known a greater wizard than this? And yet since that state does not endure for ever, it must surely have happened to us to seek for straws in his towering head once too often, had not death taken our kindly enchanter from our company, and thus spared us the bitter discovery that the one man who reconciled us to life was considered rather more than eccentric by an obtuse world. It is true that we noticed that the grown-up people were apt to treat him sometimes as if he were one of us, but we felt that he merited this distinction, and did not find it strange.

Nor did we wonder that he should tell stories aloud to himself lacking a wider audience, for we knew that if we had the power, we should tell such stories to ourselves all day long. We did not only fail to realise that he was mad; we knew that he was the only reasonable creature of adult years who ever came near us. He understood us and paid us the supreme compliment of allowing us to understand him. The world called him fantastic for actions that convinced us that he was wise, and, thanks to a fate that seemed at the time insensately cruel, the spell was never broken.

The Wool-Gatherer

When he walked down the streets with his head drooping towards the pavement and his hands thrust deep into the pockets of his overcoat the grown-ups would say, "There goes poor Mr. X. wool-gathering as usual"; and we children used to wonder what he did with all the wool and where he found it to gather. Perhaps he collected it from the thorn-bushes whereon the sheep had scratched themselves, or perhaps, being a magician, he had found a way to shear the flocks that we often saw in the sky on fine and windy days. At all events, for a while his strange calling made us regard him with interest as a man capable of doing dark and mysterious things. Then the grown-ups tried to dispel our illusions by explaining that they only meant that he was absent-minded, a dreamer, an awful warning to young folk who had their way to make in the world.

This admirable moral lesson, like most of their moral lessons, failed because they did not appreciate the subtlety of our minds. We saw that the wool-gatherer did no recognisable work, wore comfortably untidy clothes, walked in the mud as much as he wanted to, and, in fine, lived a life of enviable freedom; and we thought that on the whole when we grew up, we should like to be wool-gatherers too. Even the phrase "absent-minded" excited our admiration; for we knew that it would be a fine thing if our thoughts could travel in foreign countries, where there are parrots and monkeys loose in the woods, while our bodies were imprisoned in the schoolroom under the unsympathetic supervision of the governess of the moment. Although we no longer credited him with being a magician, the tardy explanations of the grown-ups had, if anything, increased his glamour. It seemed to us that he must be very wise.

He lived in an old house a little way out of the town, and the house stood in a garden after our own heart. We knew by the shocked comments of our elders that it had formerly been cut and trimmed like all the other gardens with which we were acquainted, but it was now a perfect wilderness, a delightful place. My brother and I got up early one morning when the dew was on the world and explored it thoroughly. `We found a goat in an outhouse and could see the marks in the meadow that had once been a lawn, where he was tethered during the day. The wool-gatherer was evidently in the habit of sitting under a tree that stood at one corner, for the earth was pitted with the holes that had been made by the legs of his chair.

Being a wise man, we thought it probable that he conversed with his goat and could understand the answers of that pensive animal, who wagged his beard at us when we peeped shyly into his den. In the long grass by the tree, we found a book bound like a school prize lying quite wet with the dew. It was full of cabalistic signs, and we took care to leave it where we found it lest it should be black magic, though now I would support the theory that Mr. X. read his Homer in the original. Taking it altogether, it was the most sensible garden we had ever seen, with plenty of old fruit-trees, but with none of those silly flower-beds that incommode the careless feet of youth. Our expedition enhanced our opinion of the wool-gatherer's wisdom.

Here at least was a grown-up person who knew how to live in a decent fashion, and when he ambled by us in the market-place, his muddy boots tripping on the cobbles, and the pockets of his green-grey overcoat pulled down by the weight of his hands, our eyes paid him respectful tribute. He really served a useful purpose in our universe, for he showed us that it was possible to grow old without going hopelessly to the bad. Sometimes, considering the sad lives of our elders who did of their own free will all the disagreeable things that we were made to do by force, we had been smitten with the fear that in the course of years we, too, would be afflicted with this melancholy disease.

The wool-gatherer restored our confidence in ourselves. If he could be grown-up without troubling to be tidy or energetic, why, then, so could we! It amused us to feel that our affronted rulers were itching to give him a good talking to and to send him off to brush his clothes and his boots; but he was beyond the reach of authority, this splendid man. And one of these days we thought that we, too, would enjoy this delightful condition of freedom, for, like many grown men and women, we did not realise that liberty is a state of mind and not an environment.

We had never seen the inside of his house, but we could imagine what it was like. No doubt he kept his servants in proper order and did not allow them to tidy up, so that his things lay all over the room where he could find them when he wanted them. He had a friendly cat, with whom we were acquainted, so that he would not lack company, and probably on wet days when he could not go out into the garden, he had the goat in to play with him. He went to bed when he liked and got up when he liked, and had cake for every meal instead of common bread. A man like that would be quite capable of having a sweetshop in one of the rooms, with a real pair of scales, so that he could help himself whenever he wanted to. Whenever our own lives grew a little dull, we played at being the wool-gatherer, but although he occupied such a large part of our thoughts, we never dared to speak to him, because we were afraid of his extraordinary wisdom. This was not our normal reason for avoiding the society of grown-up people.

When one day a funeral passed us in the street, and we were told that it was the wool-gatherer's, we shook our heads sceptically. The coffin was quite new and shiny, and all the horses had their hoofs neatly blacked, and we thought we knew our man better than that. But as day followed day and we met him no more our doubts were overcome, and we knew that he was dead. After a while his will was published in the local newspaper, and the grown-ups were greatly impressed, because it seemed that he had been very rich and had left all his money to hospitals. Secretly we patronised them for their tardy discovery of our man's worth; it had not needed any newspaper to tell us that he was remarkable. But when some new people took his house and cut down all the bushes and tidied up the garden we were really hurt, and began to realise what we had lost. Where should we play now these hot nights of summer when the hours passed so slowly and we could not sleep? They had made his beautiful wilderness as dull as our own, and our dreams must find a new playground. We never heard what happened to the goat.

Now that I am myself grown-up, though children occasionally flatter me by treating me as an equal, I revert sometimes to our earliest thoughts and wonder what the wool-gatherer did with all his wool. Perhaps he wove it into blankets for the poor dreamless ones of the world. They are many, for it is not so easy to be absent-minded as people think; in the first place, it is necessary to have a mind. It is wrong also to believe that wool-gatherers fill no useful place in life. I have shown how Mr. X., lost in his world of dreams, was yet of real service to us as children, and in the same way I think that we who

189

live the hurried life derive genuine satisfaction from the spectacle of the dreamers sauntering by. If they serve no other purpose, they are at least milestones by aid of which we can estimate our own speed, and if no one were idle we would win no credit from our marvellous energy. Also, they are happy, and the philosopher will always hesitate to condemn the way of life of a man who succeeds in that task. Perhaps we should all be better off gathering wool!

On Going to Bed

When the winter fires were burning their merriest in the grates, or when the summer sun was melting to crimson shadows down in the western fields, we, pressing our noses on the window-panes in placable discussion of the day's cricket, or dreaming our quiet dreams on the playroom floor, would hear a heartbreaking pronouncement fall tonelessly from the lips of the Olympians: "Come, children, it is time you were in bed!" It needed no more than that to bring our hearts to zero with a run, and set our lips quivering in eloquent but supremely useless protest. Against this decree there was, we knew, no appeal; and we pleaded our hopeless cause rather from habit than from any expectation of success. And even while we uttered passionate expressions of our individual wakefulness, and vowed our impatience for the coming of that golden age when we should be allowed to sit up all night, we were collecting the honoured toys that shared our beds, in mournful recognition of the inevitable.

It was not that we had any great objection to bed in itself, but that fate always decreed that bedtime should fall in the brightest hour of the day. No matter what internecine conflicts, whether with the Olympians or each other, had rendered the day miserable, when bedtime drew near the air was sweet with the spirit of universal brotherhood, as though in face of our common danger we wished to propitiate the gods by means of our unwonted merit. Feuds were patched up, confiscated property was restored to its rightful owner, and brother hailed brother with a smiling countenance and that genial kind of rudeness that passed with us for politeness.

This was the time of day, too, when the more interesting kind of Olympian would make his appearance, uncles—at least, we called them uncles—who could perform conjuring tricks and tell exciting stories, and aunts who kissed us, but had a compensating virtue in that they had been known to produce unexpected sweets. The house that

might have been a gloomy prison of dullness during the long day became, by a sudden magic, entertaining and happily alive. The kitchen
was fragrant with the interesting odours that come from the cooking of strange adult viands; the passages were full of strong men who
could lift small boys to the ceiling without an effort, and who would
sometimes fling sixpences about with prodigal lavishness; the whole
place was gay with parcels to be opened, and lively, if incomprehensible, conversation. And ever while we were thrilling to find that our
normal environment could prove so amusing, the Olympians would
realise our existence in their remote eyries of thought, and would
send us, stricken with barren germs of revolt, to our uneventful beds.

On me, as the youngest of the brothers, the nightly shock should
have fallen lightly; for I was but newly emancipated from the shameful
ordeal of going to bed for an hour in the afternoon, and I could very
well remember, though I pretended I had forgotten, the sensations of
that drowsy hour, when the birds sang so loudly outside the window
and the sun thrust fingers of dusty gold through the crannies of the
blind. I should therefore probably have been reconciled to the common lot, which spelt advancement to me, had I not newly discovered
the joy of dreaming those dreams that men have written in books for
the delight of the young. The Olympians were funny about books.
They gave them to us, or at the least smiled graciously when other
people gave them to us, but the moment rarely arrived when they
could endure to see us reading, or spoiling our eyes as their dreadful
phrase ran.

And especially at nightfall, when the shadows crept in from the
corners of the room and made the pages of the dullest book exciting,
it was inviting an early bedtime to be detected in the act of reading. As sure as the frog was about to turn into a prince or the black
enchantress had appeared with her embarrassing christening present,
the book would be taken from my hands and I would be threatened
with the compulsory wearing of old-maidish spectacles—an end that
would make me an object of derision in the eyes of man. And even
if I shut the book of my own accord, and sat nodding before the fire,
working out the story in my own fashion with someone I knew very
well to play the part of hero, some ruthless adult would accuse me
of being "half asleep already," and the veil of illusion would be torn
beyond repair.

In winter-time the bedroom would seem cold after the comfortable kingdom of the hearth-rug, and the smell of scented soap was

a poor substitute for the friendly fragrance of burning logs. So, we would undress as quickly as possible, and lie cuddled up in the chilly bedclothes, holding our own cold feet in our hands as if they belonged to somebody else. But if it happened that one of us had a bad cold, and there was a fire in the bedroom, we would keep high festival, sitting in solemn palaver round the campfire, and toasting our pink toes like Arctic explorers, while the invalid lay in bed crowing over his black-currant tea or hot lemonade. It was pleasant, too, when natural wea-riness had driven us to our beds, to lie there and watch the firelight laughing on the walls; and the invalid, for the time being, was rather a popular person.

In summer-time getting into bed was a far more complex process, for the youth of the night held us wakeful; and if the weather were warm, bed was an undesirable place as soon as we had exhausted such coolness as lingered in the sheets. Then we would devote ourselves to pillow-fighting, which was, I think, a more humorous sport for elder brothers than for younger, or we would express our firm intention of sleeping all night on the floor under tents made of the bedclothes. The best of this resolution was that it made bed seem so comfortable, when we climbed back after the first fine romance of camping-out had worn off. Thunderstorms we loved with a love not untouched by awe, and we would huddle together at the window, measuring the lightning, appraising the thunder, and listening to the cool thresh of the rain on the garden below.

There were rare nights—nights of great winds—when we would suddenly realise that fear had entered into the room, and that, after all, we were children in a world of men. Our efforts to talk resulted in tremulous whispers that bred fear rather than allayed it, and though we would not even then admit it, we knew that we were possessed with a great loneliness. Sooner or later some cunning spirit would suggest a pilgrimage to the realms of the Olympians, and treading the warm stair-carpet with our bare feet, we would journey till we heard the comforting sound of their laughter and the even murmur of their conversation. Sometimes we would stay there till we grew sleepy, and the fear passed away, so that we could tiptoe back to bed, wondering a little at ourselves; sometimes the Olympians would discover us, and comfort our timid hearts with rough words and sweet biscuits. In the morning we would pretend that the whole business had been only an adventure, and we were not above bragging of our courage in daring the ire of the grown-up people. But we knew better.

Faith

She came downstairs while he was taking off his coat in the little dingy hall, when he saw the sorrow in her face, he blinked his eyes in fear.

"Is she dead?" he asked quickly.

She dropped her head on his breast, sobbing.

"The doctor says. . . .no hope."

The man drew a deep breath, and then he stooped and kissed her.

"God—God knows best," he said with an effort, "but it's damned hard. Our only one, and some with so many."

He stood there puckering his brow, while the gas whistled drearily over his head, and his wife cried softly at his heart. Then he led her upstairs.

In her room the child was playing with her dreams, and from her small bed they could hear her talking, and hardest of all to bear, laughing to the comrades whom they could not see. The firelight seemed to have a share in her game, for it danced about the room as cheerfully as the child had in the past. The man and his wife walked into the room on tiptoe as if they feared to spoil her enjoyment. "So very little to die," he muttered, leaning over the bed, "so very little."

At the words the child opened her eyes, as if his hushed voice had penetrated to the dim garden in which she played. For a while she saw only the deep blue of the night sky, but then he realised with a thrill of unreasoning hope that she had recognised him.

"Dear!" he cried softly.

"Father," she said with a voice at once shrill and hoarse, "I want a necklace, a necklace of stars."

The woman wrung her hands by the bed.

"We have no necklaces here now, darling," she said, "Father will bring it for you in the morning."

"A necklace, a necklace of stars!" the child cried.

195

The woman looked hopelessly at the man across the bed.

"What can we do?" she said bitterly.

"I want a necklace of stars," the child repeated.

The man looked round the room helplessly, at the grapes, the medicine, and the neglected toys. Then with a strange light in his face he caught up a piece of string from the table and turned towards the door.

"I will go and fetch it for you dear," he said quietly, and he bore her cry of joy with him up the dark stairs and through the little door on to the sooty roof.

The air was very cold after that of the sickroom, and for a while he stood there in uncertainty, with the string hanging from his fingers and all the world of smoky light rolling like the sea below him. Then, with a quick, nervous movement, he tore the largest star from its place in heaven, and threaded it like a blazing jewel upon his string. After that it was easy, and when his string had become a glowing chain of stars, he tied the ends and set the moon there as a pendant. Then he retraced his steps to the child's room, but the staircase was dark no longer.

"See! What I have brought you!" he cried, and he threw the necklace on to the bed. The child laughed out in an ecstasy of delight.

"The necklace of stars," she whispered, and she clutched the dazzling thing with eager fingers.

All night the great jewels glowed on the bed and filled the room with their lovely light, and though dawn, when it came, would have it that the necklace was no more than a loop of common string, the child knew better.

Fate's Solution

Morris's buildings, Southwark, were decrepit and ram shackle in the last degree, and nothing but a continuous and expensive course of repairs saved their owner from an order for their destruction. That one was wont to swear when the builder's accounts came in, but tenements are highly profitable, so Morris's Buildings continued to exist, when a better-class house in the same condition would long ago have been pulled down.

The Authorities saw that they were safe, if not sightly, and the inhabitants held their peace because they were poor. This adjective certainly applied to Charles Anderson and Mary Wade, who each had a room near the stars in that gloomy building. They also had another feature in common—they were both highly unpopular with the other inhabitants of the tenements. Charles, because he spoke like a gentleman, and no one has a right to give himself airs in such a place—Mary because she lived alone without a "husband," and for a young woman that was not considered "respectable."

Perhaps it was their mutual aloofness from the society of the Buildings that had made them to some extent acquainted; when they met on the stairs they talked for a minute or two, and once she had mended his coat sleeve.

And that was all.

It was New Year's Eve, and Charles was making his way upstairs with a bottle but ill-concealed under his coat. On the topmost landing but one he overtook Mary. They each said good evening and paused in their upward course. And there was momentary silence.

Somewhere down below Stevens and a select party of exiled compatriots were keeping it up, and the gusts of shouting and laughter made the upper part of the house seem very silent by contrast.

This struck Charles and he spoke to Mary with a faint bitterness in his voice.

197

"It's as quiet as heaven up here tonight, and as cold."

"It is very cold," she said, and added sadly, "It is always cold."

They mounted the last flight of stairs together. "I have a fire in my room," he said as they reached the landing. "Come in and make good resolutions."

She looked at him doubtfully.

"Unless you are afraid?" he continued.

"I'll come in," she said quietly. "I'm not afraid. Why should I be?"

"With all the stars in heaven for chaperons," he said as he opened the door of his room. "It is a fine night. 'A wonderful fine night of stars.' Good **Lord**! That's Stevenson. You don't know him I suppose."

She had never seen the interior of his room before, though there was little in it to surprise her, with the exception, perhaps, of the small heap of books in the corner. The bed covered with newspapers for blankets, the broken windowpane stuffed with the same useful material, the crazy wooden table, the packing cases, the bare and rotten boards—these she had in her room; but hers was cleaner because she was a woman.

The fire, however was unusual enough, and their first thoughts were centred on that. Charles placed the bottle on the table, and going down on his knees by the fire, blew the ashes tenderly from the bars; then with a small piece of wood, and a couple of diminutive nuggets of coal, he stirred the wretched embers into something like a blaze.

"There!" he said proudly, and getting up from the floor he drew a couple of the packing-cases to the front of the fire. "Now we can talk."

Mary sat down and looked gratefully at the flames. "It was cold," she said.

"Yes," said Charles. "I'm glad I have a fire. I was lucky today. Till I was poor I never had blue blood in my veins as far as I know, but now it shows quite plainly in my nose."

"I'm never lucky," said Mary, smiling a little. "And I have always been poor. I suppose you like the sunshine more than the others though–it makes some difference."

"Properly considered we are the salt of the earth. We rise daily and overcome all the tyrants that make the well-to-do miserable. Heat and cold. Rain and fog. Hunger and thirst." His eye wandered to the bottle on the table. "Some of us have not quite overcome that last tyrant, by the way, but I, for one, never have indigestion, and I shall not die of the gout!"

"How can you talk like that," she said gently," when you feel it so?

I like to hear you joke, and yet-I suppose it is all a lie. You know what poverty really is. You know it is below laughter—-"

"No, it is above it," he answered quietly. "Above laughter, above love, and above life, for it slays them all. Dear life! what a thing this poverty is. It makes crime a virtue, virtue a crime, fools wise men, Poets Anarchists. It makes me a sot, and you a brave woman-but I daresay you would have been that anyhow. Oh! how great a thing it is to be poor. We are part of our Mother Earth, because they cannot help it, and nothing more. But, if ever I were rich, phew!"—he spread his arms round the garret, "I should be Nero. And you, you should be my empress. How we should crush them! Not the poor smallest who are so easy to crush. But those others, landlords, publicans, sub-editors if you wish! Oh, I didn't mean to say that about my empress. It was rude. I beg your pardon."

Mary had blushed at his words, but now she drew nearer the fire, and stretched out her hands to warm them. "It is cold, tonight," she said.

Charles laughed at the bottle on the table.

"I know what will warm you," he said, "Whisky. Hot whisky and water. Punch without lemons."

Mary smiled and shook her head.

"I don't like it. I'm afraid," she said.

"Nor do I," cried Charles. "I hate it. But the effect. The exhilaration. I'm a poor had literary hack, a bad one, mind you, sober. I am *Czar* of all the Russias in my cups. Not that I get drunk," he added quietly, as he thought he saw her frown. "Oh! I know it's weak. D—d weak. But I just tipple when I have the money."

"I am sorry," she said, looking steadily at the fire. "I did not know you, yet I always thought you were so brave. I saw you were a gentleman, and as poor as—as one of us, and I always found you with a smile on your face, and a joke on your tongue, and it did me good. I said to myself, 'See how much harder it is for him than for you'. And I felt more brave myself."

"I am sorry," said Charles humbly. "I did not know it mattered to anyone but me. I did not know anyone cared."

He looked at Mary interrogatively, as if to ask whether it was the fire that made her cheeks so red.

"I care," said Mary softly, and Charles saw that it was not the fire. The room was very quiet.

"I suppose—" said Charles at last—"I suppose you never guessed

199

I was thinking a little, not a great deal of you too. Well, I thought you were plucky. I think you are plucky to come in here tonight. And you came because you are good. 'My strength is as the strength of ten because my heart is pure!' It is so with you. Well, I have a certain amount of strength in me in spite of the whisky. I don't know what it is. I think that is what idiots call the problem of life. To find out where one is strong, so that one may avoid the places where one is weak. But however, that is, I know this. Here are two of us, side by side in a manner, each finding life difficult, and each trying to fly our flag nevertheless. Mary! Can't we fly the same flag? Share the same difficulties? Can't we marry? Oh! I know there is the whisky. That shall go overboard, never fear. Don't you see? I know we have had no love-making, no pleasant foolery. That's because we are not players but realities, not living but fighting for our lives. Your strength for my weakness. My weakness for my strength, Mary?"

Mary was crying a little, crying and shaking her head. "I'm very sorry," she said at length—"I am sorry. I can't marry anyone because— I am married already."

"Married already," Charles repeated quietly. "Married already. What a pity."

"He left me and the baby died," she went on. "Four years ago."

"The beast," said Charles. "The beast."

"I married him," she said.

"Oh, I'm sorry," he said. "Of course, there must have been some mistake. He could not have left you on purpose."

"Oh, but he did. He was very cruel before he went. Yet I liked him once."

"And now—" said Charles—"and now his ghost spoils all. And I don't know whether I am sorry or glad that you are so good."

"Please," she said. "Please. It is so nice to be here by the fire."

Charles got up and heaped coals in a profligate manner on the little grate.

"We may as well have a good one," he said. "It is New Year's Eve, and it will be well if I have no more troubles in the New Year than a trivial dearth of fuel!"

She looked at him sadly.

"You are so good to me, and so sorry."

"Mary," he said, "I feel like the devil. Why and why and why not? That's the song in my brain. You are good, and I want to be good. But we can't. Poor people can't be good. We have got to fight and we want

200

help. What does it matter what they say?

It matters not how strait the gate,
How charged with punishments the scroll,
I am the master of my fate:
I am the captain of my soul.

Mary, that is the thing. Captain of my soul. I know this thing isn't wrong. It is only fate would have it so. Mary, can't we master fate? You and I. Against the world. Knowing that nothing we can do is wrong, because we are ourselves the only judges. Knowing that God knows how hard it is!"

Mary shook her head again.

"It is no use," she said. "Can't you see that we should lose the one thing that we have kept? The one thing that has been given us to keep. You say I am good. That is tonight. What would you call me tomorrow? How should I judge myself tomorrow? I have only this one little thing. I have tried to be good."

"Oh, I suppose you are right," he said. "I said I was the devil. And yet I have tried to be good sometimes, and it all ends in whisky and the devil. I remember words in the play, 'If love were all!' I suppose if Love were all we should be King and Queen tonight, Mary; As it is—I know you love me."

"I—I am married, and my husband is alive," she said, looking at him startled.

"I know! I know! Why are you afraid? It is not me you fear-it is yourself," he cried, and he strode towards her and seized her by the hands.

"If I were a brute. No, I am a brute. If—if—I am the captain of my soul. Mary, Mary, you love me. Are you the captain of yours?"

She stood there looking into his face.

"Ah," she cried. "And you said I was strong. I, who am so weak."

"You love me! You love me!" he cried; and the world swam before him because she trembled so beneath his strength.

Mary was crying.

"What shall I do?" she sobbed. "Oh, why is it so hard?"

"Why! Why!" he echoed. "But there must be a way. We are not meant to be slaves. We are not meant to suffer so." He had let go one of her hands, and they stood hand in hand in the firelight like children, and like a child she cried.

Suddenly the quiet of the stairs and passages was turned to horror by the shrieks of women, and panic-stricken cries of men. Dully through the door there came "Fire! Fire!" in senseless iteration, and the street below was filled as by magic with an excited crowd.

"The house is on fire," he said to her, and with the words a film of smoke came curling under the door.

Charles clutched her arm closer to him, and went to the door. The landing was filled with bitter smoke, and there was a spit and crackle of flame below.

"It is the stairs," he said, stepping back into the room, and shutting out the smoke. He led her gently to the window.

"Dear, I think this is the answer. You are not afraid?"

"I'm not afraid. Why should I be?" she said, smiling.

"I am so glad," he said, and he flung open the window. Below them in the street he could see a mass of white faces upturned. All about lay the lights of houses and streets, with the stars over all.

"Good God! how rich we are!" he cried. "We are letting in the New Year. And I think it should be happier than the last. I see that you were right. Quite right. Still there is no harm now."

And he bent down and kissed her.

"It will not hurt much," he said.

"No, it will be very sweet, dear," she said, and she smiled into his face.

And so, they waited.

Welcome Home

He stood in Charing Cross Station, wrack cast up from the sea, looking idly at the strange faces and wondering what home meant to him. In all the years that he had spent, blown hither and thither like spindrift by the sea, he had thought of England, of London, as home. But now that he had come back from his haphazard wanderings, he realised that the thing in truth was only a name. While he had been seeking his singing rose in the weary wastes of the sea, his princess with the bright eyes and the lamp-lit hair had changed, and it seemed in the moment's bitterness as though singing roses were of no more worth.

All the faces were strange....And yet he had to make the best of it. Doubtless in time he would find another princess, not so merry with love as the old, perhaps, but with a deeper knowledge in her sad eyes. He had money, and this was a city of shops, shops of pleasure and love and sea-worn memories; and if a night or two might not restore the old wine to his lips, there was always the patient sea. He shrugged his shoulders and passed out of the station with the crowd, the crowd of strangers.

For a while, used as he was to the great sea-spaces, he could hardly breathe in the genial turbulence of the Strand. The people drove him from side to side, and though their faces were friendly he longed to stretch his loose limbs that seemed cramped by the crowd. And so, he wandered off into the quieter streets, where the stars were like those which had balanced above the tropic masts, and where he might fling about the pavements as he wished. And presently he came to the theatre.

Although the front was brilliantly lit there was not a great crowd before it, and he thought with satisfaction that he could probably get a seat, even though the bills announced that this was the first performance of a new play. And he felt that the name of the play was a good omen. *The Welcome Home.* Perhaps after all he would find the princess somewhere, the princess who pined for the singing rose. He went into the theatre gladly.

At the box office they gave him a seat at the back of the dress circle, where his unorthodox attire might be condoned. To him the lights and the glow of the theatre represented a dream fulfilled. Often, he had thought of these things at sea. The orchestra, the well-dressed men, the beautiful women, they had filled his mind when the sea had lashed at his face like a whip, and the wind had buffeted him like an angry crowd. It was pleasant to be home.

And the play, he realised that it might not be a great work of art, yet it danced with his mood as a child might dance with a doll. How long, how weary long, he had been away at sea. It was very good to be home.

When he came out of the theatre, he realised that the princess had not really changed. There was an end of the foam, and the rain, and the swift-scudding clouds. The great seas would sing for him no more. He had come back to a place of laughter, and dreams, and languorous de lights. He fell asleep with a smile upon his lips, a smile that his mother would have recognised. It is good to be home.

★★★★★★★★★★★★★★★★★

In the morning it seemed natural to him to turn his steps towards the place which had given him back his dead. As he passed down the street it broke upon him in the grey morning light, a place with broken windows and unpainted woodwork, the shattered wreck of a heater.

"Oh, the Old Frivolity!" said the policeman, "it's been shut these twenty years!"

The Fat Man

I met him first at Lord's, the best place, perhaps, in all London for making acquaintances and even friends. Even if he had not worn a light suit of clothes that drew the critical eye inevitably to his monstrous girth, he would have been conspicuous as occupying with difficulty the space provided for two persons on an afternoon when seats were at a premium. But though I own to no prejudice against flesh in itself, it was not his notable presence that induced me to speak to him, but rather the appealing glances that he threw to right and left of him when he thought to have detected that fine wine of the game which, tasted socially, changes a cricket match to a rare and solemn festival. Such an invitation is one that no one for whom cricket is an inspiration can refuse, and it was natural that thereafter we should praise and criticise in wise and sympathetic chorus.

The acquaintance thus begun warmed to intimacy at the Oval and Canterbury, and I began to seek his easily recognisable figure on cricket-grounds with eagerness, to feel a pang of disappointment if he was not there. For though to his careless eye his great moonlike face might suggest no more than good-natured stupidity, I had soon discovered that this exuberance of form barely concealed a delicate and engaging personality, that within those vast galleries of flesh there roamed the timid spirit of a little child.

I have said that to the uncritical his face might seem wanting in intelligence, but it was rather that the normal placidity of his features suggested a lack of emotional sensitiveness. Save with his eyes—and it needed experience to read their message—he had no means of expressing his minor emotions, no compromise between his wonted serenity and the monstrous phenomenon of his laughter, that induced a facial metamorphosis almost too startling to convey an impression of mirth. If normally his face might be compared with a deep, still pool, laughter may be said to have stirred it up with a stick, and the consequent ripples seemed to roll to the very extremities of his body, growing in force as they went, so that his hands and feet vibrated in humorous ecstasy.

Later, when, in one of his quaint interrogative moods, he showed me a photograph of himself as a child, I was able to give form to the charming spirit that Nature had burdened with this grievous load. I saw the picture of a strikingly handsome little boy, with dark, wide eyes and slightly parted lips that alike told of a noble sense of wonder. This, I felt, was the man I knew, whose connection with that monstrous shape of flesh had been so difficult to trace. Yet strangely I could recognise the features of the boy in the expansive areas of the man. In the light of the photograph, he resembled one of those great cabbage-roses that a too lavish season has swollen beyond all flower-like proportions, yet which are none the less undeniably roses. Others might find him clumsy, elephantine, colossal; thenceforward he was for me clearly boyish.

His voice varied more in tone and quality than that of any other man I have ever met, and over these variations he seemed to have little control; and this, too, made it very difficult for strangers to detect the trippings and hesitancies, gentle, wayward, and infinitely sensitive, of his childlike temperament. Within the limits of one simple utterance, he would achieve sounds resembling the drumming of sudden rain on galvanised iron and the ecstatic whistlings of dew-drunk birds. It was sometimes difficult to follow the purport of his speech for sheer wonder at the sounds that slid and leaped and burst from his lips.

His voice reminded me of a child strumming on some strange musical instrument of extraordinary range and capacity which it had not learned how to play. His laughter was ventriloquial and rarely bore any accountable relationship to the expressions of mirth of ordinary men. It was like an explosive rendering of one of those florid scales dear to piano-tuners, but sometimes it suggested rather an earthquake in his boots.

He dwelt in a little flat that seemed like the upper floor of a doll's-house when related to its proprietor, and here it was his delight to dispense a hospitality charmingly individual. His meals recalled nothing so much as the illicit feasts held in school dormitories, and when he peered curiously into his own cupboards he always looked as if he were about to steal jam. He would produce viand after viand with the glee of a successful explorer, and in terms of his eager hospitality the most bizarre cates appeared congruous and even intimately connected, so that at his board grown men would eat like schoolboys, with the great careless appetite of youth.

He had a fine library and a still finer collection of mechanical toys, which were for him a passion and a delight. It was pleasant to see him set some painted piece of clockwork careering on the hearthrug, stooping over it tenderly, with wondering eyes, and hands intent to guard it from disaster. It was pleasant, too, to hear him recite Swinburne, of whom he was a passionate admirer; for, though his voice would be as rebellious as ever, his whole body would thrill and pulse with the music of the poet. He always touched books softly because he loved them.

Of bonfires he spoke reverently, though a London flat hardly lent itself to their active exploitation; and I remember that he told me once that nothing gave him a keener sense of what he had lost in growing up than the scent of burning twigs and leaves. Yet if he felt this loss, what should it have been for us who had come so much farther than he!

Himself a child, he was beloved of children and treated by them as an equal; but I never knew another child who was so easily and continuously amused. The Hippodrome, the British Museum, the Tower of London, and the art of Messrs. Maskelyne and Devant alike raised in him the highest enthusiasm, which he expressed with charming but sometimes embarrassing freedom. Alone of all men, perhaps, he found the Royal Academy wholly satisfying, and it could be said of him truly that if he did not admire the picture he would always like the frame. He had a huge admiration for anyone who did anything, and he liked riding in lifts.

Though he treated women with elaborate courtesy, their society made him self-conscious, and he, who could direct his body featly enough in a crowded street, was apt to be clumsy in drawing-rooms. Perhaps it was for this reason that they had apparently played no marked part in his life, and I may be wrong in attaching any special significance to a phrase he made one quiet evening in his flat. We had been speaking of the latest sensation in our group of mutual acquaintances, of the marriage of Phyllis, daintiest and most witty of cricket-lovers, to a man in whom the jealously critical eyes of her friends could perceive no charm; but the conversation had dwindled to silence when he said, "Surely his love can make any man lovely!"

Then, as if the subject were closed, he fell to speaking of his latest pocket-knife with boyish animation; but the phrase dwelt in my mind, though the image of the brave boy with wide eyes and lips parted in wonder was all that I ever knew of the man who made it.

The Romance of the World

In past days there dwelt in a wood with her mother a maiden of youth and great beauty, by name of Ysolde. The birds and squirrels that leap in the trees were her playmates, and happiness was with her from day to day. But at length the fair lady her mother went on a journey to a far country and came back no more, and sadly in this manner was Ysolde left alone.

She did not yield lightly to misfortune, but rather sought to make the woods merry with song and a dance and passing from place to place as heretofore. But it happened that when the forest was stilled and the little birds were no longer singing, the spirit of solitude would trouble her, and her ancient joys be lost in bitter tears. And thence would come relief.

Now it chanced on one bright day that she heard the sound of a horse's feet speeding along the path towards her. And presently a most noble and courteous voice saying:

"Wherefore, sweet damsel, weepest thou so sadly?"

Ysolde plucked her hands from her face and then rose to her feet amazed, for she beheld the most beautiful youth that there has been, arrayed in silk and velvet, his mantle embroidered with the golden crown of a prince, and dominion shining in his face like a glowing light. But truly, if Ysolde was astonished at the noble countenance and magnificent apparel of the prince, no less delighted was that one with the tender beauty of Ysolde. Her hair lay drooping to her shoulders in gleaming masses of brown, while beneath, her eyes, yet moist with tears, were like two dark flowers wet with the dew of the dawn, now ruffled with gentle winds of surprise and delight.

"Oh, Prince!" she cried, and, her sorrows put off, gazed on his handsome raiment, for in that is ever a woman's joy.

But the prince answered: "Greeting, O most fair." For he was a man, and the simple white garments of the maiden, neat and comely though they were, were nought to him beside the beauty of her face, or even the whiteness of her feet like silver.

When Ysolde heard these words, the red blood was in her face, and she gazed steadfastly at the ground, for none had told her this before, and though her modesty bade her not believe it, yet in her heart she was glad.

Now did the prince utter sweet words unto Ysolde, and since it was in the time of spring her heart flew out to his, and when he asked her to come with him to be his true princess, she cried "Yes" softly but joyously. And she mounted his horse and he bore her before him out of the woods and into the glad countryside with the sun shining hotly overhead; but the birds and the little squirrel that leap about in the trees were sorry to see her go because she had played with them so often.

So rode they together through the fair fields, what time, he told her of the wide dominions she would help him rule, but ever as they went, he grew more sad until at last he reined up his horse and said:

"Now must we part for a while, beloved. But surely await me here, till I return."

Then Ysolde, perceiving by his sadness and the grievousness of his sighing that something was amiss, said in a sorrowful voice:

"Art thou weary of me so soon, my lord?"

To this the prince replied:

"Nay, even unto the grave shalt thou not weary me, O heart of mine; but I ride this way to slay a most fierce and monstrous dragon that has sorely ravaged my father's kingdom. So, I pray thee wait here till I return."

At these sayings Ysolde as in no wise afraid, but replied softly:

"Where thou goest I go, O my Prince," and though the love of the prince caused him to plead against this resolve, yet in his heart he was glad that his lady should be as brave as she was lovely.

And so they rode on, until the sun drooped in the heavens like a red blossom, and the words of love on their lips sank hushed in the quiet of the evening.

And the wearied steed trod sorely up the side of a great hill, whose top touched almost the sky itself, and there stopped; for his work was done, and now was the time for the prince to fight for his honour and his lady. And when they had dismounted they saw before them a great valley whose sides were dark with shadows of grey and purple and green. But lo! The bottom of the valley was a sea of leaping flame, red and yellow and aching white, for there lay the dragon in all his fearful greatness.

At the sight of this fearsome thing the maiden's heart fluttered in her breast, for he was an hundred times the length of a man and dreadful to gaze upon. So that she prayed the prince not to approach him.

But he, no whit dismayed, smoothed his hair with his hand and kissed her brow, and drawing his sword from its sheath, began to descend the side of the pit to approach the dragon.

At first the maid did sit as one stunned, with her face lost in her hands and great fear in her heart lest she should hear Death crying form the lips of her prince.

But *anon* she thought that if he perished, she too could leap into the pit, and go with him to those Isles of the Blest of which poets of old did sing so sweetly So finding courage in this thing, she stood upright by the horse, and gazed down the valley to see how her lord might fare. That one passed around the monster, seeking on every side for a point at which to attack him, but so thick were the monster's scales, and in such orderly manner were they placed, that in no wise could he decry a point of vantage. And so, he came to the head of the beast, all clouded with fumes and horrid smoke, and lo! In the midst there shone his two great red eyes, wide open and watchful. And the prince saw that there only could his sword strike home, but so great was the monster's head that he could not contrive to pierce him from where he stood.

So, trusting that the thick armour of the monster would save him from betrayal, and breathing the name of his beloved right fondly, he set himself to climb the head of the beast.

The sun was now set, and the valley would have been black indeed but for the flame of the dragon himself, and perchance that same was weary with the great ravage he had made that day; for truly the prince, with but one slipping, reached the summit in safety, so that he was scorched with the flame that came from the beast's nostrils below, while on either hand lay his eyes like two deep red waters.

Then did the prince, with one word to his God, lean forth from where he stood and plunge his good sword deep into the monster's eye; but there came forth from the wound such a rush of flame and boiling foam that he needs must leave his sword and cling to the scales of the beast's head.

Now the dragon beat his head desperately from side to side and from rock to rock owing to the biting anguish of the wound, and the prince was in deadly peril of his life either from being thrown to the ground or crushed against the sides of the pit. And wishing to perish like a true knight with his lady's name on his lips he called aloud "Ysolde," and again "Ysolde." And lo! He looked up and there he saw his lady standing at the edge of the pit no whit afraid of the smoke and the flame, and in her hand, she held his lance, that he had left with the horse, and though it was of great weight she flung it far and true, and it fell to his feet.

Now did the prince raise himself up and seizing the weapon thrust it down through the dragon's unscathed eye and through his very brain, so that he cried with a terrible sound of agony through the valley, and dropped his head to the earth in bitter death. Thus was the monstrous dragon slain that had ravaged the prince's father's country.

But the prince and his fair Ysolde rode blithely from the land of the shadows to the lightening sky, and it was indeed wondrous to behold how deep wounds love could make in those unharmed by a dragon.

And *anon* the dawn came over the mountains, and all was laughter and joy in the waking world.

Summer Time

Well, we are married and 'tis summer here,
We are the lovers who
Heard the birds sing.
This is the place where all the violets were;
Surely the sky is still as warm and blue—
Where is the spring?

Their pulses beat a little faster as they neared the little wood.

"After all these years," he said, with a trace of sentiment.

"Yes," she said simply; and then they came to the stile, and he gravely helped her over.

"This is the wood!" He laughed, but it sounded false. "It has not altered anyhow."

"No, it has not altered." She spoke solemnly.

"It might have been yesterday."

"A thousand years ago—perhaps. Or not at all. I wonder——" There was no bitterness in her voice. She spoke as one who states a fact.

"Dorothy. Not today. I swear not today. Dear——"

"Today and tomorrow and forever. It is no good to pretend. We didn't pretend then, Willy."

He frowned thoughtfully.

"I wonder whether it was all our fault. Perhaps it was the trees, and the flowers, and the blue sky, all in one conspiracy against us."

"Oh, it is Fate," she said. "Fate has just made fools of is, that's all. We thought it would last forever; that's folly. Nothing lasts forever. And now we make the best of it; that's brave."

He said, "I wish to God we didn't," and they walked on down the grassy path in silence. They each knew what they were seeking, though nothing had been said about it—the tree, the great oak, on which in rustic fashion, with many a loving jest, he had carved their

213

linked initials.

"They do it in books," he said. "We shall do it in real life."

And after ten years they had come back

"Anyhow, I'm glad we came," said he.

"I'm sorry," she replied.

"Why?"

"Because it proves it," she said. "That year, that year must be dead indeed, when we come like tourists to view its remains. Had there been any hope we should have stopped away. If anything, any little thing were left it would have hurt us too much to raise this spectre from the ten year's dust. But it doesn't matter, now we have only common sense, which was one thing we lacked then."

"How silly we were, and yet how wise!"

"We were people of sentiment then, we are sentimentalists now. False coin. Our raptures didn't ring true."

"Raptures," he smiled at her painfully. "This is worse than I expected, Dorothy."

"Oh, I knew it would be pretty bad," she replied calmly. "It was bound to be. But it's good for us; makes us honest, you know, teaches us our place—if we have one."

They reached the clearing, and after all it was a trifling shock to find their oak tree gone.

A peeled stump stood graceless in the centre, and that was all. Dorothy looked at it silently for a while and then burst into laughter.

"It's about the height of a tombstone," she said. Then, after a pause, solemnly, "I suppose it is a tombstone." And she walked up to it and seated herself comfortably on the top. "Perhaps that's why the lightning struck it."

"To blot out our boast?" he said.

"No, so that I can sit on the stump."

He was pained.

"Dorothy," he cried. "It may be—no, I suppose it is bad, but it isn't as bad as that. Why can't we look at the pleasant things that are behind us without tearing them so to pieces?"

"Ghosts! Ghosts!" she chuckled. "That sounds like Ibsen. I don't tear them to pieces, Willy. But when I find myself possessed of an unwholesome memory, I try to crush it; when I find a comfortable stump, I sit on it. That's common sense."

"That memory isn't unwholesome. It is we that are unwholesome now, Dorothy. And it is because you know that, that you are ashamed

214

of the past."

Dorothy looked at him steadily for a minute.

"Do you really think so, Willy?" she said quietly. "Yes, I suppose you're right. I'm trying to make the best of it. Trying to forget. And what would you have me do? Pretend? Speak with lies? Live with lies? Love with lies?"

"No, but— Oh, I think there must be a better way than this," he cried passionately. "There must be on an earth that is not hell. Your tears are not less true because you think I do not see you weeping. I am not less sorry because you prefer not to notice it. Dorothy, I have been thinking, will we not meet again in regret, as we met once before, here, in this very place, in joy? Can't we start again in a different way? A more lasting way. Then we loved because the gods were kind. Can't we love now because they are cruel?"

Dorothy shook her head. "Look at me," she said abruptly. "What do you see?"

He looked at her and hesitated.

"Precisely," she cried, "and now when I look at you, what do you think I see?"

"You are cruel," he murmured.

"Not too cruel," she said. "Because you still love the girl of ten years ago—because I still love that boy if you will—that is why there can be nothing now. Willy, I never look at you without the ghost of that boy stepping in between us. Thin and dark, and with a face like a poet."

He swore softly.

"Yes, and when you look at me," she went on inflexibly, "don't I know, don't I see your eyes looking everywhere for something? You are looking for a hat with pink ribbons. You are wondering where that girl can have hidden herself. You are wondering why she does not come running to you with outstretched hands—'*Love it has been so long!*'"

"Don't, don't. Not here. It seems like blasphemy."

"It doesn't matter. The gods are dead. Youth, Love, Romance; Common-Sense has slain them every one. We sit on top of a mountain, old and wise and ugly, and deal in facts. The gods are dead."

"Oh, let's walk on," he said. "This day has been wretched."

"It was bound to be," and she slipped down from her seat. They walked away from it quietly.

There was one more place to visit, the little hollow where he had waited for her, and where they had been wont to build their castles.

"Cupid's Cup," he said softly.

She laughed. "I expect they've sunk a well in it or something," she said.

"No, oh no!" he said seriously.

They had not. The Cup was as they had left it some ten years before, a valley in miniature, floored with grass and flowers, and with silver birches climbing up the sides, and at the bottom in *their* place stood a young man, a young man who was thin and dark, and had a face like a poet.

He had not marked their approach, being too intent on listening to the footsteps of someone who was drawing near on the other side of the Cup to his arms.

Husband and wife turned away forthwith, and walked back to the stile in silence.

He broke it.

"She ought not to have sung that," he cried.

Dorothy turned to him with a little pathetic smile.

"Don't you see now?" she said. "Don't you understand? We are moved on. That's all. We had our turn, now it is for those other glad ones. We are too old now. We shall be very civil to each other, no doubt. And happy. But glad never. I like you and you like me, I think. We are quite friends, you know. If I had known, I would not have had things go differently. It was worth a lifetime, that."

"Dorothy, if I did not think it was a lie—"

"Oh, well never mind. It doesn't matter. But that girl: she was pretty, don't you think?"

"Pretty. Yes, I suppose she was. But she ought not to have sung *that.*"

Dorothy looked at him nonplussed for a few seconds.

"Well, well," she said.

And they walked back to the station.

LEONAUR

ALSO FROM LEONAUR
AVAILABLE IN SOFTCOVER OR HARDCOVER WITH DUST JACKET

THE COMPLETE FOUR JUST MEN: VOLUME 2 *by Edgar Wallace*—*The Law of the Four Just Men* & *The Three Just Men*—disillusioned with a world where the wicked and the abusers of power perpetually go unpunished, the Just Men set about to rectify matters according to their own standards, and retribution is dispensed on swift and deadly wings.

THE COMPLETE RAFFLES: 1 *by E. W. Hornung*—*The Amateur Cracksman* & *The Black Mask*—By turns urbane gentleman about town and accomplished cricketer, life is just too ordinary for Raffles and that sets him on a series of adventures that have long been treasured as a real antidote to the 'white knights' who are the usual heroes of the crime fiction of this period.

THE COMPLETE RAFFLES: 2 *by E. W. Hornung*—*A Thief in the Night* & *Mr Justice Raffles*—By turns urbane gentleman about town and accomplished cricketer, life is just too ordinary for Raffles and that sets him on a series of adventures that have long been treasured as a real antidote to the 'white knights' who are the usual heroes of the crime fiction of this period.

THE COLLECTED SUPERNATURAL AND WEIRD FICTION OF WILKIE COLLINS: VOLUME 1 *by Wilkie Collins*—Contains one novel 'The Haunted Hotel', one novella 'Mad Monkton', three novelettes 'Mr Percy and the Prophet', 'The Biter Bit' and 'The Dead Alive' and eight short stories to chill the blood.

THE COLLECTED SUPERNATURAL AND WEIRD FICTION OF WILKIE COLLINS: VOLUME 2 *by Wilkie Collins*—Contains one novel 'The Two Destinies', three novellas 'The Frozen deep', 'Sister Rose' and 'The Yellow Mask' and two short stories to chill the blood.

THE COLLECTED SUPERNATURAL AND WEIRD FICTION OF WILKIE COLLINS: VOLUME 3 *by Wilkie Collins*—Contains one novel 'Dead Secret,' two novelettes 'Mrs Zant and the Ghost' and 'The Nun's Story of Gabriel's Marriage' and five short stories to chill the blood.

FUNNY BONES *selected by Dorothy Scarborough*—An Anthology of Humorous Ghost Stories.

MONTEZUMA'S CASTLE AND OTHER WEIRD TALES *by Charles B. Cory*—Cory has written a superb collection of eighteen ghostly and weird stories to chill and thrill the avid enthusiast of supernatural fiction.

SUPERNATURAL BUCHAN *by John Buchan*—Stories of Ancient Spirits, Uncanny Places & Strange Creatures.

LEONAUR

ALSO FROM LEONAUR
AVAILABLE IN SOFTCOVER OR HARDCOVER WITH DUST JACKET

MR MUKERJI'S GHOSTS *by S. Mukerji*—Supernatural tales from the British Raj period by India's Ghost story collector.

KIPLINGS GHOSTS *by Rudyard Kipling*—Twelve stories of Ghosts, Hauntings, Curses, Werewolves & Magic.

THE COLLECTED SUPERNATURAL AND WEIRD FICTION OF WASHINGTON IRVING: VOLUME 1 *by Washington Irving*—Including one novel 'A History of New York', and nine short stories of the Strange and Unusual.

THE COLLECTED SUPERNATURAL AND WEIRD FICTION OF WASHINGTON IRVING: VOLUME 2 *by Washington Irving*—Including three novelettes 'The Legend of the Sleepy Hollow', 'Dolph Heyliger', 'The Adventure of the Black Fisherman' and thirty-two short stories of the Strange and Unusual.

THE COLLECTED SUPERNATURAL AND WEIRD FICTION OF JOHN KENDRICK BANGS: VOLUME 1 *by John Kendrick Bangs*—Including one novel 'Toppleton's Client or A Spirit in Exile', and ten short stories of the Strange and Unusual.

THE COLLECTED SUPERNATURAL AND WEIRD FICTION OF JOHN KENDRICK BANGS: VOLUME 2 *by John Kendrick Bangs*—Including four novellas 'A House-Boat on the Styx', 'The Pursuit of the House-Boat', 'The Enchanted Typewriter' and 'Mr. Munchausen' of the Strange and Unusual.

THE COLLECTED SUPERNATURAL AND WEIRD FICTION OF JOHN KENDRICK BANGS: VOLUME 3 *by John Kendrick Bangs*—Including twor novellas 'Olympian Nights', 'Roger Camerden: A Strange Story', and ten short stories of the Strange and Unusual.

THE COLLECTED SUPERNATURAL AND WEIRD FICTION OF MARY SHELLEY: VOLUME 1 *by Mary Shelley*—Including one novel 'Frankenstein or the Modern Prometheus', and fourteen short stories of the Strange and Unusual.

THE COLLECTED SUPERNATURAL AND WEIRD FICTION OF MARY SHELLEY: VOLUME 2 *by Mary Shelley*—Including one novel 'The Last Man', and three short stories of the Strange and Unusual.

THE COLLECTED SUPERNATURAL AND WEIRD FICTION OF AMELIA B. EDWARDS *by Amelia B. Edwards*—Contains two novelettes 'Monsieur Maurice', and 'The Discovery of the Treasure Isles', one ballad 'A Legend of Boisguilbert'and seventeen short stories to cill the blood.